Running on Empty

Kat Ryan

Dedicated to my mother-in-law, Mary Jo. Thanks for being a cheerleader for my books in normal times as well as in the hospital, nursing home, assisted living, or anywhere life has decided to bring you.

And to the CNAs, nurses, and doctors out there that work tirelessly for us all, but especially those that have taken care of those I love - thanks for the work you do.

Chapter 1

Traitor

Logan

My dick was a goddamn traitor. I briefly considered texting my brother Levi to ask his thoughts on referring to it as Benedict Arnold from now on. Scratch that. The last thing I needed to encourage was anyone in my family thinking about my dick or what I should be doing with it. They already shared their opinions with me far too often.

I mean, I was grateful to have been born into the family I had been. My parents were supportive; my brother and I were close. If you'd asked me about them even three years ago, I would have said everything was fine. But then a bomb went off, shattering my world, and now they hovered in the periphery of my life. All. The. Damn. Time.

I knew they worried, and I got it. I really did. But I simply couldn't be who they wanted me to be. That version of myself was gone. Even if old BA in my pants had decided to side with them.

Fucker.

A scent of the ocean woke up my senses and told me I

was no longer alone moments before a chocolate muffin slid under my nose. Taking a deep breath, I reminded my brain —the one in my head as well as the one in my pants—that Allyson was my friend and we could all knock it way the fuck off.

I glanced up into her light blue eyes, and both brains declared I was a damn liar.

"Hey, you're looking a little mopey."

Her face was wide open, innocent. Her freckles stood out against her pale skin, and her long red hair was fighting to escape the messy bun she'd twisted it up in. She had no idea what bullshit I was struggling with—in my pants *or* in my head. Allyson made me think of being outdoors, a feeling of freedom. Part of me wanted to confide in her, but I didn't want to weigh her down. It didn't matter. Nothing could happen between us. That was something I'd already set aside. Not that she'd given any indication she thought of me as anything other than a friend. I just knew it was a no-go for me, so why bother to burden her with my traitorous dick?

I worked to make the mental shift to the friend whom she deserved and that I'd become over the past two years. Café owner and park manager. Friends. Yep, that was it. Nothing more, nothing less. The lies we tell ourselves.

"Mopey. That sounds like something my grandma would have said to me after school when I was a kid. However"—I gestured to the muffin before me—"if looking that way gets me this, well, I'll take it."

I picked the muffin up and took a bite, moaning as the first morsel hit my taste buds. Allyson knew I had no willpower around baked goods, but either the woman had been holding out on me, or these were new, because I certainly hadn't had them before.

Swallowing, I gave her a withering stare that only served to bring a smile to her face. I worked to ignore how that made me feel like I'd won some damn race. "Woman, where did these morsels of goodness come from?" I took another bite, happily drowning in the taste bursting in my mouth. Seriously, they were that good. Forcing myself to set the other half down before I devoured it all in one gulp, I looked at her with narrowed eyes. "I like your regular muffins, but there's something..." I tried to place the flavor that was making these stand out.

She was bouncing on her toes behind the wood counter, joy evident on her face. "I know, right? I found this old cookbook at the library sale last week. It was all stained, dog-eared. Who wouldn't have scooped it up? No one, that's who. Totally worth a dollar or twenty. In it, I found this recipe. It has instant coffee granules in it, though I used instant espresso, and a sugar crust on top." She gave me an impish smile. "I'm taking from your reaction that you're a fan."

I couldn't hold back. I picked up the other half and popped the whole damn thing in my mouth. "Mm-hmm," I mumbled as I swallowed the bite. "A fan that would be glad to take another one off your hands."

She arched an eyebrow in my direction. "I thought you were going with the whole 'one muffin or scone per day' resolution this year."

"I mean, I made it a whole... What would it be?" I paused to do some mental calculations. "Ninety-six days into the new year. I think that's cause for a celebration." I tipped my head, nodding toward the baked-goods case Allyson had, which I was assuming was fully stocked with this chocolaty goodness I needed more of.

Benedict in my pants reminded me there were other

things I wanted, but fortunately my willpower in that area was made of steel. I could want many things, but acting on those desires wasn't on the table for now and wouldn't be again.

"Now Logan, you made me promise back in December to sell you one baked good a day this year. You even made my employees promise too. Heck." She leaned over below the counter that her point-of-sale system sat on.

I groaned because I knew what was coming.

Victoriously, she held up a napkin. "I even had to sign this!" She deposited it in front of me in a flourish.

Yep, my handwriting, dated December 27.

I, Logan Traub, will only eat one of the damn delicious treats from the Sanctuary Café at the Park each day or I will become an old man with a giant belly.

Signed by me and Allyson. Notarized by one of her employees, Andy. Brilliant idea on my part.

I balled it up and tossed it over her shoulder.

"Logan!" She turned around and picked it up off the ground, smoothing it out.

Benedict perked up, and I chastised him to go back to sleep.

She placed the napkin on the counter. "Not happening, my friend. Everything is good in moderation. Now where's Charlie? Maybe you need a walk."

"Max stole him." I dropped my chin into my hand. I didn't want to give up on the muffin, but really, she was right. I didn't need two. Needs versus wants, however, in all areas of my life were a bit out of balance.

Allyson moved over to the espresso machine and gave me a questioning look. I nodded. Coffee might just hit the spot.

She moved as if by muscle memory, brewing my latte as

she glanced my way. "Just saying you might want to relax. Max and Emma have Poppy and Winnie, so I'm not thinking he stole Charlie. God knows they don't need another dog." She dropped my coffee in front of me and turned to the line of women who had been drooling over the bakery case, not that I blamed them.

No, Max didn't make off with my dog, though Charlie was sweet enough it would be tempting. Nah, Max had his hands full. Poppy was a King Charles; Winnie was just a puppy, not quite a year old. She was a golden retriever, though, and had passed Poppy in size some time ago. Max brought them both out to work often, and it was hilarious to see the two of them together. Size be damned, Poppy seemed to be the alpha in that duo.

Maxwell Harp was my right hand out here at Highland Woods. He was the natural areas manager and had moved back to Highland Falls, his hometown, a year ago next month. It had been touch and go at first. The man didn't like to delegate and was drowning trying to do everything himself. I side-eyed Allyson with that memory. She and Max shared that particular quality. Fortunately for Max, he'd reconnected with Emma, the sister of his closest friend, and she'd given him a new priority. Since then, it had been smooth sailing.

However, the man was always snagging my dog when I brought him out here, though Charlie was happier for it. Don't get me wrong, I did get out into the park as often as possible, but the job of park director involved a lot of work at my desk too. Somehow my goldendoodle was not as fond of office life as he was of splashing through streams, the pond, or time spent on the trails in general.

Looking back to Allyson, I watched her hand over a coffee and scone to the next customer in line.

"See something that interests you?" A voice to my left made my heart jump.

Looking at the stool next to me, I met the smiling eyes of Drew Spencer, another employee at the park, though a more recent hire than Max. Drew was just hired a little over a month ago and would oversee a new community outreach program. The position, I reminded myself, was thanks to the hours spent in my office writing grants. I was excited about some programs we were going to be able to bring to the park and the community with Drew at the helm.

However, I was also well aware that the man rivaled my brother Levi for the joy he found in giving people shit. Any time spent around him and his brother Jake had taught me that. The Spencer brothers were amazing and a lot. I seemed to enjoy some peace and quiet more than they did. And I sure as hell didn't need him knowing about this attraction I was fighting.

"Not sure what you mean, man." I picked up my coffee and took a sip, working to look relaxed as I did so.

He shook his head at me, clearly communicating his pity for the predicament he believed I was in. "You poor sap. This will be fun to watch." He gave a nod to Allyson, and she got to work making his usual.

"What will be fun to watch?" Max slid onto the stool on the other side of me, giving his own nod to Allyson in response to her unspoken question.

"This fool is still drooling over the woman that keeps us all supplied with nourishment here at the park and doing not a damn thing about it," Drew said, thankfully wrapping up his statement before Allyson brought them both drinks and took their payment.

She headed back to a woman who stood at the register, her tight gray curls standing in contrast to her warm brown skin. I recognized her as a semiregular fixture out here, though we hadn't exchanged names. She gave Allyson her order and then, to my surprise, looked over the top of her glasses at Max with an assessing glance.

"You behaving yourself?" she asked him in a tone that said she would only be accepting the truth.

"Don't I always, Mrs. T?" he replied with an innocent expression.

She shook her head with a look that said she knew him well, then took her order to a cluster of armchairs pulled together near the window that looked out at the pond. Several ladies her age were already over there with books in their laps.

"Who's that?" I asked.

"My high school guidance counselor, Mrs. T. Let's say she kept Sully and me in line for years."

"Tough job," I muttered. Sully owned the brewery here in town with Jake Spencer and was also the brother of Emma, Max's fiancée. The connections around this place were ridiculous. The slogan for small towns should be "Don't say anything about anyone because everyone knows, or is related to, everyone else."

"Don't try to dodge the conversation," Max said, making eye contact with Drew.

"Where's my dog?" I asked, ignoring both of them.

"Blake has him. Hosing him off; the river was muddy. Back to the topic at hand—when are you going to ask the woman out?"

Drew clapped a hand on my shoulder. "We're here for you, man. Max has been at this longer than I have, but you just need to lean into the feelings. Stop fighting them."

I rolled my eyes. "I don't know what you're talking about." Was it time to go home yet?

Drew leaned over, dabbing at my beard.

"What the fuck, man?"

"Sorry, you just had a bit of drool there." He sat back, laughing.

Max tapped my to-go cup with his own. "Sorry, Logan. It's hard to keep this one in line at times. I blame his siblings."

I nodded, staying silent. The Spencer siblings, Jake, Drew, and their sister Steph, were a force of nature. Steph lived in the Chicago area, which was good. I wasn't sure this town would survive all three. They were the best people but also didn't know what privacy was in any form.

"But he speaks the truth." Max was clearly ignoring my prayer to move on from this topic. He nodded to Drew. "We've both been there in the past year. And I can tell you from this side that my life is far better with Emma than it ever was without."

"Ditto," Drew said, looking smug though his relationship with Kate was new.

I looked at my coffee as an uncomfortable silence surrounded us. I knew it made me seem like a bit of an ass, but I was fighting a ton of emotions right now and I didn't trust myself not to let them all spill out if I started talking.

A knock at the window by the pond was my salvation and had us all turning to see Blake, one of our interns, standing there with a wet and happy Charlie.

"I can grab him," Max said.

"No, I'm good." I tossed a tip into Allyson's cup as she gave me a glare from where she was taking another order. She'd said more than once that I didn't need to do that. Good thing I was a bad listener.

Drew had clearly read my emotional state and caught my eye. "Logan, we didn't mean to overstep."

I shook my head. "No worries, we're good." And with a wave to them, I headed out the side door, where I thanked Blake and took all the love that Charlie wanted to heap on me as he shared his happiness for his morning so far.

Straightening with his leash, I decided to head to the pond instead of my office until I could clear my head. I was glad Max had found Emma, that Drew and Kate had finally straightened their shit out. Hell, when I'd moved to Highland Falls three years ago, the majority of the guys I'd met were single. Over the past year, many had found their life partners. And I was happy for them. I truly was.

The thing was, I'd found mine at the age of twenty. We had ten fucking amazing years together. And a drunk driver took that all away three years ago in a flash.

I was damn glad these guys had found their happily ever after. However, life had taught me that we didn't all get one, or it didn't last as long as you wanted. I'd met the love of my life in college, and now that part of my life was done.

It was just the way it was.

Chapter 2

Cheetah

A*llyson*

I was a goddamn cheetah. I repeated my mantra, *thank you, Glennon Doyle*, over and over as I filled orders at the café. I *should* feel grateful that on an early Monday morning, we had a crowd. We'd only been open in this location just shy of a year, closing in on two in the café in town, but my focus was struggling this morning. Again.

My new hometown of Highland Falls had been good to me. Moving here from Connecticut had been a culture shock for certain but one that was desperately needed. And while this small town made New Haven look like a metropolis, it was more than that. No one here knew my parents. I wasn't the oldest daughter of Patrick and Mona Murphy, sister to Maeve. Here I wasn't considered the responsible Murphy sister, the one who'd broken her parents' hearts after walking away from the family business. Everyone had expected that from Maeve; she was the free spirit. Who knew where she was from month to month? My parents hadn't put the weight of their expectations on her. That would've been a recipe for disaster. That was all for me. Well, until it wasn't.

With a glance down at my outfit today, I laughed. If my mother saw me right now, she'd certainly have something to say and none of it would be positive. My baggy jeans had a few holes in them from wear, not fashion. They were rolled up to keep the hems off the floor. My socks were rather vibrant for her taste, and she certainly wouldn't approve of them with sandals, especially Birkenstocks. I could just picture the look of disgust on her face.

And I simply couldn't find it in me to care.

"Here you go." I passed over the lemon-and-raspberry scone to one of the ladies joining Mrs. T for a book group. "Hope you enjoy it."

Having no other patrons, I grabbed a cloth and spray bottle to clean off the counter and some tables that were unoccupied. My brain was a jumble of lists, schedules, and never-ending things to do when running a business. One day I'd rest or feel caught up. Today was not that day.

As I wiped down a table near the window, I saw Logan and Charlie heading from the pond area to the door nearest his offices. Charlie gave a final shake, which made Logan laugh as he got sprayed. I stopped to admire Logan for a moment, telling myself that it was harmless. His hair was longer on top, closer cut on the sides. After he'd been out with Charlie, it was tousled and I had a strong desire to run my fingers through it or his dark beard or...

I worked to ignore the flutter in my stomach and continued wiping down the tables, with a wave to Drew and Max as they headed out, and listened to the murmur of conversations all around me. I lost myself in the repetitive swipes, but the vibration in my pocket pulled me back to the present. A feeling of dread filled me even though I didn't know for certain who it would be. However, a glance at my phone showed me that my assumption had been correct. I ignored the call and let it go to voice mail as I slid it back into my pocket. I'd deal with that later.

Another vibration from my pocket had me working hard to put my mother out of my mind. She was just under a thousand miles away, and I thanked the gods for each one of those miles daily.

Mrs. T was at a nearby table. I'd gotten to know her well since her club started using the café for their meetings. I knew she'd cut back to part-time this year, was retiring in May, and as much as she would miss the students, she was ready. She gave me an appraising look.

"What?"

"I'm just saying if I ever call you, I hope you do more than glance at the phone and slide it back in your pocket." She shook her head at me with a knowing smile.

I sighed and slid down in an armchair next to Mrs. T but on the edge of the group. "I know."

"Spill. You are far too young to have these worry lines."

I dropped my head to the armchair. "It was my mother," I said into the chair. A groan might have slipped out.

I sounded terrible. Part of me was grateful for my family. They wanted the best for me, I knew. But it was the best on their terms. Mine didn't factor in.

"And do you typically ignore phone calls from your mother, or is today unique?"

I let go with what my mother would have called a dramatic sigh. "When I can?"

"Are you asking me or telling me?"

I sat up, curling my legs under me. "Do you really want to know?"

"I asked." Mrs. T gave me a look that I was sure she'd used on high school students over the years to tell them to get to the point.

"It's just I know you have your book club." I gestured to the women in deep conversation just past her.

"They won't miss me a bit. Let it out."

"Okay." I bit my lip, uncertain where to start. "I moved here from Connecticut a little over two years ago after my grandmother left me a lot of money in her will." I teared up for a moment, thinking of her. It sucked because she was the bright spot in my family. She loved me without reservation or expectation. My grandfather had died before I was born, but my grandmother was her own person. I had no idea how she birthed my mother; they were polar opposites.

Mrs. T reached over to pat my hand. "Were you close?"

I shrugged. "I mean, kind of? Or as much as we could be. My parents are, well, reserved. They are all about appearances and high expectations, traditions. My grandmother was the opposite, so they didn't let me spend too much time with her. At the reading of the will, Grandmother had left me more money than I knew what to do with, along with a letter that told me it was time to start following my own north star and not the one that had been dictated to me. She said it was time to stop putting everyone else before me." I looked down at my hands. "Much to my parents' dismay, I gathered my courage and did just that."

Mrs. T sat with that for a moment before she asked, "What had you done for a job before you came here?"

I smiled at her. "Can't leave the guidance-counselor mode for a moment, can you?"

Her eyes twinkled. "Not until May."

"Honestly, it is ridiculous. I'd graduated and became a financial analyst at my father's firm before I finally looked around and began to question what *I* actually wanted from my life. I hadn't really had any direction, so my parents put me on one they approved of." I got lost in thought for a moment before continuing. "When Grandmother left me the money, I found an online listing for the Sanctuary Café in Highland Falls. I quit my job, packed up my life, and moved."

"Just like that?"

"Just like that. With every step, I questioned myself. Was this what I wanted or was I just being reactionary? My grandmother used to say when it felt right, it felt like warmth. Comfort. Since it felt warm, I continued moving forward. And I know I'm luckier than most. Lou's business had been established, plus I have my inheritance as a cushion."

"Don't sell yourself short. You've worked hard." She gestured at the folks sitting around the café, the line at the counter. "You've even opened a second location. Are your parents proud of your success so far?"

I snorted. My parents weren't, to say the least. If they could have gotten the will declared null and void due to Grandmother not being of sound mind, they would have in a heartbeat. Anything to keep me near them and doing exactly what they wanted me to do. Too bad for them that she'd known them well and prepared her attorneys ahead of time.

"Um, I wouldn't say so. Mainly they're pissed that I'm not there to follow the path they've dictated, to do what they need done with no questions asked."

Mrs. T patted my hand again. "Well, I bet your grand-mother would be."

God, I hoped so. I missed her terribly.

Vibrations reminded me of who I was ignoring. *Cheetah, you're a cheetah.* I ignored my phone.

"Allyson."

I turned and saw Logan standing in the doorway that took you from the café to the rest of the mansion.

"Sorry, Mrs. T. I better see what Logan needs."

She raised her eyebrows at me and tipped her head toward Logan. "You do just that, my girl."

I stepped over to the doorway. "Yeah?" My eyes skated over the zipped fleece to his Carhartts that I knew hugged his ass. *Stop*, I told myself. My grandmother's face popped into my mind, and she stuck out her tongue with a *pffft*. I fought an eye roll as I worked to remember what I was doing.

Logan continued, oblivious to my mental struggle. "I can't come in; Charlie is a mess. But I forgot to take my coffee. Could I possibly get another?"

My fingers itched to comb back his hair. *Sigh.*

"Sure, usual?"

He nodded, and I moved back to the espresso maker. I'd met Logan when I first took over the café in town. He'd been new to the area, only moving in the year before me. Actually, I had him to blame, or thank, for my business expansion. When the conversation came up at the park about how they wanted to add a spot for visitors to get something to eat or drink, he'd told me about the opportunity, suggesting I submit a proposal.

Did I pause, write down a pro/con list, consider my options, realize that I might be over my head going from zero to two businesses in the span of two years? No, I sure didn't. I dove right in.

Honestly, I loved having both locations. The vibe of each was different. My spot in town was in a former church. Here we were in a mansion overlooking a pond. But both cafés had eclectic but comfortable spots to sit and relax.

The coffee shop I had frequented on my way to work in New Haven had a similar vibe, but the seating there had been uncomfortable. To be fair, maybe they hadn't wanted people to linger all day. My thought though was in a small town, I *needed* those loyal customers who would tell their friends that we were the place to work, meet, or just contemplate the meaning of life.

So long farmhouse tables with comfortable seats, small tables as well, and loads of armchairs, a few couches. It worked and I was damn proud of it.

And the customers loved it. True, I had that cushion —*thanks, Grandma*—but hadn't needed it. We were busier than I'd dreamed.

As I'd shared with Mrs. T, my parents would not be impressed. My mother would see the decor and ask when the estate sale was starting. Well, if she'd ever seen it, that would probably be something she'd say. They'd also tell me the percentages of small businesses that fail each year, ignoring the success I'd had. However, in my two years out here, they'd yet to visit. At first because they were angry. Now on principle.

Moving on.

I finished up Logan's coffee and brought it to him at the door, handing it over and ignoring the brush of his fingers against mine or how the hair stood up on my arms. Static electricity or my brain malfunctioning, I'm sure.

"Thanks, Allyson," Logan said. He looked like something else was on his mind, but instead he took a sip of the coffee, letting out a sound of pleasure.

That wasn't helping matters.

I knew it was ridiculous to crush on this man and not say anything. I was an adult, for God's sake.

Point being Logan was one of the first people I'd met, along with some women in town. He didn't think it was weird that I tended to be more comfortable on my own because he was too. He had a different reason than I did. He'd lost his wife three years ago. Me? Nothing that drastic. I just didn't love large groups.

If I was at a party, I found one or two people I knew and talked to them. Larger groups exhausted me, and honestly, after a long day at work, I just wanted to go home at the end of it. At the age of thirty, I envied the schedule of Mrs. T and her friends. I bet no one thought they should be living it up past eight in the evening. Logan hadn't asked me to be anything beyond who I was, the person who gave him coffee and one baked good a day.

And we'd become friends. Well, like work friends because, until recently, I didn't really see him outside our role as park director and caffeine supplier.

I hated that he'd lost his wife, and I knew he hadn't dated anyone since then, which was why my infatuation was completely inappropriate. He wasn't ready to move on, and there was no indication he ever would be.

And yet here we were.

I looked to Charlie. "Who is the best dog? Hmm?"

Charlie gazed at me with such adoration I wondered if I should go out and get a dog. At least it would give me a reason not to go out with Emma, Grace, or Maggie next time they tried to cajole me into a night out. I bent down to give him a few pats, not too much because he really was a mess. As I rose up, Charlie showed that a few pats were not enough as he started to jump up. I tried to side step him. As much as I loved the pup, I really didn't want to be covered in eau de dog, and my clumsy nature took over as I tripped over my own feet.

While I tried to right myself, knowing I was probably going down and looking like the klutz that I was, Logan reached out to steady me. Coffee in one hand, he snaked his other arm around me, pulling us together.

My chest hit his with an *oof* as I looked into his widening brown eyes, my arms naturally wrapping around him for stability.

I lost the ability to breathe. We both seemed frozen together, eyes locked, and he parted his lips, his tongue running over the bottom one. Gracious, that was nice.

Did I pull back? Jump up and wrap my legs around him? Christ on a cracker, I was powerless. I shifted, and holy moly, I didn't think I was alone in my attraction here.

"I'm sorry," I whispered.

He tilted his head. "For what?"

I glanced down to our connected bodies, then back up to him. "Um, well."

His face flushed, and he took a step back, looking anywhere but at me.

"Logan?" I wanted—no, needed—to get us back to where we were.

And where was that again?

He cleared his throat and looked out the window, still avoiding my gaze.

I glanced at the time, then back to him. Maybe I'd just move ahead like we hadn't just been locked in an embrace that I wanted to continue in a more horizontal fashion. Fake it till you make it, right? "Hey, are you still up for a run after work?"

I saw something flash in his eyes, and whatever it was, I didn't love it.

His voice sounded strained when he replied. "Sure. Meet you here." And with that, he whistled to Charlie and went out the door.

Well, shit.

Chapter 3

Sibling Love

Logan

I'd woke up with one thing on my mind, or shall we say one person? While I often rethought many of my decisions revolving around the redhead currently occupying my brain space as well as the coffee shop in the mansion, becoming her running partner might be my biggest regret. Clearly, it had not been a well-thought-out decision.

A few months ago, Allyson had seen me running on the trails. When I came in for some caffeine, she'd mentioned she'd always wanted to run a marathon and had signed up for one in late spring, started training months ago, but was concerned she wouldn't be ready. Before my brain caught up with my mouth, I'd offered to train with her even though I didn't want to consider the last time I'd ran a race, much less a marathon. Some things are meant to stay forgotten, even if they really aren't.

Much to my dismay, she'd taken me up on my offer.

I'd gone so far as to suggest an upcoming half marathon at the park as good practice for the marathon coming up next month. She'd enthusiastically agreed to it, and now we were committed.

We didn't run together daily but made it out on the trails around the park a few times a week as well as a long run on the weekend. It had brought us closer, which wasn't something I wanted to think much about right now.

Two more weeks until the half, then the marathon just weeks after that. I could do this.

Charlie let me lose myself to my thoughts as we trudged up the lawn to my place. He raced back to the dry creek bed that ran parallel to my cabin, then back to our place, then to my side, happiness evident in every fiber of his being. If only I could move through life with the joy Charlie felt in everyday life.

We reached the door, and I ran a hand over him, knocking off some loose dirt he'd picked up from the tilled fields he had chased a rabbit into on our morning walk. Crazy pup.

As I came into the open cabin, my eyes caught as always on the wall of windows across the back looking into the woods where I spent most days. When I'd been debating the job downstate at Highland Woods, Nola and I had talked about the type of place we'd like to buy. Nola had been adamant that we needed to live surrounded by trees. She often joked that trees watched over us; they were our protectors. Her ideal day involved a walk in the woods, talking to the trees and animals as she went. She'd love this place.

After her death, I'd accepted my new job and moved down, mourning her loss and wishing that everything wasn't new around me, but I did pick a cabin that faced Highland Woods because it made me think of her. Three years out, I knew living somewhere new had likely saved me. I didn't have a house that felt like a shrine to an old life—no part of this cabin had been touched by Nola, but the nod to her was there. And while that was hard some days, it was also healing on others.

Charlie barked to let me know he was ready for breakfast.

I made quick work of feeding him, then grabbed some breakfast for myself. The layout of the kitchen—hell, the whole house—was perfect. But lately it felt empty, like I was missing something. I felt lonelier than I had in years. Since I moved to Highland, I'd been focused on grieving, but now maybe I was ready to do more than go to the brewery one out of every five times Max asked?

Maybe. Maybe not.

Since the day was rather warm for early April, I took my plate and coffee to my back porch where I could hear the birds calling to each other. I left the door cracked so Charlie could join me when he was done. I'd just settled in when I looked down to see my phone lighting up with a call from my brother Levi. I propped the phone against my coffee cup and clicked to accept the call.

Levi appeared to have recently woken, a crease on his cheek likely from a pillow and his hair, longer than mine, a mess.

"Yo, baby bro. Woke up thinking of you—how goes it?" He reached for something off-screen and came back with a coffee mug that, I squinted, read WOKE UP SEXY AS HELL AGAIN.

Yeah, that tracked.

"Ten minutes older, dipshit. And I'm good. Just got back from a walk with Charlie. Eating breakfast before heading to the park."

"A walk? That pup I bought you is ready for more than

a walk. He's got retriever mixed up with poodle in there. Charlie is begging for a run, aren't you boy..." Levi's voice dropped into a baby-talk tone that was so annoying, it must be to blame for the words that spilled out of my mouth.

"Allyson and I got six miles in yesterday after work, so chill. He runs plenty." I shoved a forkful of eggs in hoping against hope that Levi wasn't awake enough to catch what I'd just said.

Judging by how he sat up straight and looked alert, luck was not on my side.

"I'm sorry, baby bro, back that truck right on up. You were running, which is great to hear, but unless you've changed the name and gender of the dog, I think you have some explaining to do."

I fought the urge to drop my head to the table or hang up on him so I could go about my morning in the peace and solitude I was accustomed to. Even if I wasn't sure if it was healthy for me anymore.

Instead, I tried to brush it off. "Allyson. I'm sure I've talked about her before. You've just forgotten. Owns the café in town and the one out at the park."

Levi was watching me intently, which was never a good sign. The man knew all my tells. All of them. We were twins, but he was my best friend. Had been forever and knew me better than I knew myself.

"Have I met her?"

I thought back to when Levi had visited me in the past two years since Allyson had moved to Highland Falls. He usually made it down once every few months, but he typically worked during the day remotely from my place while I went to Highland Woods and we met up after my day was over. The café would be closed, and I didn't think he'd ever been there.

"Nah, I don't think so."

"Describe her."

Allyson's face flashed in my mind. God, she really was gorgeous. "Long strawberry-blonde hair, freckles, pale skin, blue eyes, short—maybe right at five foot or a bit taller?"

Levi cleared his throat, and I focused on him. He looked, well, pensive. "No, I don't think I have met her." He watched me for another beat, then with a soft voice, he asked the question I knew was eating away at him. "So you're running."

I couldn't lie to him. I knew the past three years while I worked through my grief had been hard for him too. "Allyson and I are friends. She is running her first marathon and was nervous about it, so she asked me if I'd train with her."

Levi put his coffee mug down and watched me with an intense look. "So you're helping her train..."

"And running a half marathon and a marathon with her." I rushed through the words, thinking it might make this entire conversation easier.

"I'm sorry, repeat."

I took a cleansing breath, staring at the brilliant blue sky as the birds called to each other only feet from where I was sitting.

"I don't want to make a big thing of this, Levi."

"Does this Allyson know about Nola?"

"Yes. Some." My throat threatened to close up.

"Does she know how she died? What she's really asking of you?"

"No. I've talked to Ashley, my therapist. She says that I can pick when to share my stories, there are no rules, so I really don't want to get into this, but thanks. I know you are only worried because you care."

Ashley would actually be damn proud of me for speaking up. Boundaries and all.

Levi was quiet for a moment, which was, quite frankly, a modern miracle.

After a bit, he looked at me with some serious consideration. "You okay?"

I let the past few weeks roll through me and thought of how I'd been feeling. "Yeah, I think I'm okay. Really."

Levi watched me, then nodded like he was making a decision. "Tell me more about Allyson."

So as I headed back in the house, dropped my dishes in the sink, and got ready for work, I shared with my brother how I'd met Allyson and how worried I was about her overworking herself. "...I mean, she just texted today to cancel on an easy run we were going to do after work because someone called in at the park location. She needs to hire more staff but is stubborn and wants to do it all herself."

Levi looked up from where he was pouring some more coffee, his phone still propped somewhere on his counter. "Sounds like you two know each other well."

"Yeah, I guess we do." I grabbed everything I needed for work, including Charlie's leash, and started pouring a thermos of coffee, though I knew I'd get more from Allyson in a few hours. "You coming to me next or me to you?" I asked, patting down my pockets for my keys and wallet.

Levi still looked lost in thought—maybe he just needed to wake up—before saying, "You're up here for Mother's Day, right? Or are we coming down this year?"

Levi lived in the same town as my parents, Aurora, a suburb of Chicago. I loved our parents fiercely, but I did enjoy the three-hour cushion. Otherwise, Mama Traub would likely be dropping in all the time.

"I can't remember. I'll ask Mom next time we talk. Got to head to work. Thanks for the call."

"Love you, baby bro."

"Love you, asshat."

Clicking to end the call, I noticed that, as always after a call with my brother, I felt lighter. On that note, I headed to work.

Chapter 4

Those Kinds of Friends

Allyson

The coffee shop was finally quiet for the first time all day. While I knew starting a small business could be stressful if you were operating in the red, I was blessed with the opposite problem. Since taking over from Lou, business had exploded. I credited some of our success to teaming up with Kristine for yoga before she had a studio of her own. She'd rotated between the community building at my spot in town until I opened this space at the park, which was then added into the mix. The after-yoga crowd grew, and through word of mouth, people came in droves.

I was grateful.

Even now that she had a studio with Kate and no longer had classes in the café, either of them, she made sure to send people here after class. We ran specials for the morning yogis and business was still booming.

The truth was I wasn't sure how I could sustain this. Between the two locations, I was draining myself dry. Hell, as a last resort, I'd turned to running. Was I a runner? No.

When I took it up this year, did I think I'd enjoy it? No, no I did not. Honestly, I'd known that I had to do something to help clear my mind, and several of the regulars in here were runners.

So last summer I'd lost my damn mind and signed up for a marathon this May. It had been almost a year away and felt doable, which was a laugh now. However, there had been benefits. It gave me something else to focus on, and quite frankly, I was shocked to find that I somewhat enjoyed running. I know, I know, it surprised me too. Turns out being out in nature and having no bigger decision to make than what trail to take was a relief. Who knew?

I ran all late summer and fall on my own, just building up some endurance without following a plan, but the start of the new year made me doubt myself and I lost steam. I'd never as much run a 5K, much less a full marathon. What was I thinking? I envisioned myself pulling into the parking lot for the race and seeing cars with those 26.2 stickers on them. I didn't have a bumper sticker on Bessie, my beautiful Jeep Cherokee Classic—RIP best model out there—but if I did, it might say I Brake for Coffee. Sure as shit wasn't going to be about distances I'd run. So yeah, suffice to say I was feeling unsure.

Talking to Logan had helped my mindset. He'd shared that he had some experience with racing, and I'd asked him if he wanted to run with me. He'd said yes, and the heavens rejoiced. He even suggested I compete in a half as one of my long runs in mid-April in preparation for the real thing in May, which would allow me to get a feel for running a race with other people. Good idea, right?

Running with Logan got me back on track, and I looked forward to every minute of training with him, which was not something I wanted to examine too closely. It was nothing, really.

The lies we tell ourselves.

So running was helping, I might or might not be prepared for my upcoming race, and I was still overwhelmed at work, and if I kept having to watch Logan's shapely ass in running tights like I did last night when we ran after work, I might go mad.

That about summed it up.

"Earth to Allyson."

I looked up to see Max watching me with some amusement and a touch of concern. Beyond Logan, Max was likely my closest friend in Highland Falls. I'd met his wife Emma first, back when Max was only a childhood crush of hers. Then he'd moved home almost a year ago, and they'd had a whirlwind romance, the kind books are written about. Their wedding was on tap for this summer, and I was thrilled for them.

And just a smidge jealous.

While I missed seeing Emma as much as I did pre-Max, I'd found a friend in the tall Momoa look-alike once he started frequenting the café at the park. He came in for a bacon, egg, and cheese biscuit most mornings. Since he usually waited to stop in until the morning rush was over, we often caught up on his life, which was far fuller than my own.

I longed for what they had together.

"Sorry, Max. Usual?"

His green eyes watched me with concern. "Sure." I watched as he scanned the counters of the café littered with dishes. The plastic bins placed strategically around the space were filled to the brim.

The place, to be frank, was a bit of a mess. Kind of like

my brain. It didn't help that one of my few employees, Caydence, was out with strep throat, which was going around. Fingers crossed I didn't get it; I couldn't afford to be sick.

I ignored the mess in favor of getting Max's order together. Maybe another few miles added to the tally this week would make everything more manageable. Sure, sounds good, but when would I find the time? My sigh was audible.

"Allyson..." The breath Max let out after he said my name spoke volumes. "When are you going to hire more help?"

My gut clenched. I knew we needed more help. Heck, the café in town was just as busy, if not more. It just seemed like such an expense. "Max, you know small businesses have to watch the bottom line. I'll look into it soon, I promise."

He shook his head at me. "You need to hire at least another barista for here *and* for the Sanctuary in town. And most importantly, a manager. Emma has told me that downtown is just as slammed, if not more, and you simply cannot do it all."

"I know, I know. I plan on being in town tomorrow to help out." I passed him his coffee and got to work on the breakfast sandwich he often had as a late-afternoon snack. "Maybe I'll find time to get there this afternoon after I close up here..." I thought of what wouldn't get done here if I took the time to go into town. What ever happened with that sheep? Dolly, was it? Maybe cloning would be a viable option in the future. If you cloned yourself, did all your knowledge get cloned too? Or would I just have to explain everything that needed to be done to another person? Because that wouldn't be any help whatsoever.

"Where'd you go now?" Max asked, bringing me back to reality.

"Cloning."

"Are we for it or against it?"

Valid question. Where should we stand on a moral ground here? Probably against, right?

I sighed, again, sliding Max his sandwich, and braced myself on the counter to look at him. "I'm just so tired, Max. I took up running, hoping it would wash some of the stress from my body, and it does, but then I come back in here and have to catch up from being gone for an hour. It's like it's a vicious circle and never ending."

Max gave me a knowing look. "That's because you're *understaffed*."

"But do you know how much work it is to train someone? I mean, in the time I explain to someone what I need them to do, I could be done myself."

"Short-term work for long-term gains, my friend."

I dropped my head to the counter and rested it on my arms as I muttered out a reply into the wood surface.

"Didn't catch that." Max's voice came from above.

I picked up my head and looked at him. "I need more coffee."

Fine, I whined a bit. Or a lot. Yes, I sure did.

"Fortunately, you're in the right place for that need to be met."

He was right. With a thought to what type of coffee I was in the mood for, I got my shit together and quickly whipped up a mocha.

The grind of the beans was soothing to my soul, and within minutes the siren song of the scent of fresh coffee permeated the space. One sip and I felt my body relax.

Better. The hot caffeinated beverage was exactly what I needed to ward off the damp spring day.

Andy came behind the counter, fresh from her break. Her hip popped into mine as she nodded toward the group of armchairs beside the window, indicating that I should take a break.

It was like my employees were conspiring with the giant man in front of me. I mean, sure, I knew they were right. I also knew I needed to cross several things off my to-do list today, and they would only get done if I did them.

Andy, however, would absolutely say something if I didn't take at least ten. Her displeasure would be known far and wide. While only thirty-five to my thirty years, her maternal instinct often kicked in and she tried to take care of me. She was a single mom, but maybe she needed more kids. Or a pet or two. Because right now she got off on bossing me around, and I wasn't here for it. I gave her an assessing glance. She raised a pierced brow at me with a pointed look at the window again.

Fine, I couldn't stand up against the woman. I mean, it didn't help that I knew she just wanted the best for me, but did she have to be right all the time? The unmitigated gall.

"I've got it, I've got it," I muttered as I looked down at her arm where the flowers and vines weaved around with a cardinal here or there. "Your sleeve is coming along nicely," I said, working to distract her with flattery. Although in this case, it was the truth. Her tattoos were badass. I pondered if I could pull her look off. Probably not.

"One, of course it is. My tattoo artist is the best. And two, I know what you're doing. Break. Now." She pointed across the space.

I did the only thing I could. I grabbed a chocolate chip

scone and headed for the armchair, trailed by Max who was laughing like the traitor he was.

I plopped down into the leather armchair, pulling my legs up and under me as my gaze drifted to the pond outside the windows. The sight of water did its job to relax me, as always. I loved both cafés, but this location tugged at my heart, largely due to the view. And quite possibly the company in one gorgeous park director, but we weren't acknowledging that. While I was ready to date someone—it had been a hell of a drought—I could tell Logan wasn't, and I wasn't here to push myself on him. So I friend zoned myself. It was fine. Everything was fine.

"So you ready to admit you need some help?" Max propped his foot up on the rustic coffee table. Where it might be considered rude in other places, here we worked to make the vibe one where kicking your feet up was encouraged. Thus the sturdy-as-shit coffee tables where you could stand on one and there would be no worries about a collapse. Wipeable surfaces and you were good to go.

"Allyson..." Max apparently wasn't in the mood to let me ponder the furnishings of the space. Whatever.

I refocused on him. "I know, Max. What can I say? I promise I'll think about it?" A childish urge had me wanting to cross my fingers behind my back. I met his gaze, and the guilt filled me up. Here was a friend telling me he was concerned about me, and I just wanted to distract him. I dropped my head against the back of the armchair and looked to the ceiling, searching for the words I wanted to share.

"Want to tell me why this is so hard for you?" Max's words were gentle, like he was talking to a horse he didn't want to spook.

I closed my eyes, wondering how much I wanted to get into.

"In the spirit of honesty, I should say that your struggle isn't unknown to me."

I rolled my head to the side to meet Max's eyes. "Yeah?"

Max nodded. "Yeah. Your pal." His right eyebrow went up at that word and waggled at me. Waggled, now that was a weird word, but waggled it did. "Logan got on me when I first came to the woods. I was complete shit at delegating, and he was concerned I might burn out." Max's gaze dropped to his hands as he flexed them for a moment, seeming to be lost in thought. After a moment, he looked my way. "He was right."

"So we're going to be that kind of friends?"

"Come again?"

"The ones that lay out honesty and call each other on our bullshit? Is that what you're telling me?"

Max's green eyes twinkled as they crinkled around the corners, and he brought a hand to his beard to smooth it down as he considered me. A wide smile met my look, and he nodded. "Yes indeed, Allyson, we are that kind of friends."

"Super." I worked to control my enthusiasm. It wasn't difficult.

Before I could get my thoughts together to respond to Max's concerns, he got a lapful by the way of Emma dropping in with a laugh.

Max lifted his arms so that she could snuggle closer to him and then wrapped them around her waist, resting his chin on her shoulder. "Hey, Em," he murmured.

"Hey, Maxwell, Maggie dropped me off out here so I could ride home with you." Emma leaned back to kiss the underside of his bearded chin. Turning toward me, she gave me a beaming smile. "Allyson, I've missed you! Heck, Maggie and I were just talking about you the other day. Now that yoga is in the studio, which is lovely, we don't see you enough."

I shook my head at her. "Em, you both get coffee often in town almost daily..."

"And speaking for myself, I don't see you enough there. You are either swamped and can't visit unless it's six in the morning or you're out here." She gestured around the space like she blamed it, giving a glare at my shelves of my snow globe collection like it was their fault. "You need to take a break and come hang out with us more."

Max, like the traitor he was, spoke into Emma's ear in a voice that was purposely loud enough that I could overhear. "I've been telling Allyson that she needs to learn to delegate and hire more staff."

Emma looked excited. "Absolutely!" She looked thoughtful for a moment. "Actually, I could recommend some teens from my book club at the library."

Max moved a lock of her hair off her shoulder to wrap it around his fingers. "Gabe?"

Emma nodded. "And maybe Henry? Sam?"

Max watched her, then lowered his voice, but I could still hear him. "You'll never stop trying to save them all."

Emma leaned forward and kissed his nose, then looked my way. "Gabe and Sam are great. Henry is too. He had some poor choices last year and started a fire out here but is on the right track now and needs people to believe in him."

I nodded, mentally wondering if I could take on teens. Would that be more or less work for me? "Maybe I could hire some help..."

Andy chose this moment to drop Emma's coffee off. "From your mouth to God's ears, but we all know that isn't happening." With those words of wisdom, she headed back for the counter. Good call. Maybe I could fire her for being insubordinate. Then again, without her I'd really be screwed.

Emma, however, took up the cross. "You could absolutely use more staff in both locations. If you don't want to hire teens, do you need me to ask around and see who needs a job? And I have a resource I've put together on the library's website with jobs available locally. I could add your listings there if you'd rather have adults..."

"Whoa, whoa, slow down girl." My head was spinning. "I'm not there yet. I need to think about it."

Emma gave me a look and then swiveled to Max, matching his ridiculous whisper that I could hear. "Max, Allyson needs you to be her Yoda here."

Maxwell Harp looked at Emma as if she was the only person on earth, just as he always did. "Whatever you say, sunshine. I'm working on it."

Jeez, these two. They kept up the lovey-dovey eyes at each other and then said their goodbyes, waving to Andy with promises to talk soon.

I checked my watch and was glad to see it was time to wrap up our day. Andy began closing behind the counter as my ever-growing stack of dishes in the nearest tub threatened to tumble. Finally, I gave in and told Andy I was taking five, knowing she had to leave in a few to get to her appointment in Champaign. I'd get a quick catnap before finishing up around here. It was a great idea.

I grabbed my headphones and lay down on the couch near my favorite cluster of armchairs with my favorite playlist pumping. I was going to close my eyes for five minutes, and I would be refreshed to finish up on my own. Just five minutes.

Opening my eyes, I wiped away a bit of drool that was snaking down my chin. I'd only lain down on this couch ten minutes ago—fine, likely closer to thirty or more—but I couldn't find it in me to get up. My headphones were pumping in my favorite Taylor Swift songs, and I was here for it.

I wondered if Taylor had trouble delegating. Likely not. She was superwoman.

With a sigh worthy of a stage performance, I pulled myself to stand up to get started on the mess. As I stood, I stretched and willed my body to be happy with the work ahead of us. Heck, I thought I still needed to gather all the dishes, then start on washing and prepping for tomorrow. I stood and opened my eyes, then blinked, then looked around again.

Was I dreaming?

I rubbed my eyes. Late-afternoon sun shone through the windows facing the pond. White lights strung in trees on the far side were already turned on even though sunset wasn't for an hour or more. Visitors were mostly gone, and I'd hazard to guess most park employees were off too.

There was magic in the air.

Um, let's make that magic in the air *and* the café was spotless. I turned around in a circle trying to wrap my brain around what was right in front of me.

I tugged my headphones out. "Is this an elves-and-the-shoemaker situation?"

A voice from the counter threatened to give me a heart attack. "I'm guessing you're the shoemaker in this scenario?"

You always wonder if you are a fight-or-flight person. Apparently, I'm neither. I screamed loud enough to raise the dead and jumped straight up in the air because that would be helpful.

"Shit, sorry, Allyson." Logan ran toward me from the counter, a towel thrown over his shoulder, his hair completely disheveled. Why I was noticing this in my panic, I cannot tell you. What I can tell you is that he looked good. Lickable. Who knew that was a thing?

It's entirely possibly I was having a dream. Maybe it was one of those fever dreams? But those were bad, right? Logan came to a crashing stop in front of me.

"I'm so sorry. I didn't mean to startle you." His hands reached out to rub up and down my arms. Goose bumps rose in his wake. I wondered if I could pull him closer, but that was likely not a great choice. *Friends, Allyson.*

I tilted my head back to meet his eyes. They were warm, brown, and held a touch of concern. If I had to hazard a guess, I'd say he was over a foot taller than me easily, which wasn't saying much with my five-foot-two frame. Usually I didn't mind my height, or lack thereof, but right now I really wanted to climb him like a tree and check out those eyes a bit closer. They looked like melted pools of chocolate, but maybe I did think about chocolate a lot...

"Allyson, are you okay?"

I shook my head to focus my thoughts. "Yes, I'm sorry. I wasn't expecting anyone in here." I looked around again, making sure I wasn't making this up. "Did you clean the café?"

Logan took a step back, which only served to make me want to step forward. I restrained myself, shockingly.

"Yeah. I was coming in to see if you wanted to run a different trail tomorrow, and you were zonked out on the couch." His head nodded to the space behind me.

"Excuse me. I was just resting my eyes."

"Or snoring."

"I beg your pardon; I do not snore." Mortification

washed over me. Did I snore? Darn my pale skin. I was certain a flush was working its way up my neck to my face.

Logan laughed lightly. "Sorry. No snore, but you were clearly out. I used my key to get in. Thought I'd help out." He shrugged like it was no big deal when truly, it was the biggest.

My eyes watered as I thought of when the last time was someone tried to take care of me. It said a lot that I couldn't think of a time since my grandma had passed. Hell.

Logan bent down to meet my eyes and squeezed my arms again. "Allyson, are you okay? Did I overstep?"

I bit my lip as I shook my head, working to hold back the emotions welling up inside.

He watched me as I struggled to find words and then did the best and worst thing he could do, he pulled me against him and wrapped me in the best hug I'd ever felt.

At first, I froze. But then I sank into his embrace. And without words, without commentary, I wrapped my arms around his waist, and we swayed back and forth together to some silent melody only we could hear.

And I never wanted to let go.

Chapter 5

Intimate Conversations

L*ogan*

Twenty-four hours later, my brain was still scrambled. A full day of work had me thinking of Allyson far too much. I'd barely been able to give Max and Blake's reports on upcoming projects the attention they deserved. Once afternoon hit, I was grateful to slip into my running clothes and lean into the direction my brain had been trying to take all day.

Walking toward Allyson outside the mansion, I questioned at what point I'd become a sadist. There she was, leaning against the building, leggings and fitted, long-sleeved T-shirt hugging every curve of her small frame, and I wondered how I would keep from tripping over all the branches and roots on the trail. Again. Running with this woman was a perfect kind of torture, one I wasn't sure if I wanted to escape from or not. And yet here we were.

My brain chose that moment to remind me of how *right* it felt to hold her in my arms last night. Honestly, seeing her crashed on the sofa when I'd passed by the café, the instinct to sweep her into my arms, bring her home, and take care of her had roared to life. That wasn't something I'd felt before. Cleaning up had taken no time at all. But when she stood, dark circles were under her eyes, confirming her exhaustion even if she wouldn't own it. When she realized what I'd done and her eyes welled up, I was helpless against her. Why did this woman press every button in me? I was consumed.

I'd held her, and everything felt right and so very wrong at the same time. I didn't know what to do with that.

"Look at that. It's my knight in shining armor. Swoop in and save anyone yet today?" Allyson's voice was light, but her eyes belied her feelings. She looked reserved, embarrassed. Whether it was the fact that I'd done her job or that she had shown emotion like a regular human being, I wasn't sure.

Coming to a stop in front of her, I kicked at her sneaker. "Enough out of you." I scanned her face. The dark circles were still there, though not quite as dark as yesterday. "You sure you want to run today?"

She shook her head at me and headed toward the river trail. "Ignoring you for now. Of course I'm sure. T-minus ten days until the half. I need to get out there." She turned and picked up the pace. My only choice was to follow.

The trail was quiet; our footfalls on the soft and muddy ground were muffled. Early April in Illinois still warranted layers. Right now it was cool, but I knew I'd shed my top layer for just a T-shirt before too long. While the air held on to the winter chill, we had come far from the stark days of winter. Any day now, the trees would begin to bud. The birds were calling to each other, our quiet run against the soundtrack of the animals of the park.

I didn't say anything for our first mile. Running with Allyson, while stirring up old demons, did relax me. It reminded me of why I took up running in the first place. I'd still run over the past few years, just not regularly and no races. Until now.

Allyson didn't fill up the air with conversation, especially in the beginning of the run, which was perfect. The first mile was almost always my least favorite. It was like my body needed to wake up and decide we were, in fact, doing this, and Allyson said she was the same. As a result, we often ran in silence, at least to start, until the cadence felt natural.

This afternoon, however, felt off. Allyson had gained so much endurance in the past three months. She'd done well on her own, but running together had pushed her to do more. She'd said she was apprehensive about the half coming up and the marathon following, but I knew she had it in her. Whether I did or not, time would tell.

Her turnover was good, as was her breathing, but there was tension in her frame. I let it go, trying to decide whether I should speak up or not.

We dug in, avoiding the worst of the mud to head up a slight incline.

"Want to pause by the river?" Allyson asked, a bit breathless.

"Sure." She'd picked my spot without knowing, not that it was too surprising. It was a great spot on this trail, high on a bluff, allowing you to see the river in either direction. Far and away my favorite place in the park, I'd been coming back to it since first starting work here at the woods. It helped the darker memories I struggled with become background noise when I was in the presence of such beauty and surrounded by the trees that Nola always said held the wisdom of the ages.

Within minutes, we reached it after a steady incline for

the last quarter mile. Allyson immediately placed her hands on her head, working to catch her breath.

"Good?" I asked before glancing at my Garmin.

She nodded. "Still more breathless than I'd like to be at this point."

I held up my watch so she could read it. "Pace is up quite a bit today. Your half is on flat land, and you won't go out like this." I considered her expression. "Want to tell me what's eating at you?"

She walked toward the edge, leaving her arms elevated as her breathing began to slow. "My mom called earlier, and I stupidly took it. I should know better."

Damn. I knew her relationship with her parents was far from ideal. I'd hazard a guess that with her emotions close to the surface for whatever reason last night, a phone call with them today would have been hard.

"Want to talk about it?"

"Not much to talk about, really. She just expects me to drop everything in my life to fix things for her even though there are many people that could do what she needs. She wasn't happy when I said no." She paused, then continued, "Seems like I am continuing to be a disappointment."

Allyson's body language was rigid, her arms lowering to wrap around her waist. She looked lost, forlorn. As if drawn in by a magnet, I moved to her side. I wanted to sweep her into my arms, but that wasn't where we were. Instead, I stood by her side and felt her lean in. I wrapped my arm around her shoulder, figuring the least I could do would be to give her my presence, let her know she wasn't alone.

"Sorry your parents are such asses."

She let out a huff of a laugh. "That's a good way to classify them, though I feel guilty for even saying it. It's like, they provided for me growing up. I never wanted for much. I just won't conform to their vision of who I should be, and I guess I always had before. They're confused."

I tightened my arm. "Pretty low bar for parenting if them providing for you means they were decent."

"Well, to be fair, some kids don't even have that."

"Truth."

We stood side by side in silence as I debated what else to say when our serenity was interrupted by footfalls and a loud shout. Looking back over Allyson's shoulder, I saw the Spencer brothers racing each other down the trail. Clearly, they saw us at the same time, because they turned and headed toward our spot at the river with Drew reaching us first. I dropped my arm and stepped away from Allyson, instantly regretting it, especially as I felt her turn and look at me.

"Hey, stranger," Drew said with a mischievous glance in my direction. "Where's our pup?"

"Charlie is lounging with Max back at the mansion. I don't want to deal with an unplanned swim today." I chose to ignore the looks he was shooting my way.

Jake laughed. "And you trust Max not to let that happen?"

I gave a small shrug. "Not usually, but he and Emma are taking some pictures out here today with Winnie and Poppy. Not sure if they're engagement pics or what in preparation for their big day coming up. But Max is on orders to keep Winnie and Poppy clean, so I think Charlie is safe by default."

"For today," Allyson murmured with a small smile, as if she was amusing herself. Then she focused on Jake and Drew. "How far are you guys running today?"

"On our way back now after ten," Jake said. "We've

finally decided to go ahead and register for the half next week. Little late, but we're just in it for some fun."

Her smile widened. "You're kidding! Logan and I are running that too so I can prepare for my first marathon next month."

Jake held out his hand to high-five her. "Your first marathon. I'm impressed."

"Have you run one?" she asked.

Drew spoke up. "Nah, neither of us has." He looked my way. "You?"

I cleared my throat as that familiar feeling hit my gut. "Yeah, I've run a few."

"You guys should swing by the brewery tonight. Max and Emma will be there as well as Ivy and Kate. We've got an amazing local band. Should be packed," Jake said with a glance at his watch.

"Absolutely," Drew said.

I looked at Allyson who appeared to want to burrow in the ground.

"Um, I actually already asked Allyson to come over for dinner to discuss strategy for the half." The words were out of my mouth before I my brain caught up.

Allyson's head swung my way in surprise. I met her gaze with a raised brow and watched as relief washed over her features. I'd do anything to keep her looking like that. Her brows smoothed out from the tense expression that she'd worn, and she turned to the Spencers.

"Thanks for the invite, though," she said with far more enthusiasm that was warranted in this situation.

Drew and Jake both gave me a look that indicated we'd hit upon this topic later and then headed down the trail, leaving me to face Allyson and deal with the repercussions of committing her to dinner with me.

Did I regret it?

No.

Did I know what I was doing?

Also no.

"So dinner?" She turned her face up toward me, her freckles highlighted across the bridge of her nose.

I'd dug my own grave.

"If that's okay with you." I paused, then decided to address it. "Didn't look like you were too thrilled for a night at the brewery."

Allyson bit her lower lip, which led to me wanting to tug it down and smooth my finger across the abused flesh. And possibly kiss it. My mental state was so conflicted. Maybe one day my heart and my mind would be in the same place.

"Do you like crowds?" she asked, surprising me.

Looking at her expression, I gave her question careful consideration. "Like? Maybe. Love? No." I thought of how to explain what I meant. "I mean, if you told me I could get tickets to one of my favorite bands at Red Rocks, I'd race you to Colorado—"

"And your favorite bands would be..." She gave me an impish smile; her entire being was lighter than it had been ten minutes ago. I wanted to keep that going.

"Let's see." I considered. "Nathaniel Rateliff and the Night Sweats, Jason Isbell, Avett Brothers, Mumford & Sons, Hozier. I'm an equal opportunity music lover. Not much I won't give a listen. I could keep going... Do you want more?"

"Nah."

I tugged her elbow over to the bench that faced the river and dropped down. She took the hint and sat down next to me.

"So how about you? Favorite bands?"

Allyson braced herself on her hands positioned behind her so she could lean back, soaking in the spring sunshine or what there was of it. With her eyes closed, she replied, "I'm a Swiftie."

"Taylor Swift, huh? Anyone else?"

"Stevie Nicks is a goddess." Her eyes hadn't opened as she spilled out her truths.

"Wow, pulling back into the vault, are you?"

"My grandma loved her." She peered at me from an eye that was barely open. "She said Fleetwood Mac was amazing but gave most of the credit to Stevie."

"As would be appropriate."

She nodded like that sealed something with us.

"Brandi Carlile is also at the top of my list."

"I don't know her."

Both eyes were open, and she pulled her legs up to spin in my direction. "Oh my goodness. If I had my phone here right now, I'd play you some of her music. I mean, 'Mama Werewolf' alone is magic."

"Well, maybe that can be on the playlist tonight." She gave me a blank look. "Dinner?"

"Oh yeah." A more reserved expression was back.

"I didn't finish answering your question." I watched her carefully. "So Red Rocks, I'd be down for. I can handle a night out at the Homestead. If I'm in the mood, a sporting event. But honestly, I like small groups better."

Her face cleared. "Me too. I mean, I could do Red Rocks, especially for a favorite artist. But I'd need a lot of downtime afterward."

I got that.

"So a night at the Homestead with a local band and a crowd doesn't quite compare?"

That lip was under her teeth again. There's no describing how I wanted to fix that. To tug it down and... maybe better not to go there.

"I mean, I'd need to gear up for that. It could be fun, but..." She looked to the river.

I squeezed her knee, wanting for reasons I didn't understand for her to share more. Her gaze shot from the river, to my hand, to me. I didn't move though my gut clenched.

"But?" I prompted.

Her cheeks flushed. "But a crowd can be exhausting. It's not that I want to be home by myself—"

"Got it. You like more intimate conversations." Yep, I used that word on purpose to see if I got a reaction, and I absolutely did. The flush deepened. Then a look came over her face as she gave me a glare filled with humor.

"Are you just trying to embarrass me, Traub?"

"Depends. Is it working?"

She gave me an impressive eye roll and then stood up, holding out her hand to pull me up off the bench. Sliding my hand alongside hers, I worked to ignore the tingles that traveled up my arm.

She spoke to our hands, which, I'd note, were still joined. "Did you really want me to come over for dinner, or were you just giving me an out for the night?"

"Can both be true?" I exhaled and squeezed her hand before letting go. "I knew you weren't comfortable, so I didn't want you to feel like you had to go, but I'd also love to have you over for dinner. I was just thinking about the fact that I haven't had anyone over since I moved here, which was years ago."

"What I'm hearing is that we're both recluses."

I laughed. "Maybe. How does pork stir-fry sound?"

"Delicious. What can I bring?"

"Yourself." I turned to the trail with a glance back to Allyson. "But before we can eat, we have eight miles left. Loser does the dishes?" I watched her eyes widen as I took off, listening to her shout and the pounding of her feet coming after me.

Chapter 6

Dinner Date

Allyson

Looking up at the rapidly darkening sky, I debated my life choices. The front porch of Logan's cabin faced wide-open fields where the sun would be setting in a few hours. A glance to my right showed a window-enclosed room that looked like an excellent spot to curl up with a book. Yep. I was doing this. I was spending the evening with Logan Traub. No expectations. Deep breaths. I had this.

And I kind of wanted to puke.

Instead, I raised my hand to knock and had to smile at Charlie's bark in reply along with a gallop that got louder as, I assumed, he got closer to the door. Before the butterflies could completely overtake my stomach, the door swung open to Logan, who looked, I must say, delicious.

Choosing not to focus on that, I decided to address something that didn't make my core pulse with desire.

"Does that creek bed I drove over ever get water?" I jerked a thumb back at the long drive I'd driven up in my

Jeep. I'm not one to go off-roading, and that drive had felt dangerously close to something like that.

Logan looked over my shoulder at my vehicle. "Aw, you know Bessie probably loved it." With a step back, he ushered me in. "And yes, that's why I have a 4Runner."

I was at a loss for words, so I stepped past him and took in his space.

Holyyyy shit.

While the cabin's front porch faced tilled fields that were waiting for crops to be planted as well as a small, currently dry creek bed running across the front yard, the back of his cabin clearly faced Highland Woods. Whoever had built this place decided to capitalize on that view. As I walked in through the door, the living room opened directly in front of me with floor-to-ceiling windows looking out onto the park. It was breathtaking. Large wood beams outlined the ceiling and broke up some of the windows. On the far left was a large fireplace with a sectional in front of it, a hall to the side. On the right back was the kitchen with another hall leading, I assumed, to the windowed room I'd seen on my way up.

I wondered if he'd noticed if I moved in. Probably?

Before I could get my bearings, Charlie jumped up with a paw on each of my shoulders like we were going to do a slow dance. I mean, to be honest, not the worst offer I'd had.

"Charlie, down!" Logan tugged on his collar to encourage him to let go. "Sorry. He's a brute. Sweet pup with a bark that could wake the dead and zero respect for personal space. He loves a good cuddle."

"Me too, Charlie," I replied before I could think better of it. I could feel my cheeks immediately flush and chose to ignore my idiotic comment. Thankfully, either Logan did too, or he hadn't heard me.

Charlie dropped to a seat and looked at me with a clear longing to embrace once again. That poor pathetic expression made me laugh.

"What can I get you to drink?" Logan headed toward the open kitchen, and I followed, allowing myself one quick moment to look the man over with what were far from friendly intentions.

His jeans were worn, with a hole at the corner of one of the pockets. He had on a gray thermal shirt that was snug across his shoulders. His hair was slightly damp, like he'd gotten out of the shower not long ago. And his feet were bare. Why in the hell was that sexy? Normally, I was not a fan of feet. I mean, eww. However, this felt like another layer of intimacy, and I didn't hate it. Not one bit.

"Um, what are you having?" It was ridiculous, but sometimes I struggled with the easiest things. Like what if I said I wanted a beer, but Logan hadn't meant alcohol? Just one more thing my parents had blessed me with, the constant worry that I was being judged for my decisions because, with the people I grew up with, you were.

Chalk up one more reason that I preferred small group situations to large ones, you weren't on display to as many, though clearly decisions could be difficult even here.

Logan's head was in his large fridge. "I grabbed a few packs from the brewery of a few of their current selections. I also have wine, water, and iced tea."

Relief washed over me. If I'd asked for a beer, it would have been fine. Good to know. "Which beers?"

Still looking in the fridge, he rattled off the names. "Barn Owl Stout, Fire and Rain, Black Hole Sun, and Evolution."

"One of those is their West Coast IPA, right?"

"Yep. Fire and Rain."

"I'll take it."

He came out with two cans. "Glass?"

"Yes please."

Upper cabinets lined the wall next to the fridge. Logan grabbed a beer glass from one and set it and the can in front of me before pouring his own.

I glanced at the island and had a second take when I saw his set up. "Is that an electric wok?" I pulled out a stool and settled across from him.

He held his filled glass in my direction and leaned over to tap mine to his as we both took a drink. After he put his down, he nodded toward the red wok. "You mean you didn't grow up with one of these beauties?"

"Um, no."

Logan laughed as he began cutting an onion in thin slices, making a pile on the cutting board in front of him. "Yeah, it's ancient. My parents used one similar to this when I was growing up. Mom somehow found two of these vintage beauties for Levi and me when we moved out on our own."

I raised an eyebrow. "Vintage? Like is it safe?"

He shrugged. "As much as anything is, I suppose. It's from the eighties near as I can tell. Works great, so no complaints there, and I use it pretty often."

I watched as he scooped the sliced onions into a bowl set to the side and began pulling down soy, teriyaki, and some spice jars. "What can I do?"

He nodded toward my glass. "Relax, drink that, kick back." He lined up his ingredients near the wok before crossing to the fridge. He pulled out something wrapped in white paper before coming back and unwrapping what looked like a pork butt.

"Sounds perfect," I said. It had been a long week, so I didn't have to be told twice. "I think you said pork stir-fry?"

"Mm-hmm." He was cutting the pork into bite-sized pieces. "Mom's college roommate was Japanese American. She taught her this dish and"—he nodded toward another countertop appliance—"the importance of rice cookers and good rice."

"There's such a thing as good rice?" This was definitely unknown territory for me.

"You bet there is. I buy mine in Champaign at an Asian market. You need to wash the rice before cooking, let it sit, cook it, let it rest, then stir."

"No steps can be skipped?"

"Not if you want good rice, young lady." He looked down his nose at me with an air of superiority.

I laughed. "So if I ever meet your mom, I shouldn't mention that I use Uncle Ben's?"

"Better than Minute Rice."

I relaxed, leaning on the counter with an elbow to prop my head up. Hanging out with Logan was easy. If I could just get the pesky attraction to vanish, all would be well.

"Mind turning on some music? My hands are contaminated." Logan nodded toward his phone.

"Sure." I reached across the counter to grab it. "Code?"

"Six nine six nine." His cheeks immediately flushed.

Laughter bubbled up before I could even speak. "I'm sorry. Are you thirteen?"

His eyes briefly closed like he couldn't handle looking at me, the mortification evident on his face. "I'm so sorry. I hadn't even thought about that when I asked you to put on music."

"So your code is not named after a sex position?"

"Oh, it totally is, but my brother programmed it in there

to fuck with me. And"—he shrugged—"I just haven't changed it back."

I laughed as I typed in his code, opening in his music app. "So you haven't changed it because secretly you love it?"

His eyes on me were vulnerable at first before he blinked it away. "Well, I don't hate it, but it's more like it reminds me of Levi whenever I have to type it in, and it makes me laugh." He gave a half shrug. "I guess I feel like a little extra humor in my day is never a bad thing."

"Makes sense. I've told you about my sister, Maeve. I miss her a lot too and wish I saw her more." I held up his phone. "What do you want to listen to?"

"I downloaded that Brandi Carlile album you were talking about. *In These Silent Days*. Want to listen to that?" His eyes were on the cutting board, but my heart did a little skip. He remembered?

I navigated to his library and saw the album. "Did you listen to any of it yet?"

"Nope, wanted to wait."

"Do you want to hear it all or just the song I was talking about?"

Logan met my eyes with a half smirk. "Are you going to think I'm weird if I tell you the first time I listen to an album, I need to hear it straight through?"

"Well, I already know you're weird, so we're good." I clicked song one and put his phone down. "Right on Time" poured out of his speakers that were placed around the room, and I hopped down from the stool. "Bathroom?"

He nodded toward the hall behind me, off the living room. "First door on the right."

I moved in that direction, noting the picture frames on every flat surface I passed. I didn't look closely—Logan could see me from where he was stationed and I didn't want to look like a creeper—but it looked like pictures of a young Logan with his brother. They must be close in age. At a glance, they appeared to be the same size with a striking resemblance.

What I didn't see, I noted, were any pictures of his wife. He'd told me she was killed three years ago in a car accident but never any more details than that. I didn't bring it up; it was none of my business. But I hoped he and his family were close. I couldn't imagine what that had been like for him. My heart hurt.

Coming out of his half bath, I saw Charlie outside the door, waiting for me. I gave him a good rubdown, which he leaned into. This dog was always the same, soaking up any attention he could get. He was absolutely insatiable.

"Come on, pup." I stood up and headed back toward the kitchen. A step out of the hall had Logan's eyes coming up from whatever he was concentrating on to meet mine. A whimper slipped past my lips at his focus resting on me. Fortunately, it was quiet, and I think only Charlie knew my humiliation. The aroma of the pork cooking was already filling the space.

"Smells good."

"Thanks." Logan laid down his knife and stepped around the counter, moving my way.

"Did you think I needed an escort?" I asked, trying to inject some humor into the situation when all I could think about was the hug he gave me last night. Could I ask him for another? Too much? I didn't want to push, but I was getting some vibes that maybe this wasn't a completely one-sided attraction. I didn't know anyone who was widowed though. I would hate if I overstepped and made him feel weird. Nope. Needed to move at his pace, if at all.

He glanced down at Charlie, who was now sitting at my feet because somewhere in my journey across the room, I'd frozen. When? Why? No idea.

"You might need that escort; you seem to have forgotten the way to the kitchen." He came to a stop in front of me. If I reached out, I could pull him to me, but I resisted. For now.

Looking up, I muttered, "Damn, you're tall."

"Please don't ask if I played basketball."

"Random aside."

"My brother and I used to get that all the time," he said by way of explanation.

"Sooooo, you came across the room because..." My subconscious begged for him to declare his undying love for me, toss me over a shoulder, and take me to bed. Logic said I probably had something on my face, and he was letting me know.

"I'm not sure," he said. His voice was strong, but I also heard confusion in it. Some sadness. Uncertainty.

That would not do. Did I want to jump this man? Yes. Yes, I sure did. Was I going to when he wasn't ready? Nope. Not happening. Whatever else we were, Logan was my friend. Nothing was worth pushing him, no matter what the pulse going on below my waistband was saying.

Hush.

I reached out and put a hand on his forearm, giving it a squeeze. Oh geez. Tingles raced through me. No, focus. *Focus.* It was a friendly squeeze. Hand to God.

I needed to get us back on track. "Logan, it's fine. Truly. Are you done in the kitchen? Do you still want to listen to music? Or did you want to watch a movie? I could—"

"Allyson," he interrupted. "I wanted to—"

The front door opened with a joyful shout. "Honey, I'm home!"

I turned and was immediately confused. Was this a seizure? Had I hit my head? What was happening?

My head swiveled from Logan, with his expression that was a combo of surprise, irritation, and resignation; then back to the man who had just walked in, who looked startling similar to the one that I was standing across from.

When I say startling similar, I clearly meant almost identical.

"Um, you failed to mention that you're a twin," I whispered. "Unless I'm seeing double?" I mean, the framed picture that I'd rushed by had them looking similar, but awkward teens in a photo had nothing on two gorgeous grown men in the flesh.

"Aww, are we keeping secrets again, baby bro?" Our newcomer had a smirk that wouldn't quit stretched across his face.

"Ten minutes, asshat, ten minutes younger."

"So what do we have here?" Logan's brother waggled his eyebrows and gave a pointed look to my hand, still on Logan's forearm.

Shit. I jumped back, then met Logan's eyes. He shook his head, then turned to his brother.

"Levi, meet Allyson. Allyson, this shithead is my twin brother and constant pain in my ass, Levi."

Levi moved in and pulled me to him, kissing each cheek like we were living in France. Logan growled in the background, which only served to make more tingles race through my body while Levi laughed.

"Oh, Allyson, we're going to become fast friends." Levi stepped back, his eyes absolutely twinkling with mischief.

Then he turned to Logan and pulled him into a tight hug. "Missed you," I heard him whisper in Logan's ear.

Logan's eyes were closed as he appeared to relax and soak in their embrace. His face was more peaceful than I'd seen him in, hmm, I think ever.

"Missed you too," I heard him say. "Even if you are a shit."

Levi laughed as he rocked them back and forth.

Well, tonight just got a little more interesting.

Chapter 7

Twin Language

Logan

Levi was standing in my kitchen, stirring my pork, adding the onions and seasoning all while talking to my girl. Yeah, strike that. I was well aware that Allyson was not mine. *Well aware.* And yet that didn't change the fact that I wanted my brother as far from her as possible for so many reasons I didn't know where to begin.

I mean, let's start with the fact that he knew every embarrassing moment I'd experienced in my life and found joy in retelling each and every one of them. I couldn't hate him for it—I'd do the same—but still.

Also, let's not overlook that if Allyson was remotely attracted to me, something I both longed to be true and feared at the same time, here stood my exact replica without any of the trauma surrounding him of losing his wife with no idea how to do the relationship dance once again.

Not that Levi would go there, if—and here was the big if —*if* he knew I wanted to. Did he? After our conversation the other night, he might.

Ummmm. Damn it.

Shoving all this baggage to the side for now, let's return to what in the hell my brother was doing in my house instead of at his place in Aurora.

It all boiled down to the question of what the fuck he was doing standing in my kitchen.

I worked to ensure my voice was measured. "Levi, think you could come outside with me for a minute?"

He looked up to meet my gaze and his narrowed. "Nah, I'm good." The fucker looked back to Allyson.

"Levi, outside." I might begin frothing at the mouth if I wasn't careful.

Levi put down the wooden spoon and took a breath. "Logan, we're not going outside. We both know that you want me to go out there so you can grill me on why I'm here when if you'd simply read Mom's texts, you'd know." He spoke with a tone of voice like he wasn't trying to spook a small child.

I glared at him. *I'll kill you later*, I thought as I reached for my phone on the counter.

He gave me a glance back that said, *I'd just like to see you try*.

Asshat.

"Whoa. Are you guys communicating through your thoughts?" Allyson's gaze was pinballing from him to me, then back again.

"You bet, babe. We have since we were kids. Freaky, right?" He nodded at her glass that was getting low. "Want me to grab you another one?"

I growled. Again. I know. Neanderthal, party of one. However, I hated that he was being the host. I hated that I felt so out of sorts.

"Read your texts," Levi sang as he moved to the fridge. "Which one, Allyson."

"Fire and Rain."

I looked at my phone, then up to Levi. "I don't have any texts from Mom."

He looked over his shoulder from the fridge at me. "Seriously?"

I held my phone out in his direction, not that he could read it from there. "Nope. None since a message about her gardening club two days ago."

"Yeah, she has been on a rant about this year's garden walk planning committee for the past week. Doesn't think the new leadership is looking ahead as they should." He shook his head, grabbed a beer for Allyson, and nodded in my direction, asking me if I wanted one. I jerked my chin up, and he grabbed one for each of us before returning to pass them out.

"So—" I started, but he held up a finger, putting his phone on the counter and tapping a few things before the sound of ringing filled the air.

Within seconds, my mom's voice was there, then a video of her on his screen.

"Levi, we've talked about FaceTime. Why can't you just call like a normal person?"

"Because I like to see your beautiful face. Sue me." He gave her a smirk that made me want to hit him on the top of his head. Such a kiss ass.

"I like your face too, but I'm in the garden center and it's hard to hear without putting the phone to my ear. Can I just call you later?"

"No, you forgot to text Logan, and now he's pissed that I'm here."

The bastard turned the phone in my direction.

My mom's face went from a smile when she saw me to a frown when his words registered. "Logan Michael

Traub, why are you not welcoming your brother to your home?"

"Jesus," I muttered before dropping my head into my hands.

"Hi, Mom. So great to see you," my mother quipped.

I lifted my head to meet her gaze from Levi's phone screen. "Hi, Mom. So great to see you," I parroted.

She ignored my tone, as she often did with the two of us growing up. Survival skills. "Now son, I asked Levi to come visit you."

"Why?" I wasn't proud of it, but that came out as a whine for sure.

"Because I'm worried about you. So it was either him or me, and my garden club meets this week and you know what a mess it is right now. But if you'd rather I came, that can still happen."

"No, no. It's fine. *I'm fine.* I'm happy to see Levi." Christ. I loved my mom, but if she came down, she'd bake up a storm, I'd gain ten pounds, and she'd want to talk about my feelings twenty-four seven, and I was just not in the mood.

"Promise?" Her stern expression was one I remembered well from childhood.

"Promise." I dropped my head again. I was exhausted.

Levi turned the phone back toward him. "Thanks, Momma Bear. I'm on it and will be back in a few days."

"Thanks, Levi. Love you two. Have fun."

And silence gloriously filled my cabin.

I lifted my head to look up at him. "Seriously? You couldn't have given me a bit of warning?" Honestly, regardless of my mom's words, I wasn't absolutely convinced he hadn't come somewhat of his own accord. It was convenient that he trekked down here after our call the other day.

Levi slid his phone onto the counter and resumed stirring the pork. "The way I see it, you owe me."

"How?"

"Well, one, I'm here instead of Linnie. You know she wasn't joking; she was adamant on one of us coming down here, and you don't mess with Mom when she thinks something is amiss with her boys."

"Truth."

"And two..." He nodded to Allyson who was watching us while she sipped the beer like this was the most fascinating part of her day. She just needed some snacks and could watch this shit show unfold. "I could have let the video call show Allyson over here."

My groan wasn't as quiet as I thought judging by the look Levi gave me. He was right. If my mom had seen Allyson, all bets would have been off. The woman would have rounded up my dad and broken all speed limits to get down here.

Allyson lowered her glass. "Sorry to butt in where I'm not needed, but why would it have been bad for your mom to see me?"

Levi's gaze met mine across the counter, and I knew he was waiting to see what I wanted to share. I'd already told him I'd shared some about Nola, but not all. I tipped my head from side to side, meaning not much had changed in the past day or two.

He nodded, telling me he got it, and moved to look like the relaxed life of the party that everyone believed him to be. "Well, Allyson, it's like this. Linnie, our mom..." He gestured in my direction and back to him with the wooden spoon he'd been using to stir. "She swears on all that is holy that she won't rest until we are settled. She doesn't care who that's with, how they identify, what their religion, race, or political party is—"

"Um, I think she'd have some thoughts on the alt-right," I interrupted.

"Well, who wouldn't?" He gave me a look like I was an idiot before continuing. "At any rate, she wants us both settled. I'm fighting that with everything in me, just not there yet. And Logan here was on that path, as I think you might know, but tragedy struck three years ago. Linnie is certain that the path to healing leads through the bedroom with a stop afterward at the kitchen, so she's a bit concerned about Logan's lack of movement on that front."

Both Allyson's eyebrows shot up so high that if she'd had bangs, they would have vanished. "I'm sorry. Are you saying your mom wants you to have sex?"

Yep. Mortification, party of one. Dying. I dropped my head back to my arms and decided to let Levi handle this.

"Well, sex would be a good starting spot. Honestly, she'd take any progress for this one. She's very concerned that he's so grief-stricken that he will be in this depression forever."

I lifted my head to protest, but Levi was already there with his hands up.

"Her words, not mine."

Allyson put her glass down and turned on her stool to face me head-on. Or side-on, because I was still looking at Levi. This was a lot and not what she signed on to when I invited her over for dinner tonight. Hell.

I felt her small hand on my thigh, tapping me. Taking a deep breath, I turned her way.

"Is this too much, Logan?" She worried her lip, which only served to make me want to trace the path of her teeth with my tongue.

Instead, I took a cleansing breath and leaned on my friend, denial. "How do you mean?"

She looked unsure, which wasn't a look I loved on her. Allyson typically spoke her mind with me, which meant she was tiptoeing around the loss of Nola. I knew it sucked, but people never knew what to say, which put a lot of pressure back on the person that was grieving.

Meeting her eyes, I spoke up. I liked this woman. Whatever else, I wanted her as a friend. That meant we needed to be able to talk. "It's okay to talk about Nola. I hate when people hold back around me." Didn't mean my gut didn't clench, but I'd rather be honest, for the most part.

Still biting her lip, she then charged ahead. "I mean, you had me over tonight to talk about the upcoming race. And now here I am with your brother, your mom on Face-Time, and we're talking about personal stuff, including your wife. We're friends, but I want to respect your privacy. If you'd rather we just catch up at the coffee shop tomorrow, I am absolutely fine with that. This might have been more than you bargained for with a Wednesday-night dinner."

She'd left her hand on my thigh and squeezed in a gesture of comfort.

My cock perked up because of course he did. Mental note to go ahead and ask Levi if the name Benedict Arnold was too much attention for my lower brain, though it fit. I mean, Levi was already in my business, might as well go all in.

"I'm sorry. Did you say you two were having dinner to talk about an upcoming race?" Levi's glance from Allyson to me indicated that he was indeed curious about my return to running thanks to this woman. This visit was all Mom's idea my ass.

I gave a negative headshake which he interpreted and then let me know that would be a later conversation.

Shockingly, he immediately worked to lighten the mood and turn the conversation in another direction. "Well, the pork needs about ten more minutes. So beautiful, let's start with how you came to know this Grumpy Gus and didn't run away at first meet cute?"

Hours later and too many embarrassing childhood stories to count, Allyson was conked out in my house. We'd had some wine. Strike that. Levi and Allyson had some wine. At first, she'd said she couldn't; two beers were her max. But Levi, mastermind that he was, pointed out that it was a little foggy outside with the crazy spring temps fluctuating the way they had been and why not crash in one of my guest rooms? Levi knew, without a peep from me, my thoughts on any impaired driving. So two glasses of wine, some stories, and a terrible movie later, Allyson begged off to the guest room, leaving me to my doom.

Otherwise known as my brother.

Levi's eyes were narrowed on me as he sat. Waiting. Watching. We were each propped into a corner of the sectional. I sipped my beer, choosing to ignore him. I was sure it wouldn't work, but I was taking the coward's way out as long as I could.

After ten minutes, a throw pillow hit my face. I mean, to be honest, that was longer than I thought he'd last.

"Are you seriously going to sit there in silence? Time's up, baby bro. Spill."

"You want to spill? I'm thinking that Mom isn't the only reason you're here." I sank farther into the couch, wishing I could just go to bed but also wanting to spend some time with Levi. He had my back a few times tonight, after all. "What else do you want to know?"

He brought his fingers together like a criminal mastermind. "So many things, but let's start with the fact that you're signed up for a race and haven't shared with the vision of Ireland in the guest room what truly happened with Nola?"

I cleared my throat, fighting some emotion that was still present. "She knows she was in a car accident."

"But she doesn't know that Nola was hit by a drunk driver when you were training for a race? Or that you were in Boston for the lead-up to the marathon? Or that she was off to get you some fuel that you'd forgotten to bring? Or that while you used to dream of running a marathon in every state, you instead haven't run *any* race in three years?" Levi's gaze wouldn't leave mine. It was constantly assessing, making judgments.

I shook my head and looked away.

"So she doesn't know that just by training for another race, you are likely having a metric ton of shitty memories as well as demons come up? That you shoulder the guilt for something that is absolutely. Not. Your. Fault?"

My gaze swung back to meet his.

"You don't think Mom and Dad realized what you were doing? You don't think *I* realized what you were doing? Logan, that's why we've been so worried about you." Then he looked away. "And I couldn't get you to talk to me."

Guilt swarmed up, though it was nice to have it directed at my actions toward Levi instead of Nola for a change.

"I'm sorry." It came out as a whisper, like I couldn't bear to give voice to my words because I knew I would be swallowed up by all this if I wasn't careful. I had been and had only clawed my way out in the past two years, piece by piece.

Levi's face swung back to meet mine. "No. No apologizing for bullshit that you're dealing with."

"Shut it. I'm apologizing for locking you all out. Well, Mom and Dad included, but especially you."

"Nope, you don't need to apologize for that either. Grief sucks. I miss Nola. We all do. You know that. But I lost a sister-in-law, a friend, not my wife. I have no idea how you've dealt with that, and however you have, you don't have to apologize for it. You don't have to apologize for the way you choose to deal with your grief, that's personal. But don't get upset when we worry about you because—and I hate you for making me say this—but we love you, you dumbass. If you need me planted on this couch every weekend to drink beer and play Warzone, I'm here. If you need me on the trails as a running partner, done. Hell, I haven't run a race for some time either, but I'm happy to lace back up for you. If you need me to get Mom's recipe for her chocolate peanut butter cookies, well, she might kill me, but I'd do it. What I'm trying to tell you, what we've all been trying to tell you for three damn years, is that you need to lean on us. We love you, we're here for you, and want to go through this with you. You don't have to grieve alone." Levi sat back and took a breath.

It was like a punch to the gut, but in the best way possible. It wasn't that I didn't know all of this, that I didn't know I always had my family's support, but for whatever reason, my idiot brother actually made the words somehow sink in. Not that I could tell him that. Sarcasm, as always with Levi, came in my retort. "That was an Oscar-worthy speech."

Levi looked at me for a moment, and I knew he was deciding what my mindset was. "You don't think I rushed it a bit in the middle?" He'd assessed correctly.

"Nope, it was perfect." I took a sip of my beer to gather

my thoughts. Levi, uncharacteristically, gave me the time. That, more than anything else, told me how worried he was. As hard as it was, I needed to share.

"You know I've been seeing a therapist."

He nodded.

Deep breath, then I let the words flow. "It's helping. She's helping. I'm not saying I'm not still harboring guilt. Honestly, I'm not sure that will go away. But I'm working to move through it." Tipping my head back, I considered what was weighing on my heart. "I still miss her. It's like a bullet to the heart sometimes and takes me back. But..." My voice trailed off.

"But...?" Levi watched me for a moment, then the corner of his mouth kicked up. "But... some gorgeous red head is making it all a little easier? Making you reconsider bullshit like never running races again?"

I looked his way, and I knew he could see the emotions swirling inside. "Something like that. Like I'm not sure I'm ready to move on, but I don't know if I can *not* move on anymore. Does that make any fucking sense?"

Levi reached a foot out to kick my leg. "I don't think I need to tell you how completely pissed off Nola would be if you just became a shadow of your former self. She had the biggest heart of anyone I've ever met."

"I know."

"And if that Irish beauty in your guest room is *at all* responsible for some positive movement in your grief journey, well Nola would be leading the parade of celebration. So don't let fear hold you back, dipshit."

"Hey." I let the air clear, then went for the jugular. "So I've decided my dick is a traitor."

"Hmm. I like it, I like it. Maybe call it Benedict Arnold or BA for short?"

I exhaled a laugh. "Exactly."

"And if old BA is a traitor because he's perking up at the notion of Miss Murphy, I wouldn't say he's a traitor, but maybe the smartest part of you right now."

I rubbed beard. "Hmm, you might be right." Looking back at Levi, I spoke the truth. "I'm glad you're here."

"Even if I crashed your date?"

Interestingly, my gut didn't clench at that phrase, but excitement did wash over me. "Even if."

Chapter 8

Flat Max

A*llyson*

I crept down the stairs, hoping that I wouldn't wake anyone. I'd been out of sorts when I woke up, looking around after sleeping on a ridiculously comfortable bed. Not that mine was bad, mind you, but waking up with a pile of blankets with the cozy cabin vibes—well, I loved it times a million. Give it to me every day of the week, thank you very much. The only possible way it could have been better is if a certain bearded park director had been curled up around me. However, his pup had been, so it was okay.

Charlie gives good cuddles. Noted.

But now it was the ungodly time of five in the morning, and my internal alarm clock, which rarely let me down, woke up my slightly hungover self, reminding me that I was opening the café in town today.

Fabulous.

Cue the internal debate that went on for more than a few minutes. Cozy bed, fluffy dog, gorgeous man somewhere in this cozy cabin versus being a responsible business owner and getting my tail out of bed.

Clearly you can see what won. Geez. It's so much fun, this adulting.

Reaching the living room, I figured I was home free. In the low under-the-cabinet lighting from the kitchen, I tiptoed over to the couch to find my shoes that I'd kicked off somewhere between beer two and glass of wine number one, otherwise known as the turning point where I wouldn't be driving home. And honestly? Not mad about that. Spying those shoes, I turned and saw the heavens open up in front of me. If the sun was up, surely a beam or two would be shining down on this tableau.

Jesus is real because he allowed me this vision.

There, on the sectional, were Logan and Levi, sound asleep. But the adorable sight, the reason-I-now-knew-I-had-ovaries-because-they-might-have-exploded sight, was that their heads were at the midpoint of the sectional. Each of them had a blanket somewhat haphazardly tossed across them, like they began covered, but kicked that baby off in the middle of the night to let their feet breathe. Logan's head was on a pillow near Levi's torso. Levi had an arm tossed over Logan's shoulders and back, Logan had one on Levi's stomach.

Images of the two of them sleeping over the years popped into my mind like a vision. Surely, I was becoming a psychic and had just seen the past, or my happy version of it. How damn sweet to be that close to a sibling that you sought them out when you slept? I was both jealous and wondered if I should call Maeve. Was she in California? Colorado? Connecticut? *Shudder.* Surely not, but I was almost ninety percent certain she was somewhere that began with C, at least last time we talked.

Still, I grabbed my shoes and debated pulling out my phone and texting a picture of these two adorable men to Logan so that he could send it to his mom. I felt like a loving mom would want this—I mean, I could assume. My mom? Probably not.

Moving on.

Reminding myself that privacy exists, I didn't snap a photo. I did give Charlie a good rubdown and said a little prayer that this wouldn't be the last time I got to hang out with the Traub brothers and have too much to drink. A girl can dream and all.

I headed for the door and Bessie. Boy, did I have a story for my girl on the way to work this morning.

A little under an hour later, plus one deliciously warm shower, I was at the Sanctuary in Highland Falls. I stood behind the wooden counter, looking over the space with some peace in my heart. Owning a business was stressful, true, but tucked in these quiet moments, I sometimes had the chance to appreciate the enormity of what I'd accomplished.

In truth, Lou Williams had started off this place and given me an excellent foundation. Even so, I knew my fingerprint was on this in so many ways. Right now, not long before sunrise, I simply appreciated the peace.

Low lighting made up for the lack of sunlight for the moment. I had my seventies playlist going right now, heavy on Fleetwood Mac, Neil Young, and Van Morrison. Maeve had grown up certain she'd been born in the wrong generation and had indoctrinated me into some great older bands as a result. I grabbed the materials to make two drinks to go for what I knew would be my first customers of the morning, Maggie and Emma, and set them so I'd be ready when they arrived.

This duo had been loyal customers of mine since day one. And while they'd gone through a lot of changes in the past year, most notably Maggie having baby Ellen around Christmas, they still tried to get in here for coffee at least once a week before Maggie headed to school, Emma to the library. Though Emma was right, I'd been rushed the last few times they'd been in. It had been far too long since we really caught up because I was always multitasking and only taking a moment here and there to talk.

I had to be honest. I was a little jealous of their lifelong friendship at times. Not that they weren't inclusive; they absolutely were. It's just the people I'd known in elementary school were not people I'd want to spend any time around now. Heck, I didn't then. And while I enjoyed these women, I often bailed when they invited me out after work. I much preferred quiet time like this morning to get to know them. It was just easier. The question was why I didn't just sit down and visit with them but instead hovered on the periphery far too often. I promised myself here and now to work on that today.

I suspected they knew I struggled with crowds because they'd started coming at six instead of seven this year when I theoretically had more time to chat with them between customers. They'd text on the mornings they knew they'd be in, and I looked forward to the visits, even when brief. And while I still talked to Max more regularly than Emma since I saw him almost daily, I felt like a true friendship was beginning to develop with these two.

Just as I plated the scones for today in the front case, the bell over the door rang.

"Hello, Allyson!" Maggie's voice rang out. "Little Miss El slept like utter crap last night. Thank God she's adorable. Let's add an extra shot of espresso today."

"Ivy would tell you to thank the goddess," I called back as they came up the steps into the former nave of the church. "More to the point, I'm on it, Mama."

Humming, looking over what I'd already set out for their beverages, I grabbed the portafilter and set about making two honey oat milk lattes. The two of them fluctuated on their beverages of choice occasionally, but this had been their go-to for a few months. Maggie was exclusively nursing Ellen, and when she'd been a newborn, she'd noticed that El wasn't tolerating dairy in Maggie's diet well, so she'd cut back for a few months. Now she wasn't as strict with her diet as El's digestive system had changed, but the drink had remained a favorite.

I turned my back to the two of them as I got the machine to work, churning out their beverages. The hum relaxed me as did the smell of the espresso. "There are fresh chocolate chip scones if you want them. Serve yourself."

Milk steamed, I assembled the drinks, humming along to Van Morrison's "Days Like This" as I did, swaying in place. Turning back to the counter, beverages in hand, I jumped.

"What the literal hell?" I croaked, placing their drinks on the counter before I could drop them.

Emma and Maggie both howled with laughter from their place on either side of...

"Um, is that Jason Momoa?"

"Hilarious, right?" Maggie grabbed her coffee with both hands, cradling it as she brought it to her lips. She took a huge whiff. "Ahhh, Allyson. You are a maestro."

"Should that be maestra?" Emma asked, grabbing her coffee and taking a sip.

"We're in the twenty-first century. One would think

we'd move past this gender binary at some point," Maggie grumbled.

"Happy to have that convo," I interrupted, "but can we talk about why you two are carting around a six-foot-tall cardboard cutout of Jason Momoa?"

Emma laughed and swung her arm around it. "Doesn't it remind you of Max?"

A snort escaped. Yeah, her fiancé did resemble the actor. "Sure. Does that explain anything?"

"Well, Max is concerned about you," Emma began. I noticed her voice was the one I'd heard used during story time with preschoolers, like she was trying not to spook anyone with any sudden movements.

No worries here—I wasn't easily spooked—though I knew why Max was likely concerned. Sweet, but I didn't really want to delve into it. Maybe the innocent route was the way to go. "Why would he be concerned?"

"Because although I'm the one with a four-and-a-half-month baby who likes to throw a rave around three in the morning, you're the one who has been walking around with a pair of dark circles under her eyes. What gives, lady?" Maggie asked between long drags of coffee, sighing happily after each one.

I gestured at the scones and nodded toward a grouping of chairs near the counter. I was going to be present this morning, no multitasking allowed. The three of us headed that way, Maggie carrying a plate of scones and her coffee, Emma her coffee and the cardboard cutout, and I brought up the rear.

Sinking into the nearest armchair, I started with the elephant in the room. "So a giant cardboard cutout of Momoa is to help me how?"

"To be fair, we did overnight it from Amazon two nights ago after a few drinks." Emma shrugged.

"I really used to have better tolerance," Maggie muttered. "Had to pump and dump that night, not something I'm willing to do often. Breast milk is gold."

I nodded like I was following along, which was only partially true. "Continue."

"Well, Max had told Emma here that he's been on you to get some help. Then apparently, he saw Logan cleaning up the café out at the park when you were snoozing on the couch, so he shared that with us, and one order later, we had a stand-in Max for you here in town. We figured it would be a visual reminder to have some damn boundaries and maybe hire some more staff." Maggie sat back and kicked up her feet on the coffee table, looking pretty proud of herself.

"To be honest, this might have sounded a bit better after three blueberry margaritas," Emma mumbled.

"No, no, let's go with this." I mean, this was kind of amusing and, weird as it was, very kind. "So Flat Max will be my visual reminder here in town—"

"Flat Max?" Maggie asked.

"You know, didn't you have Flat Stanley in elementary school?" I asked.

"Ah, yes, continue," Maggie said.

"So I've got Flat Max, a la a cardboard Momoa, in town. What is my reminder out at the park? Chris Hemsworth? Ryan Reynolds? Tom Holland?"

"Huh-uh. Let's go Flat Ryan," Maggie said with a wicked smile.

"Well, you've got the real Max when you're at the park," Emma pointed out. "We figured he was the reminder out there."

"Not opposed to a Hemsworth. Just saying."

"No one in their right mind would be," Maggie replied.

"Truth." I held up my cup, and she knocked hers against it.

Snagging a scone, I sat back. "Seriously ladies, thanks for thinking of me. I know I need to work on this, and I'm going to figure it out. I need a way to streamline some of the business. And that might mean promoting or adding more staff, but I need to make sure I can afford it. Even though we're just a coffee shop, I want to pay a living wage. Anything else is just bullshit, so I have to do some number crunching to figure out how that will look."

"That's why the people you have working for you are loyal, chickie." Maggie kicked my foot. "Well, that and your baked goods are to die for."

"Amen," Emma mumbled around her bite. "Remember my offer to get you some names and/or post something on the library's website."

"Thanks. Still pondering."

Behind us, the bell chimed again. I pulled myself out of the comfortable chair to move to the counter as I hear the former owner Lou's voice ring out.

"My, my, my, I'm liking the eye candy as part of the decor," she said, eyeing up Flat Max.

I shook my head as I took my place and faced Lou and a few of her gray-haired friends. "Morning, Lou. The usual?"

"You bet, sweetheart." Lou ogled Jason Momoa and then turned back to me. "Think they have one of Sean Connery?"

I glanced over to Maggie. "Look what you started."

Maggie's wide grin indicated how much she was enjoying this. "Lou, I'll look into it."

"Thanks, girlie."

The portafilter hissed, coffee began brewing, and while exhausted, I felt like I was right where I belonged, under the steady gaze of Flat Max.

Chapter 9

Head Full of Doubt

Logan

Charlie and I weaved down the trail with the afternoon sun slanting light through the trees, some of which were starting to sprout. I tossed a stick ahead of us to let him run off some energy. I'm sure my therapist would have something to say about the fact that I knew I wasn't living in the moment. She often told me that I needed to focus on where my feet were planted, not look ahead to the horizon or to days that I'd left behind. Was I on this trail, or were my feet three years in the past? Months in the future?

I think we all knew the answer to that.

Charlie knocked into me with the branch, not giving one damn where my mind was. Dogs were excellent at mindfulness. We could learn a lot.

I threw it down the path again.

A whistle from behind us had both Charlie and me turning to look back down the trail. Levi was heading our way at a good clip, and my dog was, as always, ecstatic to see one of the people he loved. The pup bounded toward him, hopping up to try to hug my brother the best he could.

"Thought you were meeting Allyson for a run." Levi shoved Charlie down and grabbed the branch to toss it down the trail for him.

"I am. We're meeting up at the mansion when she wraps up at the café for the day." I glanced at my watch. "I need to head back there in about twenty. But more to the point, why are you here and not on Interstate 57 headed home?"

Levi grabbed the branch from Charlie and tossed it down the trail again. "About that, how would you feel about a roommate for a few weeks?"

I came to an abrupt halt. "I'm sorry. What?"

Levi shrugged as he watched Charlie get distracted by some excellent scents on the trail. "Figured I could work here as well as I could at home. Maybe spend some time with you?"

I noted he didn't meet my eyes. My gut clenched. I hated the feeling that my family was still this worried about me. It was unnecessary. I mean, I knew I wasn't where we'd all consider healthy, but I wasn't depressed. It was just grief, and at times, it was still all-consuming. People say you need time, and that's true. But that makes it sound like after a certain time you're "over it." Nope. Never, or not as far as I can tell. I think it was more like you learned to live with it, as depressing as that sounded.

"I'm good, Levi. I don't need a babysitter."

"Not saying you do, man. It's just—" He looked uncertain, which wasn't Levi and made me pay more attention. "—I had fun this week. Forgot how much I missed your ass."

"It is a nice ass." Charlie sat in front of us, waiting for someone to grab the branch for him.

Levi did just that and nodded toward a bench on the trail. "Sit for a minute, and then we could head back?"

I glanced at my watch. "Yeah, I've still got a few."

Side by side, we stretched out our legs in silence. There was still a bit of a chill in the day. Warmer temps weren't really going to hit until the end of the month, and today was still in the fifties. I waited, not sure what to say to Levi. Luckily, he didn't make me wait long.

"I don't want you to think I want to stay here out of pity or that I'm worried. Hell, I should also mention this wasn't Mom's idea to stay. She doesn't even know I am considering it."

"You mean unlike your original visit which was absolutely not just because of Mom?"

He had the decency to look a little apologetic.

"What's calling you to Highland Falls?" Not that I didn't love my brother, but a suburb this town was not, and certainly not Chicago where Levi had always said he'd end up. I couldn't imagine why he'd want to be down here.

I felt him shrug, and I tried to get a read on him. Usually, it was effortless. Not today. My concerned-brother radar went up. I was worried that he wanted to stay because of me, but maybe there was something else going on. "Are you good?"

He cleared his throat as he rubbed Charlie's head. "Yeah, just feeling a little aimless. Freelance editing is great but pretty solitary. This winter was so dreary up north and, to be honest, lonely."

My brain quickly thought through our conversations over the past few months while I wondered if there had been any red flags. "Depression?"

"Nah, but lonely, nonetheless. And sometimes I feel like we've grown apart. I mean, I know we can't live together forever, but it's different, right? I wasn't in a place that I could uproot when Nola passed, even though I wanted to, but with my job now? It's possible." He kicked my foot with his own. "So is it cool if I hang down here a bit? Don't want to cramp your style, but as shocking as it sounds, I wouldn't mind some time with you."

I swallowed a lump in my throat. "Of course. My place is yours. You know that."

He nodded. Standing, he stretched for a minute, then reached out a hand to pull me up. "I'm going to head to Aurora and pack up a bag or two as well as my monitors and computer. If I get on the road now, depending on traffic, I might be back late tonight or tomorrow. Need anything?"

I pulled him against me for a hug. God, he was a pain in the ass, but also, I was grateful for some time together. It would be good for us if we didn't kill each other. "Nope. Safe travels."

Pulling back, he gave me a shit-eating grin. "Enjoy your run with Allyson. Don't think that part of my desire to stay here isn't also because I want to encourage this attraction to grow."

I flipped him off as he walked backward, laughing on the way to the trail.

"Maybe we can get some runs in while I'm here. I think I might be close to catching you here lately in speed and distance," he said walking away from me.

"In your dreams," I called his way, laughing. Looking to my pup, I called out to him so we could head back to the mansion.

* * *

I stared at Allyson's ass in front of me as she went around a narrow curve on the trail in a pair of leggings that should be illegal in at least forty states. Jesus. BA wanted to perk up, but I was in some running shorts and a long-sleeved top that wouldn't disguise shit, so prayers were sent upward that I could keep it in check. As the path opened up, she slowed down to run by my side and I was able to focus on the woods instead of her body while wondering how it would look under me. Above me. Beside me.

Good Lord, had I mentioned it had been a while?

"We haven't talked much since Levi showed up. Is everything okay?"

Allyson's conditioning had improved drastically since we started training together. She could easily carry on a conversation as we ran, which was something I had mixed feelings about. I liked getting to know her better, but that didn't help my budding attraction. It made it worse. There was no question about it. I had a head full of doubt when it came to this woman. Where on earth was this going? Anywhere? Did I want it to?

"Yeah. He went back to Aurora today to bring some stuff down here. Said he plans on working remotely from my place for a few weeks, I think."

"You think he's working remotely, or you think it will be a few weeks?" We leaned into the small hill we were headed up as we rounded the bend to take us back to the mansion.

"A few weeks."

"Can I ask why?" She stretched out her stride as I did as we came out of the trailhead and increased our speed for the last quarter mile up the trail by the meadow.

I ran alongside her until we reached the end at the pond. As we stopped, she automatically reached up to rest her hands on the back of her head to catch her breath. We walked, as always, around the pond toward the mansion and the coffee shop where I knew we'd grab water and, if I was lucky, a leftover baked good or two.

Allyson interrupted my food fantasy. "It's okay if you don't want to talk about it."

I turned to look at Allyson. Her face was flushed from the run. "Sorry, I was lost in thought as to the possible baked goods waiting for me in the café."

She grinned and looked at me with her nose scrunched up. "Um, I believe you've had a scone already this morning."

I fought the urge to kiss the tip of her nose. "That was at eight this morning, and we just ran ten miles. I think I've earned a muffin."

"Well... I don't want to break the contract I signed—it's super official on a napkin and all—but I *did* try out a new recipe for a caramel cinnamon roll, and I think there were a few left."

It's quite possible I growled.

Allyson tilted her head to the side. "So if I give you a cinnamon roll, might you be willing to talk?"

"Yes, but my brain cannot form any more words until I have food in my belly."

She reached forward to tap my abs, and prickles of electricity seemed to radiate from her touch. Damn.

If Allyson felt anything, however, she didn't let on. She just looked at me with an impish grin. "Don't want to add to the belly you've got going on with my cinnamon rolls."

I gave her a look that belied my shock as I lifted my shirt. "Um, what belly is this you speak of, ma'am?" Was I doing it just to see if I got a reaction? Maybe. What would I do about said reaction? Likely nothing and continue to live like the coward I was.

Allyson's finger reached out to graze my skin, heating a path of need everywhere she went. "Wow, an honest to goodness V in the flesh. I thought these were the mythology of the romance books I read."

I slapped her hand away—playfully, I hoped. It was either that or tackle her to the ground, and I wasn't ready for that. "Feed me, woman."

"Caveman. I like it." She nodded toward the door to the café, and I followed her.

"So Levi is headed back..." She moved behind the counter and slid a plate my way with a thing of beauty on it —a cinnamon roll that was nearly the size of a grapefruit dripping with caramel sauce. "Water, Gatorade, or coffee?"

"Water," I said and picked up the roll. Taking a bite, I let out a moan. That was unreal. "I hope this is going to become a permanent part of the menu."

"Debating. They are rather time-consuming."

"Worth it." I wiped off my mouth and set the roll down. I wanted to savor it but was tempted to devour it in a few bites. "Levi says he's coming down because the winter was long and a bit lonely."

"But you don't believe him?" Allyson slid my water in front of me and took her own bite of her roll.

A drip of caramel was at the corner of her mouth. A large part of me wanted to lick it off. Mixed feelings, party of one. BA put in his vote for a taste, but I ignored him. Smaller brain and all.

Moving on.

"Part of me does, and that makes me worry about how he's doing. Another part of me thinks that he and my parents don't think I'm over Nola's death."

Allyson's eyes met mine. She set down her roll and took a breath. She looked to me with a soft expression. "I'm sorry if this is insensitive, but I don't think you get over losing someone you love, especially losing them when it was so unexpected."

An ease settled over me at the idea that she'd understand. I cleared my throat. "Are you talking from experience?"

She looked toward the window to the pond and shrugged. "I don't mean I've lost anything compared to what you have, just my grandma. We were close, and I felt like she was one of the two that understood me in my family. Now I have Maeve who is there, but I miss her. Still, not the same."

"Not a contest, babe."

"*Babe?* Are we friends with pet names for each other now?"

Well, fuck, that slipped out. "Did you want to be?"

She pursed her lips, tapping them with her finger. "Hmm, the possibilities for you are endless. I'll need time."

"Take all the time you need." I picked up my roll for another bite.

"Roly-Poly? Muffin Man? Scone Slayer?"

I simply shook my head. "You think you're pretty funny, don't you?"

"Sure do, *babe.*" She stared down at her cinnamon roll, unrolling a piece before looking up to meet my eyes. "Can I just say that you're welcome to talk about Nola anytime?"

Emotions threatened to overwhelm me, so I went for levity as I cleared my throat. "I believe you just did."

She took a bite off the end of the piece in her hand. Damn, her lips wrapped around that were not what I needed right now. "Avoidance, Logan. If you don't want to talk about her, just say it. I'd never push you."

I looked down at my roll. Ashley had been encouraging

just this in my last session. But there was no way in hell I could do this looking at Allyson. I'd get lost in her eyes and break down. Picking up my plate, I nodded toward a pair of leather armchairs facing the pond window. "Can we sit?"

The expression she gave me was guarded, clearly because she had no idea where I was going with this. *You and me both.* But to her credit, she simply nodded, grabbed her plate, and followed me.

As we settled down in the chairs, I chose specifically to look out the window even though I could feel her gaze on me to my left. I didn't want to be rude, but this was the only way I'd be able to say anything.

I took a breath and began. "Remind me. What have I told you about Nola?"

Allyson's voice was soft and surrounded me in warmth. "Not much. Just that you were married for ten years, and she died in a car accident three years ago."

I leaned up to put my plate on the coffee table in front of me. I'd lost my appetite. Sitting back, I rested my feet on the table and closed my eyes, going back. "I met Nola in college our sophomore year. Levi actually met her first and brought her home, saying he'd found my future wife." I snorted for a moment, remembering his drunk ass had been at a party and met a girl, brought her home—not to hook up but because he thought she was perfect for his brother. Jesus. It was one of Nola's favorite stories when we met people. "The two of them were in the same major, and he'd spent the night at a party getting to know her, for me."

"Excellent wingman, even if you weren't with him."

"Exactly. And from that point, we were inseparable. She was beautiful, kind, and funny as hell."

"So perfect, in other words." Allyson's words were soft, but I heard them.

I rolled my head to the side to meet her gaze. "No, no one is perfect. She had flaws, just as I do."

"But gone too soon." Allyson's hand squeezed my forearm as her eyes filled with tears, mirroring my own.

"That she was." I looked away.

"Were you up by Starved Rock?" Allyson knew I had been up there before Max, and ironically, we'd both ended up here.

"Nah, by that point we'd made our way to the suburbs. I was doing some work at a park up there while getting my master's in business."

"That's good that you were at least by your family when it happened..." Her voice trailed off.

"Boston." My voice was a whisper.

"You were in Boston?"

Mutely, I nodded. I had no more words. I wanted to tell her about that day. I wanted to share the guilt that was eating me up inside when I let it out of its cage. I wanted to share my fear about our upcoming race. But I could say none of it.

And somehow she knew I was struggling. Instead of pressing or saying anything, Allyson's hand slid into my own. She squeezed mine, and we sat there, watching the sun come down over the trees and pond as I wondered if I'd ever be able to think of Nola without my heart being torn in two.

Chapter 10

Broken Promises

A*llyson*

I glanced once again at the running watch that Logan had required me to purchase just a few months ago though the time hadn't changed since the last time I looked. Where in the hell was he? The race was starting in thirty minutes, and we were supposed to meet at the start line, near the blue dog statues. Was he here? Nope.

I searched the crowd milling around. My nagging worry was becoming ever present. He'd been different this week. Somewhat distant. Levi was back, so I figured I was seeing Logan less because of it. But even our runs were more quiet than usual.

Last Sunday at the café he'd cracked open a bit of his past. I thought it was a good sign, that we could build on it, and I made sure not to push for more. And yet. Crickets. Did I understand it? No, I did not. Did I ask him or do anything about it? That would also be a no.

On a daily basis I sang the word *friends* in my head over and over as a reminder to myself. I mean, I was a fun person. I was kind. I was a catch. Did he call me babe? He sure did. Did we have an embrace a time or two? Yep. Longing and/or heated looks? Check and check. Did it mean anything? Nope, apparently not. And that was fine. I wasn't pushing. If he wasn't ready, he wasn't ready.

However, my parents had already done a number on my self-esteem in my lifetime. I didn't need to analyze this relationship a million times a day. We were friends times a million. I delighted in our relationship. I treasured it. It was enough.

Sure. Moving on.

All of this was to say, where in the hell was this man? I didn't have all the confidence in the world that I could do this race. I needed my cheerleader. Sure did. I wanted to do this race for me, but I felt pretty exposed out here watching all these people do a warm-up run of a mile. I'd been right; mileage bumper stickers abounded in the parking lot. Looking at the people around, it was like an advertisement for a REI store. And I'm sorry, a warm-up run of *a mile*? I mean, why waste that energy? There was a good chance I might need it later. And what in the hell was energy goo? Did I need that? What happened if I needed to pee on the course?

And thus I needed Logan. Damn it.

"Allyson," I heard my name and turned toward the voice. Coming toward me was Jake, Drew, and Logan.

A second glance told me it was Levi, not Logan. I looked beyond them, searching for the man.

Before I could find him, the guys reached me and Levi put a hand on my shoulder, bending down to look into my eyes. His own expression was indescribable. Regretful was the closest I could come.

"Allyson, I'm sorry. He isn't coming."

My gaze shot to him. "What?" Yep. Gut churn. I was going to puke.

Levi grabbed both my shoulders and got right in my face. "Breathe, Allyson. You've got this."

My eyes welled up as I met his warm brown ones that looked so much like his brother that I kind of wanted to punch him. Somehow, he knew I was *this close* to hyperventilating. "I don't, Levi. I really don't have this. I need Logan."

His hands came to cup my face as he locked gazes with me and took an exaggerated breath in, then out, then repeated. Before I even realized it, I was mimicking him. My lungs thanked him even if my mind couldn't escape the single thought of *where was Logan?*

"Sweetheart, you have this. Logan has told me several times that you were going to slay this race." He gestured to Drew and Jake standing behind him before continuing. "And the three of us will be right beside you."

I looked from Levi to the guys, then back to Levi before asking what I felt to be the pertinent question of the day. Dropping my voice to a whisper, I grabbed Levi's wrists, still framing my face. "But Levi... *Where is Logan?* Is. He. Okay?" My stomach churned, my heart raced, my armpits were sweaty, and I hadn't run a step.

Levi's expression was pained, which didn't help my worry one iota. "He texted to tell me that he couldn't make it. Allyson, you're just going to have to trust me that he'd be here if he could. It's not my story to tell, but I'm hoping like hell that he shares it with you later." Levi closed his eyes and took a deep breath before looking at me again. "He's trying, Allyson. I swear he is."

Well, hell. None of that seemed great. I vacillated

between being super pissed that he wasn't here and worried that there was something majorly wrong. Levi leaned forward to whisper in my ear. "Shove this shit to the side for the next few hours, Allyson. Logan would want you to rock this race. We're here to cheer you on too. You ready to kick some ass?"

He pulled back and met my eyes. I looked into his, wondering why I couldn't have a crush on this Traub brother. One day he'd make some person pretty lucky, but unfortunately my heart was drawn to his brother even if that was a no-go. Did I want to run this race? Not really. Was I going to anyway and then go find my friend and kick his ass while also checking on his emotional state? Yes times a million.

Taking a cleansing breath that Kristine and Kate at Nomad Yoga would be proud of, I looked at these three gorgeous men in front of me. "Well, gentlemen. Let's race. I sure hope one of you can double as a pack mule if we reach the back of the park on the second time through and my legs are out of gas."

Jake shook his head at me, and Drew laughed and gestured toward Levi. "This one has the biggest ass out of all of us. He can give you a ride if needed."

Levi appeared insulted. "I'm sorry, my ass is not big. And even if it is, how does that make me a better option to carry Allyson?"

"One, then she has somewhere to rest when you piggy-back her through the back part of the course. Two, Jake and I haven't even trained much. Who knows if we can finish either. And three..." Drew spun to show us his butt. "I mean, look at your ass compared to mine."

I marveled at the easy friendship that Levi was clearly developing with these two guys. I knew he'd met them before his impromptu temporary move to Highland, but it was good to see.

Levi stood back and actually seemed to assess Drew's backside while Jake stood there shaking his head. "Okay, man. I have to agree. My ass is bigger than your flat one."

"Hey—" Drew began to interject, but Jake held up a hand.

"Allyson." Jake gave me a serious look. "Don't listen to these bozos. You've got this. You've done the work. Now is the time to go out and have fun. All I want to say is don't let us hold you back. If you want to go on, do it. We'll catch you at the end."

I looked from one of these giants hovering easily a foot over me to the next. With a slight nod, my confidence began to grow. I had this. I did. My heart ached a little for the fact that Logan wouldn't be by my side, but that was a future-me issue. Right now I had to get my mindset where it needed to be to go run this race.

I had this.

With a nod to them, I leaned forward. "Okay, boys, let's do this. We need a team name."

Levi's eyes lost the sad look he'd had since he joined me as he rubbed his hands together. "Yes. I am here for this. Can we go dirty?"

"Hell, no. This is a small town, man." Jake shook his head. "We'd never live it down."

"So Big Unicorn Horns is a no-go?"

Levi waggled his eyebrows as I groaned and shoved the big idiot. "Dude, if you're talking about the horn in your shorts, how does that fit me as well?"

Levi shrugged with a good-natured smile. "I mean, we could be Big Unicorn Horns with a Couple of Coconuts..."

Laughter and head shakes.

Drew spoke up. "What about Kiss My Asphalt?"

"Fo Shoe?" Jake suggested.

"Blazing Glory?" Levi spoke up.

"I've got it," I said. "Sweaty Bettys."

Drew raised his hand. "Um, point of order. None of us are named Betty, and three are male."

"Doesn't matter. We're running this beast in honor of Betty White," I decided with zero idea where that logic came in, possibly a video I saw the other day on social media, but I was embracing it.

"That woman was a riot," Jake said. "You ever see her interviewed?"

"National treasure," Levi agreed.

"So it's settled?" I asked. "Hands in on three?"

The four of us stood in a circle and put our hands in. "One, two, three, Sweaty Bettys," we yelled and moved toward the starting line.

It was time to race.

The start was chaotic. While not as big as even the marathon was slated to be in a few weeks, there were still close to a thousand runners. I got caught up in the excitement of the start and quickly found myself ahead of my planned pace. In a few weeks, Logan had explained there would be pacers on the course to help you stay at a comfortable speed. Now my watch told the story, and I worked to slow down.

Much like our training runs, the first mile sucked, the ones after it a bit better. Levi, Jake, and Drew were excellent running companions. They cracked jokes when needed and kept my spirits up in general.

At the halfway point of the race, I'd been running for about an hour and was drenched with sweat but feeling good. My three companions and I were going strong as we ran around a giant statue that the park was known for, some type of Greek god that's worshipping the sun.

"Look, it's a giant cock," Drew huffed out, pointing to the statue.

I could feel Jake shrug on my right. "Not impressed," he huffed out.

"I mean, if that's to scale, maybe he's cold?" Levi said as we made the turn and headed back.

I shook my head. At least this race was anything but dull. And while my mind was still on Logan, I was beginning to believe I'd actually be able to finish this thing and, more importantly, the race coming up in a few weeks.

An hour later, I was on my on my back in the grass, looking up at a cloudless blue sky.

"Maybe we should have trained more," Jake moaned.

"I'm dying," Drew said to my right.

"I think I pulled a hammy." Levi spoke up from my left. "Or maybe a glute. Want to rub it, Sweaty Betty?" He attempted to kick my leg with his own, but instead dropped his leg into the grass as he whimpered.

"I did it," I whispered to myself, closing my eyes to soak in the feeling as I gripped my medal in my hand. "I actually did it."

The warmth of the sun left as a shadow hit my face.

"You absolutely did it, babe."

Unless Levi was now throwing his voice, that was Logan. My eyes shot open as I looked up to see Logan staring down at me.

"You're late," I scowled. "And I don't know if I'm speaking to you right now."

I moved between being supremely pissed while also noting that he looked like he'd lost his best friend.

Levi sat up. "Male Sweaty Bettys, our work here is done. Who's buying me a beer at the Homestead?"

Drew and Jake rushed to get up and head off with Levi. As they were hurrying, or limping, away, Jake looked back and shouted, "If you two are still speaking when whatever's going on is over, come to the brewery when you're done. We're all meeting up."

Ugh. Did I want to celebrate with my Sweaty Bettys? Yes. Did I want to be with people after being in this mass of humanity today? Not really. I hazarded a glance at this fool still hovering above me as I debated if I even wanted to be in the same zip code as him. Quite frankly, that remained to be seen.

Logan looked up to meet Levi's gaze. "I'll keep you posted."

Levi pointed two fingers at himself, then to Logan, then pointed at me. Then he addressed his brother. "Talk. I don't want to see your ugly mug until you do."

Logan nodded.

I watched all this from my prone vantage point. Logan looked miserable. I felt a smidge of concern mixed with a whole lot of irritation with a dash of exhaustion. It was an interesting combo. But what were my thoughts about this mess of emotions filling me up? No stars given; I didn't recommend.

Meeting my gaze, he held out a hand. I grabbed it and was hauled up, only to crash into him instead of standing steady on my own two feet.

"Warning, my legs are jelly." I spoke to his chest where my lips were smashed. I was too tired to even feel excitement, which, quite frankly, was saying something.

He tugged on my ponytail so that I had to tilt my head. "Want to walk a bit and get some feeling back into them?"

His expression was abashed, not one I was used to seeing on him.

"Only if you're prepared to carry me." I only spoke the truth. We'd done many training runs racking up at least thirteen miles, if not more. Today, however, that faster pace to start the race was biting me in the ass now. Lessons learned.

"Fair, fair. How about we walk to the café? I'm assuming your stuff is there." He gestured in front of himself for me to go first.

I nodded. "Yeah, Andy's working."

We walked through the dwindling crowd of runners that were lingering about. The midmorning sun was warm, but not hot, thank goodness. I looked at families gathering in small groups over the meadow and caught sight of Jake's soon-to-be stepdaughter, Addie, sprinting to his open arms with her mom, Ivy, laughing behind her.

Addie had cheered us on at multiple spots along the route. She'd been dressed in a rainbow tutu, polka-dot leggings, tall rain boots, a unicorn hoodie, and heart sunglasses. She really hadn't needed the pompoms to draw attention to herself, but they'd been there as she encouraged Levi, myself, and her boys each time we passed her. Ivy and Kate, Drew's fiancée, did their best, but they were completely overshadowed by Addie in every way.

I knew Kate and Ivy through Emma and Maggie. Part of me wanted to go to the brewery and chat with them. Another part of me wanted to go home and stand in a warm shower until it was time for bed.

Logan brought me back to the present. "So..." He seemed unsure as to where to start.

I fought an eye roll. "Seriously? You're going to make me ask?" I murmured under my breath as I led him up the path to the café and in the door at the back. I waved Andy away and moved to make my own ginger-and-honey tea.

"Your cardinals are looking kick-ass." I looked at the filled-in birds on her tattoo sleeve. Her recent appointment had the sleeve nearing completion.

"Thanks," Andy said as she wiped down the counter. "How was the race?"

"I finished, so I guess we can call it a win," I said as I got my drink together.

"More than I did today," she said with a wide smile. "We've had a lot of customers grabbing sandwiches and pastries to go. Folks think it's too nice of a day to spend it indoors." She gestured at the empty café.

"We're going to sit a bit. Let me know if you need anything."

"You're off today, lady. Relax."

Logan grabbed a muffin and nodded over to what was quickly becoming our spot near the window. I followed him and curled up in the armchair, bringing both hands to cup my tea as I took a sip and worked to relax.

Clearing his throat, Logan picked up from where he'd left off. "So... I owe you an explanation."

I interrupted, needing to get this off my chest. "I've been thinking—did I push you into this? Did you not want to train with me? Maybe I read you wrong. If so, I'm sorry." I'd had some time to think as I ran thirteen miles this morning, between the comedic acts that ran alongside me, and had landed on wondering if I wasn't the person that fucked up.

Logan took a deep breath and dove in. "Nola died when I was training in Boston for the marathon. She was hit by a drunk driver while driving to the store to get me some fuel because I'd forgotten to pack what I needed." He laid out the words in a clipped manner, like they hurt to even give voice to.

I took a breath to process, then moved to set my tea down. Before I could even process what I was doing, I found myself kneeling between his legs. I took the muffin and moved it to the coffee table behind me.

Logan stared beyond me out at the pond. His eyes were scarily vacant.

"Logan."

He looked to me, and his expression broke me. The turmoil. The guilt. The grief. It was all there to be seen, walls down, vulnerability out in the open.

"I know, Allyson. Deep down I *know* that it's not my fault. But that's here." He tapped his head. "Not here." He tapped his chest. "I haven't raced since that day. Hell, it took a while to even run again, but I needed that for my mental health, so I made it happen. But racing"—his voice cracked—"seemed like a selfish thing for me to do when, if I hadn't been training for the marathon, if I hadn't sent Nola to get supplies I should have packed, she'd be here."

A tear tracked down his cheek. Then another and another. I leaned forward to wipe them away.

His gaze locked on mine, and it was like I could see to the depths of his soul. Was it my place to have this conversation? Well, if not me, who? Knowing what I knew about Levi, I was willing to bet I wasn't the first to try, but dammit if I didn't want to be the one that finally got him to let it go.

I cradled his scruffy beard-covered jaw with my hands and brought our foreheads together. Looking deep into his eyes, I spoke from my heart. "Hear me now, Logan Traub. I didn't know your Nola. But I know you. I know the kind of woman you would have married. And I know she'd be kicking your ass for carrying this guilt that is *absolutely not yours to carry.*"

His voice was barely above a hushed whisper. "Ally, I know you're right. Truly, I do. But why can't I let it go? I wanted to run with you today, but I woke up with a pressure on my chest and guilt gnawing its way through my gut like I was betraying Nola even by considering coming to the race. I didn't want to detract from your day; you've worked so hard. But then I went and broke my promise to you, and it felt even worse."

"Do you think Nola would want you to race?" I wished Levi was there to let me know if I was on the right track. I was talking about a woman I'd never known, for Pete's sake. But I was certain she would be pissed as hell about the half-life that Logan was insistent on living.

"Yes. Without hesitation, yes." His gaze didn't waver.

My fingers were itching to caress every inch of this beard I held in my palms, but I held firm. "Would you have answered that way a year ago?"

He closed his eyes against a clear wave of emotions as another tear escaped. My thumb caught that one too. "No, I wouldn't have," he said in a whisper.

"Look at that, my friend. You're making progress. And quite frankly, being rather hard on yourself." My voice caught as I told him what he must already know. "Logan, if you had told me about Nola earlier, I would have been more sensitive to you. I wouldn't have pushed you to race—"

"You didn't push me to race. Hell, Allyson, I'm the one that convinced you to sign up and then bailed." He sat back, my hands dropping to his thighs, and hung his head.

"No, no, Mr. Traub," I chastised him. "Not acceptable. You've been an amazing training partner. And if you still want to run the marathon with me, we're doing that. And I will help in any way I can to pay tribute to Nola along the way. You've got this; we've got this. Do you hear me?" I stood up and put my hands on my hips, hoping he knew that I meant business.

Logan stood too, meaning I had to take a step back to look up. "You forgive me?" His voice trembled but had a note of hope.

"Of course I do. You fucked up, but I understand why."

He moved in a flash, sweeping me into a full-body hug where my feet left the floor. "I'm so damn sorry, Ally. I promise not to flake again."

I buried my nose in the crook of his neck, soaking in the feeling for just a moment, pretending we were more than we were. "It's fine, I swear," I murmured.

He pulled his head back, studying my face as my heart hammered out a steady beat. Was this happening? Was he ready? Was I?

My answer came as he lowered his mouth, brushing my lips with his as sensations raced through my body on a runaway path to my core. I held on to him tightly, trying to buoy him with whatever strength I could. He brushed his mouth against mine again, nibbling on my lower lip, before dropping his head to mine. We stood, locked in the embrace, soaking in the feel of each other in a slow dance that had no movement.

I inhaled his scent, feeling both at home in his arms and heartbroken for all that he had confessed.

A throat clearing behind me stopped my racing thoughts, as it did Logan's suddenly rigid body when he lifted his head from my own.

"I think we might need some introductions, Logan." A woman's voice floated from the door.

"Mom?" Logan croaked.

Well, hell. Logan's mom? The person Levi had purposely made certain wouldn't see me on the video call because she would see too much into it? The reason Levi visited because their mom was worried about Logan? The person that Logan didn't want worrying about him or she'd move in and bake so much that he'd gain ten pounds?

How on earth did I help this situation?

Chapter 11

Web of Lies

Logan
    I'd looked over at the door and wondered if I was in some type of wonky dream. A few blinks as well as the solid feel of Allyson against my body told me I was fully awake, though this might be more akin to a nightmare. My mom and dad were standing inside the café door with my brother behind them, who was grinning like he was preparing to watch a show, and all I wanted to do was return to what we just started. I knew damn well that if given time to rethink this situation, doubts would have a way of creeping in.

Damn.

Levi mimed eating some popcorn and tipped his head in my direction as if to say *game on.*

I thought he had been headed to the Homestead. I wondered where he'd met up with these two, because God help him if he'd known they were coming and neglected to share with me.

Mom was on the move, and my dad trailed her to me,

shooting me a look that let me know I'd stepped in it. Big time.

No shit, Dad. Clearly Mom wasn't down with witnessing me embrace a woman she knew zero intel about, much less kissing her, though that wasn't much of a kiss, to be honest. Not that Mom would be mad if she thought I was moving on, but she'd be pissed as hell if she thought I was holding out on her. And hurt, which would be the worst.

Several scenarios raced through my head as I debated what would be best to reassure Mom that nothing was going on, have a nice visit with her and Dad, and then get them headed the hell home before she upended my life with her concern. I was just deciding to go with the old standby, the truth, when she reached my side.

"Now, Logan, we would have been here earlier, but the construction on 57 was not to be believed." She stood there with her neck cranked up to look in my eyes with her hands on her hips like some superhero that had dropped down in the café. Unlike her personality, Mom was small. She, like Allyson, hovered just over five feet. Levi and I got our height from Dad.

Mom's gaze shot to Allyson, still in my arms because apparently my body had malfunctioned, and I had no idea what to do with this entire situation.

"Um, Mom, did I forget about this visit?" I lowered Allyson to her feet because that was the first step to untangling myself from this mess, I told myself.

My dad coughed to cover what I was certain was a laugh. Not helping, old man. I glared in his direction, and he proceeded to raise an eyebrow in response.

"No, we didn't tell you. But where else did you think we'd be when we heard you were signed up for a half marathon today? How did it go?" She beamed at me, then looked to Allyson who stepped back from our embrace. "And who is this?"

Allyson looked from my expression of what I'm certain was panic, to my mom. Shit. It had to be Levi who told her about the race. What the actual fuck was he thinking? She was going to move in and never leave when she heard about today. I worked to swallow my fear and face down Momma Bear.

With an apologetic glance toward Allyson—she was going to want to run far as possible from this circus for sure —I gestured from her to my parents to get this part over with. "Mom, Dad, this is Allyson. She owns this café. Allyson, these are my parents, Linnie and Frank."

My mom looked like the cat who ate the canary, I'm sure seeing future grandbabies in just the mere presence of Allyson. Looked like I'd be crushing all sorts of hopes and dreams today. "Well, Logan, you didn't tell me you were seeing anyone *and* racing again!" She glanced over to my dad. "Frank, did you know?"

Hell. I knew it. "No, Mom, you see...," I started.

Allyson walloped my stomach. "Logan, you didn't tell your parents about us?" She slid her arm around my waist and squeezed before holding out her right hand to my mom. "So sorry, Mrs. Traub. It's lovely to meet you. And you too, Mr. Traub."

What was happening? I looked at Levi only to see him raise an eyebrow and give me a thumbs-up. I gave him a sarcastic look that communicated my gratitude—or lack thereof.

"Oh no, you darling girl. Linnie and Frank to you." Mom pulled her away from my side to give her a huge hug, rocking her back and forth while making big eyes at me.

"Levi," she called to my brother. "Should I be mad at

you too for holding out on us?" She stepped back to allow Allyson to shake my dad's hand.

My dad, who I noted had a bigger smile than I'd seen on him for years and looked like he'd reverse aged since walking in the café. It was like a punch to the gut every time I realized how much stress they'd gone through on my behalf. It wasn't just me who'd been changed three years ago, but my whole family.

So often I'd just wanted to move past the trauma. To move on. To feel normal. And yet it felt like I was marinating in the grief.

Allyson stepped back to my side, sliding her arm around my waist again, and I was struck with the feeling that life *had* felt like that, but not lately. Interesting. That was something to think about.

"Sorry, Momma Bear." Levi's joy was clearly evident as he stepped forward to kiss our mom on the cheek. "Had to let you learn about Ally here from Logan."

Did I growl when he said Ally? Judging by the looks he and Allyson shot me, I sure did.

I was in hell. That was the only answer.

"So Allyson, did you run today with Logan?" Mom had moved to stand by Dad with a glance at the bib number and medal Allyson still wore.

Levi glanced in my direction, conflict evident on his face.

He should feel bad, but now I had to deal with the fallout. "Well—"

"He couldn't," Allyson interrupted, undoing the safety pins pinning the bib to her shirt quickly like she was erasing all record of her race. "Logan strained his hamstring this week and needed to take it easy. So he sent Levi and our friends, Jake and Drew, in his place." I noted she didn't meet my eyes as she spun her web of lies and put her number facedown on the table like that was the end of the conversation. As she reached to take off her medal, I stilled her hands. She'd earned that, and I wasn't willing to let her toss her accomplishments aside because I didn't have my shit together.

Levi nodded as if to say he approved of her fabrication. Hell, I did too. Not that I wasn't a fan of honesty, but right now we were so far from anything that resembled the truth, what was one more fib? And if it reassured my parents and got them to have a quick visit and then hit the road, what was the harm?

Well, one could say it wasn't great that I was quickly growing to enjoy Allyson's body anywhere adjacent to my own.

Yeah, I know. We'll work on that realization later. Back to the present situation.

"Logan, you're hurt?" Momma Bear was unleashed as she scanned me. "You know, running is a great sport, but look at how often you two were injured during cross country and track when you were competing. All those miles just wear on your body, and you don't have athletic trainers looking out for you anymore. Do you think you should see a doctor? Do you need treatment?"

Yup. She was in full protect her cubs mode.

"Mom, I'm great." I fibbed. "Just needed to take it easy this week."

"Hmm." She looked like she was debating if she should just call my old doc and get me in. Really, Mom was awesome. She and Dad were not what Maggie Sullivan called helicopter parents that Maggie had to deal with at our local middle school. Our parents had let us figure out a lot on our own, but when they were worried about us,

Linnie tended to go into overprotection mode. My dad typically sat back and watched from a distance, only intervening if needed.

Hence my concern that she and Dad would be moving in and filling my freezer with meals if she knew I bailed on the race today. Jesus, what a mess.

"Seriously, Mom, I'm good. I'll be running next week so we can get back to training for Allyson's marathon in May." The words were out of my mouth before I'd realized what I'd done.

"Frank, did you hear that? A marathon." Mom was breathless with excitement, her eyes shining with joy. "Logan, you're running a marathon again?"

Dread filled me up. I'd agreed to train with Allyson all the way until the race, but I hadn't fully committed to running the marathon with her but left that option open as a possibility. Hell, I'd thought it had been a big step to run the half, and we all saw how well that worked out. Still, what was one more lie in the scheme of things? "Yep. Super pumped. So you and Dad want to get some lunch before hitting the road home?"

I saw Levi turn his back to us while his shoulders shook with laughter. Maybe I wasn't being subtle, but Linnie Traub didn't do subtle.

Dad decided to drop the truth bomb. "Sorry, son, you're stuck with us this week." He shrugged like he was apologetic, but not really. "With Levi coming down here, your mom wanted to check in on you two." His expression was the one I saw on my brother often. He was not sorry at all and enjoying this.

"Are you two crashing at my place?" My mind reeled a bit. Levi was already there. I mean, there was another spare room, but I needed some space or Mom would take over. A week? Panic flooded my veins. And they thought I was dating Allyson? Should I just tell them? I should tell them.

"No, we booked the carriage house in town for the week," my mom said, moving to stand next to Dad. "We thought we could give you a little space and spend some more time in this lovely town. You haven't had us down much, and from Levi's descriptions of the brewery, deli, bookstore, and more, we thought we were missing out."

My glance to Levi was filled with my thoughts on all that he'd shared with Mom. His reply came with one look: *not my fault, bro.*

Moving on.

Mom gave me a pointed look before continuing. "And if I'm being totally honest, we were worried about you. I know you think I worry too much, but one day you will understand. But now that we know about Allyson, I feel so much lighter and am doubly glad we booked the Airbnb. You certainly don't need your parents invading when she's over for the night."

Hell. I couldn't tell her the truth. We'd just have to make it through this week, and then in a month or so, I'd just tell them it hadn't worked out and Allyson and I'd stay friends. Maybe it would be a good thing. She'd think I was back on the dating scene, and they could stop worrying. However, that meant navigating this week with my parents who, unfortunately for us all, were pretty sexually progressive and didn't have much of a filter while doing this dance with a woman I was fighting a losing battle of attraction against. Kill me now. Allyson's shoulders were shaking with laughter she was clearly trying to hold back. That was good, right? Hell, we'd just kissed and now, well, I didn't even know what now was.

"The Homestead," Levi practically shouted. All eyes

swung his way as I wondered if we were now just throwing out random asides.

"Son, are you okay?" Mom asked.

Levi gave me a look that told me to get with the program. "I mean, some of Logan's friends and their families were gathering there after this morning's race. We could head over and get something to eat."

Yes. More people, less focus on all that I wasn't ready to address. I nodded at Levi to say that I got what he was putting down. "Yeah, do we all want to meet there in twenty? Mom, Dad, do you think you can find it?"

"I'll ride with them," Levi interjected. "Jake picked me up to come here, so I don't have a car."

There was a flurry of action as my parents kissed and hugged Allyson and myself, Levi whispering that I owed him—I reminded him that he was the reason they were here—and then within minutes, blissful silence descended as Allyson and I stared at each other with expressions that asked what in the hell just happened.

Allyson sank down in one of the armchairs we were still standing by before she could speak, so I joined her.

"So that was my parents."

She nodded, her fingers on her lips.

My voice softened. "And we kissed."

She looked over at me with a soft expression. "Yep. I was there for that."

"Was that okay?" I hesitated, not sure what to say, but not wanting to lie. "I'm not sure what that means yet."

She reached a hand to me and squeezed mine before taking it back to turn and sit cross-legged in the armchair and give me an appraising glance. "How about we don't put pressure on it to mean anything yet?" Her cheeks flushed. "Especially since I just made this so much more complicated." She took a deep breath. "You must think I'm deranged. I'm so sorry I just blurted out we were in a relationship."

She bit her lip, and I fought the urge to reach over and tug it. "Not deranged, but I'm curious as to why you did."

Her gaze left mine as she looked out the window. "I just thought about some of the stuff you and Levi said, especially the other night at dinner. I didn't want your mom to worry about you because I knew you wouldn't want that. I mean, I don't think I told you I thought about your mom the other day..."

"What?"

Allyson's freckles stood out against her reddened cheeks, and I was suddenly very interested in what she had to say.

"Last week when I stayed at your house. I woke up, and you and Levi were crashed on your couch. It was cute."

"I'm sorry. Are you saying I'm cute?" My heart was thundering in my chest. I mean, I'd really like drop-dead sexy, but we all have to start somewhere. More signs of any attraction toward me was something I was willing to take.

Allyson scrunched her nose up in the way I'd grown to love. "Cute. Like the two of you had drifted together as you slept and I—" She broke off whatever she was going to say, that flush I was growing to look forward to spreading down her neck as she slowly sank in the armchair.

"Nope, spill. You what?" I asked, mentally telling BA to stuff it.

"Ialmosttookapicture." She spit all the words out without a breath to be found.

I sat with that for a minute before a smile spread across my face. "Was that 'you almost took a picture?' Of me? And my brother? While we were sleeping?"

Allyson immediately sat straight up and looked at me,

remorse wiped clean off her face. "Yes. I almost took a picture because, while the sight of you two did threaten to make my ovaries explode, all I could think was that your mom, though I didn't really know her, would probably love the picture. I mean, I assume she would. I don't have a mom like that to speak of, but I'd assume if I had twin sons and, as adults, they still loved each other so much that they sought the other out while sleeping, I'd love it. So yes, I almost took a picture of you two. But I didn't. Because privacy." Her hands fluttered as she finished her speech.

"Let's go back to your ovaries almost exploding."

"Let's not. At any rate, I had no idea she and your dad would be in town for longer than the day or I wouldn't have said anything. I thought we'd pretend today and that would be that." Looking at me, she whispered as she deflated before me, "I can tell them I made it up."

I reached out and grabbed her hand. "You're a good friend. I don't deserve you after letting you down today."

"Seriously, Logan, after you explained what you were going through, I completely understand."

"Thanks, but I feel like you're letting me off easy." I squeezed her hand, not wanting to let it go, but I did before she noticed. "And don't worry about my parents because you're right, it will be easier, so thanks. Think you can fake an attraction to me for a week? How are your acting skills?" I mean, I knew I had this in the bag. It would be more work to hold myself back and remember it was all fake. One kiss didn't automatically equal more. I didn't know where any of this was leading, and that wasn't fair to her. Allyson didn't deserve someone who was still just contemplating dipping their toe in the dating waters. Attraction was one thing; I needed to be ready for more. Anything less was simply selfish on my part.

Allyson scrunched her nose at me. "I mean, I guess I can deal with the chore that would be pretending to like you."

"And how do you feel about braving the crew at the Homestead? If you want to go home and soak in your tub after your race, I totally understand." *Do not think about her in a tub, BA.*

"My place just has a shower, no tub. And I can do the Homestead for a bit. I really should thank Jake and Drew for running with me today."

"You sure?" I knew from experience she tended to avoid the crowds when possible. Running in one might have been enough for a day. She nodded, so I focused on the rest of her comment. "And what's with no tub? How do you deal with long runs, woman? You can borrow mine later if you want." Okay, now I'm just inviting images I'll never get out of my brain.

"Seriously?"

"Consider it my payment for dealing with my family."

"Your family is great, Logan. It is no hardship to spend some time with them."

"You say that now. Let's see how you feel in a day or two." My gut clenched. Let the games begin.

Chapter 12

Oscar-Worthy

Allyson

Walking into the Homestead, I braced. A spring Saturday could either mean crowds galore: a baseball game on TV with the volume jacked up as the patrons debated the merits of the closest teams to Highland—Cubs, Cards, or White Sox, whom were always sadly forgotten. Or we could walk in the door to blissful silence, which was my preference. Logan pulled open the door for me, gesturing for me to walk in, and I entered to... a low murmur.

I could work with that.

I needed the distraction of this crew, or the tingles in my lips and racing through my body *still* were going to drive me mad. I worked to remind myself that it was one small kiss; we were caught up in the moment. I mean, for the love of God, there wasn't even any tongue. I really needed to forget about it and focus on the task at hand.

It was lunch time on a Saturday, but as we'd seen at the park, the day was gorgeous. Judging by the empty tables, most people had decided against spending the day indoors.

Their loss, my gain of a brewery that was relatively peaceful. We wound through the dining room, heading toward the bar area where I could already see familiar faces. Levi had texted that they were swinging by their parents' rental first, but Jake and Drew's families had arrived ahead of us. They'd commandeered two lower tables. Addie, Ivy's daughter, was stationed at one end, coloring and talking to Maggie and Sully's baby Ellen, who was in a sling on Sully's chest. El was a whopping three months old, so I doubted she was getting anything from Addie's seemingly nonstop dialogue. Heck, the babe looked to be sound asleep, but that didn't stop Addie. As we drew near, I could hear her conversation.

"El, do you want pink or purple ponies?" Addie looked to Sully's chest where the baby didn't move or utter a peep. Didn't faze this girl; she continued on like they were communicating. "Rainbow stripes? Brilliant." She began coloring, with the tip of her tongue poked out in concentration.

Max Harp walked over at that moment with a beer in each hand, passing one to Sully. "Evolution," he said before glancing in our direction. "You guys want a beer? Daryl needed a few hours off, so Sully told him we'd take care of the bar. I've got you."

Logan looked in my direction. "Beer sound good?"

I noted that Maggie and Emma were sitting at a table with Kate and Ivy. Kate waved and patted a seat next to her. Jake and Drew had joined the other table with Sully and Addie, and now Max. I could handle this crowd, but they weren't the ones I was most worried about. That award went to Logan's parents who would be showing up at any moment with Levi. "I think it might be necessary to survive this afternoon with your parents," I said in a low voice.

Apparently, it wasn't low enough because eight sets of eyes swung my way. All the eyes of the adults, at any rate. Addie wasn't distracted from her rainbow pony that appeared to be drawn in a world where cupcakes fell from the sky. Sounds good. Could I go there? Now? And El, as we've already covered, slept because of course she did.

"Oops?" I said, looking at Logan. His reply was a shrug like he wasn't worried in the slightest about any of this. Actually, he was looking so much better than he had been at the café with his parents. When I'd spit out my inane comments about our relationship, it was because that pinched spot between his eyebrows had been back. When we'd first met, it had been there. He'd been tense those first few months, always, which I hadn't realized until he wasn't. Perspective of time and all.

Today, after he'd shared the horrible information about Nola and how she'd passed, that divot between his brows had returned. Heck, I was kicking myself because now that I thought about it, it had been back for a week or more. Probably because in training for this race with me, I'd inadvertently stuck him in the time of grief that he wasn't ready for.

So I'd publicly claimed him. And now here were our friends. And any moment Logan's parents were going to walk in with his brother, and these yahoos were going to have to deal with the fallout and support our asses like I knew they could.

Better to rip that Band-Aid right the hell off.

I took a deep breath and spit it all out. "Logan's parents are in town, and I kind of implied, or directly stated, that he and I are dating, and it's a long story, and we just need you all to roll with it and not make a big deal about any of this for the week they're here, and then everything will go back to normal, so hush about this, and act like this is typical for us all. Got it?"

Exhale. Sure. That's fine. Looking to Max, I replied to his earlier question. "And I'll take a Black Hole Sun, thanks."

I took a step toward the girls' table before Logan tugged me until my back was pressed against his chest. He dropped his mouth to my ear and murmured, "Way to spit it out there, Ally."

I waved a hand at him as he rested his chin on my shoulder. "They don't care." My heart was thundering in my chest. Ignore, ignore, ignore.

"Take a look," he said.

I turned my head from looking at him to our group and saw that everyone seemed to be frozen. "Um, are you all okay?" With a glance to Max, I noted that he hadn't moved. "Did you want me just to get the beer myself?"

Maggie spoke up from the girl's table. "So what you're telling us is that for the next week the two of you"—she pointed to each of us—"are going to pretend to be dating when his parents are around?"

Why was that so hard to comprehend? And quite frankly, could someone else take the focus of the conversation? This was making me feel itchy.

And yet I kept talking. "Yep. And they'll be here any moment, so let's wrap this conversation up. It's no big deal." I said this while working not to hyperventilate because my body was on fire at every single point of contact between Logan and me, but that was totally normal, and as long as I didn't act on it, I'd be one hundred percent fine. It would go away soon. Like a week from now.

Maggie turned to Emma, Kate, and Ivy. "This is going to be fun to watch."

The four of them put their heads together as I looked to Max. "Beer?" Max shook his head at me and then looked to Logan. "Boss?"

"Same as Ally."

"*Ally*," Emma, Maggie, Ivy, and Kate sang in unison.

Super.

"The party is here." Levi's voice boomed from the front of the brewery. Looking past the bar area and the dining room to the door in the corner of the former barn, I saw Levi and his parents headed our way.

Butterflies took flight in my belly.

Logan slid his hand to my hip, wrapping it around so that his palm was against my belly. The butterflies developed their own pulse, and I worked not to swoon like some nineteenth-century heroine.

"You okay?" His voice had texture; it was delicious. His lips moved against my neck as he spoke, causing goose bumps to rise in response. Yep. Sure. Fake relationship where we'd kissed and just decided to roll with it. This had disaster written all over it.

"You bet. I'm fabulous. Never better." I worked to make my voice sound light and carefree. Didn't work. I squeaked out my reply and ducked from his arms to find safety in the seat that Kate kicked in my direction.

"So doing okay?" Ivy asked, putting her hand on my own while Maggie positively cackled.

Maggie handed me a board book from her magical bag of crap. "Need this to fan yourself with?"

I ignored her and glanced to Logan only to see his heated expression locked on me. Dropping my head to my arms braced on the table, I mumbled, "I think I'm in trouble."

"She thinks?" I thought that was from Kate.

I tipped my head back to note that these four women had scooted into the table to form a sort of barrier around me.

Maggie shook her head at me like I should have known better. "Chickie, you are in for it. That man is looking at you like he's been starved in the desert for a decade, and you are the oasis in front of him."

It always amazed me that Maggie spent her days with middle schoolers; the woman's mind was positively dirty.

"Let's talk about anything else please," I begged. I couldn't delve into all that was this fake relationship between Logan and me. I didn't want to address the feelings I had. I didn't want to tell them about the hugs, small touches I craved, or hell, the barest of kisses that I couldn't get out of my mind. More than that, I didn't want to get in a position where I'd potentially have to say anything about Nola because I didn't know who Logan had told what, and that was absolutely not my story to share.

As a group, we looked over to Linnie and Frank. We had a short reprieve before we needed to be polite and say something to them. Linnie had plucked Ellen out of Sully's sling and was rocking with the sense of ease that could only be found in a woman that was born to be a mom. Frank was sitting next to Addie who was describing her illustration to the two of them. The rest of the guys were huddled around Logan, giving him shit I had no doubt. Levi glanced in our direction and gave me a thumbs-up. I'm sure I didn't know what that was about.

Maggie sat forward and said, "If you need a distraction, I have a great school story from Friday."

We all leaned in to hear what she had to say. I'd told her multiple times she should write her stories from the class-room down because they were magical, and she hadn't even been back from maternity leave for that long. Seventh graders were a trip.

"Well, you all know about how some romance authors have gone viral on social media with videos shared over and over, making sales of their books go through the roof?"

We all nodded. Heck, Emma ran a romance book club through the library in partnership with Ivy at the bookstore, and many of us were in it. We'd read several of the best sellers that had gained popularity through social media.

Maggie hesitated, letting the anticipation build, then she dropped the bomb. "It seems my students—current class and last year's crew—have seen the same videos the rest of the world has, and they've started reading them."

Whoa. Those books were, hmm, let's just say spicy. "Where are they getting them?" I asked knowing damn well that Maggie wouldn't stock them in her classroom library, nor would the school librarian. Not that they were about to police book choice, but YA romance was one thing; these were books for adults. I didn't want anyone at school to get in trouble for handing out books to the kids that weren't written for their age group. I looked to Emma.

She raised her hands. "I'm not here to censor book choice. If they come to the library and check them out, they'd be allowed to, though I might suggest some great young adult books first. That being said, we have such long waiting lists for the best sellers, I doubt they're from us."

"Oh, they're not," Maggie replied. "This is the best part. One of the eighth graders moved out of her locker and into her friend's. They've essentially set up a little free library in the locker of all the romance books that have viral videos. A few girls got the books from their moms. The locker number and combo is shared among the girls, and if you take a book you have to sign it and leave a Post-it note review in the locker." Maggie raised her brow with a satisfied expression, knowing what our response would be. "They also leave sticky note flags on scenes they love and annotate some of their thoughts into the book for the next reader."

"Ingenious," Kate said in a hushed awe.

"This is Gen Z, right?" Ivy asked. "Brilliant. I'm glad they're going to be taking care of all of us in our old age. Maybe they'll actually figure out everything the generations before them screwed up."

"I mean, I'd love them to read Nicola Yoon, John Green, or Jeff Zentner, or any of the other great YA authors, but I also love that your school has an underground market for books," Emma said with a satisfied expression.

"Can I fund their library?" I asked.

Maggie laughed. "Nah, they're well-funded as is. And they don't even know that I know. I heard through the school librarian, who was told in secret by one of the girls. I feel like more adults involved will spoil the specialness of what they've accomplished. Make sense?"

"Sure does. I love this." My heart was lighter thinking about these kids sneaking around, reading books, and laughing at the parts that would make many adults blush.

"So enough of a distraction?" Ivy asked, looking in my direction. "I want to know what you're going to do with that yummy man over there now that you have a week with a great excuse to rub up against him as much as you want."

"Ivy!" Emma looked scandalized, which was surprising considering she was friends with Maggie.

"Sorry. I'm still in my first trimester, remember? Hormones are not helping me," Ivy said with a shrug and a pat on her still-flat belly.

I groaned, remembering my situation. Zero stars, I didn't recommend. Hot-mess express, party of one. What made me think this was what Logan needed? I had a flash of insecurity that he hadn't wanted to go along with it but did because he'd already bailed on me once today. That wasn't right, was it? Looking at the women around me, I decided to try some of that vulnerability that I hated but likely was needed here. "Guys, what am I going to do?"

"Well, you're going to grab that fine man and climb him like a tree," Maggie started before she was interrupted with a call from across the bar.

"Allyson." Levi was looking at me with a mischievous expression. With one glance, I knew for certain that every gray hair in his mother's head was the direct result of his choices. Don't get me wrong; I enjoyed Levi, but this focus on me made me wish I was curled up on my couch at home.

Or in Logan's bath. Yum. Okay, wrong train of thought there. Let's get back to the matter at hand.

I looked up to find Levi by my side, pulling my chair out to lead me to the group of guys. Logan looked abashed, which didn't bode well for this convo. Levi led me right to his brother's side. Whatever had happened, Logan still wrapped an arm around me immediately. It felt protective, claiming, and I liked it too damn much.

Well, why not dive in and see what's what. "I was paged?" I asked.

Levi spoke before anyone else could get a word. "So Max and Logan were reminiscing about their time at Starved Rock State Park in the northern part of the state. Did you know they both worked there?"

"Um," I replied cautiously, wondering if whatever answer I gave was going to lead me down a path I'd rather not be on.

"Have you ever been there?" Linnie interrupted with no care as to what my answer was to the first question.

I looked from her to Frank, who had a twinkle that was also seen in Levi's eyes. Danger, *danger*, is what that twinkle was saying. Even so, I proceeded to shake my head in the negative.

Linnie squealed and clapped her hands. I looked from the Traub family to Sully, who had El back and was swaying as he patted her little butt in the sling to the rest of the guys to the girls who were beaming happily over at me to Logan over my shoulder, who whispered *sorry* as he squeezed my waist and slid his hand to my belly once again.

Focus, Allyson.

Looking at Logan, I said, "What am I missing?"

"We're going camping!" Linnie sang out.

My eyes widened as I refused to look away from Logan, keeping my gaze locked on his, anxious for anything that would explain what I was hearing.

He didn't keep me waiting for long. "My family loves to camp, and my mom decided that next weekend would be a perfect time to go to Starved Rock on their way home and that the three of us"—he gestured to himself, Levi, and me—"should go with. I believe she said it would be nice to get to know you better."

Camping. With the Traub family. When they thought Logan and I were a thing. Holy shit. I took a breath. And another one.

"This is awesome," Maggie called.

This would be fine. Surely, it would be fine. Right?

Chapter 13

Cozy Cabins

Logan

"See you tomorrow," I called out the door to my cabin, waving to my parents as they pulled away after the longest dinner known to man. I'm not exaggerating. Or maybe a little.

We'd spent a few hours at the Homestead. The guys had given me copious amounts of shit for this fake-dating thing I had going on with Allyson. I played it off like it wasn't rattling me to my core, which might have been the best acting job I'd ever done. Why? Because anytime the woman pressed up against me today, my heart had threatened to thunder right out of my chest, and BA perked right on up. Or, God forbid, when I'd made the foolish decision to get closer to her. I had no idea what I was doing here.

Levi had met my eyes every damn time. His laughter could likely be heard all the way to the state capitol. Somehow, the man knew the train my thoughts had hopped right on, and I wanted to hate him for it.

After things wound down at the brewery, my parents made it clear they wanted to keep the party rolling because they just had to get to know Allyson better. As a result, dinner plans at my place were made because they just assumed she'd be coming home with me. Dad and Levi took charge grilling some steaks; Mom and Allyson joined forces on some salad and roasted sweet potatoes. I took Charlie for a walk after being cooped up in the house for hours once Allyson assured me for the umpteenth time that she was fine and could hang with the family. However, walking into the kitchen and seeing the two of them cooking together? Gut check. Maybe I was the one who wasn't fine. Scratch that. I knew I wasn't.

Dinner had been filled with highs and lows. Well, Allyson had rocked it. I was the weak link, wanting to run away and avoid any and all parts of this awkward situation. Levi's ongoing glances told me he was analyzing my mental state. I knew he'd figure it out with no lengthy conversation needed, but that left me at a loss as to what to tell Allyson. The woman had willingly entered—hell, created—this scenario because she wanted to protect me. She was acting from a point of friendship, but I know she hadn't bargained on a week of entertaining my family followed by a camping trip. I mean, did she even camp? Nola hadn't been a huge fan, though she'd gone on the rare occasion. Not that I gave a damn if she hadn't loved it, she had encouraged me to go, and that had been enough. Allyson hadn't said no to the trip, but did she know she could? That I didn't expect it of her? I would never commit her to all this Traub-family togetherness my mom was so fond of. It could be a lot. We could be a lot. I had years of experiences to back me up.

Closing the front door behind me, I leaned back and took a deep breath for the first time since that morning. Dropping my head, I shut my eyes and soaked in the quiet.

"Beer?" Levi's voice invaded my peace.

Opening my eyes, I saw his head poked out from the opening to the kitchen. He spoke softly, a rarity, because Allyson had crashed on the couch about an hour ago. The woman was running on fumes on the regular. Add in her first half that she'd absolutely killed, and well, she'd hung on longer than I thought she would. It was somewhere during Dad's stories with Levi about their favorite trips to the Boundary Waters that I'd seen her eyes begin to droop. Mom had also caught it, and in true momma bear form, she grabbed a throw and covered Allyson while she gave me an assessing glance. That look spoke volumes without the need for words or a link with a twin. It said sit back, let Allyson lean against me, and take care of her. Now.

Linnie didn't mince words, even when she didn't speak them.

Now Mom and Dad were off to the Airbnb for the night. Allyson was curled up on my couch in the spot she'd nestled into when I got up, and Levi was standing in front of me with a beer and a look that meant he wanted to talk.

I nodded toward the deck that ran along the back of my cabin and followed him out the door. It was crazy that it was just under two weeks ago that I'd talked to Levi on the phone, leading him to come down to visit.

My Adirondacks were placed to give you the best view of the woods beyond the property. It was peaceful here, and the sky was starting to darken as we approached dusk. We stealthily made our way to the chairs with Charlie staying behind where he was curled up by Allyson's side. Dropping into the chair, I let out the tension that had filled me up all day or, hell, for the past few weeks.

Levi passed me a beer, and I took it with a tap to his can. We both took a sip as we stared off into the trees beyond. My heart rate was settling, and I felt myself relax.

"So," Levi started, and I worked to breathe through whatever direction he was going to take this conversation. "Your text this morning was telling."

Fuck. Yep. No holding back there; we were diving in. I'd woken up in a cold sweat knowing with complete certainty that there was no way I could run with Allyson today. I hadn't been able to face him and headed out the door in the opposite direction of the park to go on a run that had ended up being far more than the half marathon that I was supposed to be at, just to prove how screwed up my mind was. Mid run, I'd texted Levi and told him to go to Allyson because, while I couldn't be by her side, I also couldn't leave her alone. I knew he'd understand, and that he'd run enough that he'd be able to do it. I'd even messaged Jake and Drew. They didn't understand it all, but true to form, they'd shown up because I'd asked. That was Highland for you. You show up.

Levi didn't let me get away with that. His text was more to the point, that I would regret this. He was right. I knew that then; I knew it now. Yet I couldn't go. And I hated myself for it.

I cleared my throat and refused to admit it. "Yeah, how so?" I refused to look in his direction.

In my peripheral, I saw him pull out his cell to read from it. "Need a favor. Can't make the race. Allyson needs someone by her side. Please run it with her. Talk soon."

Swig. "Yep, I'm aware of my text. My fingers typed it."

He laid his phone on the arm of his chair face up. "You said please."

"I'm not an asshole."

He snorted, apparently disagreeing, but I wasn't going to dive into that.

"Spit it out."

He made me wait while he considered his words, taking another swig. "She means something to you."

Everything inside wanted to riot, to fight what he was saying. But I wasn't enough of an asshole to lie to Levi. One, he wouldn't believe me. Two, he already bailed me out today.

"I don't know where I'm at with this yet," I said because while it wasn't enough, it was a start.

"You essentially told me that ten days ago when I got to town." Levi wasn't mincing words, not that I blamed him. If the roles were reversed, I'd kick his ass if he didn't let me help him. And hell, he already told me how hard it was when he felt shut out of my grief.

So I bared my soul, or what felt like it. "I kissed her." My voice was barely audible over the breeze. Emotions choked my throat as the feelings of lust and betrayal went to war in my gut.

"Fuck, seriously? When?" His sarcasm was highly evident.

I sensed Levi's focus narrowed in on me, but I refused to meet his eyes. "You know, dipshit. You brought our parents in to be the witnesses."

He laughed and looked at the trees beyond. "Well, as I told you at the brewery, I had no fucking idea they were coming. I was shocked as shit when I saw them headed toward the café. And yeah, walking in to see that little tableau in front of us was a welcome surprise, but it's not like you guys were making out." His voice trailed off, then he knocked his beer into my hand. "You okay?"

I let my head rest against the chair as I closed my eyes and worked through my feelings. "Not exactly."

"Talk."

I worked on those centering breaths my therapist was so fond of. "I feel like I've betrayed Nola."

"Because there's been no one else?"

"No one else and no attraction to anyone else." The confession, or what the confession *didn't* say, hurt. I was attracted to Allyson, but I didn't know what to do about it.

"What does Allyson say?"

"She said that we didn't have to put any pressure on it to mean anything." It was both a relief and a punch to the gut when she'd said that. One, I'd felt relief. But two, when it felt like that kiss turned my world upside down, I needed it to mean *something*.

"Well, how about you follow her lead?" Levi was still facing ahead, giving me space in this conversation to feel like I wasn't under the interrogation lamp.

"Say more."

"Don't put pressure on yourself or Allyson to make this mean something yet, but maybe use this week when you *have to* be close to her because of our parents to see if your body—and mind—are telling you that you are ready for more. We already know the traitor in your pants is. And it seems like your lips are too."

I sat with that for a minute. Could I just relax and go with the flow? I was so tense, but maybe, just maybe, I could give myself the next eight days without analyzing my feelings to death.

I looked to Levi. "I can try."

"Here's to trying to accomplish the bare minimum." He raised his beer to mine. We clinked the cans and enjoyed the silence.

Thirty minutes later I was facing a sleeping beauty on my couch. Levi had headed upstairs to get some work done and told me I needed to bring her up to a bed. His suggestion had been my bed, but of course Allyson would be headed to the guest room, though the visual of her on my bed was one that was currently playing on repeat in my brain.

Charlie looked up as I moved toward the couch. Reaching out, I brushed her hair from where it had escaped her ponytail and hung in her eyes. She'd made a stop at her place before coming here since she'd been in her race clothes. Her choice of joggers and a T-shirt had messed with my brain. She hadn't dressed up to impress my parents or be anyone but the woman I'd been friends with for the past two years.

"Ally?"

She blinked several times before looking up to meet my eyes. "Logan?" She glanced around, noting, I was sure, the empty couch. "Oh my gosh, I nodded off. I'm sorry; that was so rude." She worked to get up, and I lightly pushed her back into the couch. No need to run off yet.

"Babe, it's totally fine. Everyone knew you'd had the race today, and we both know that your job doesn't allow for much in the way of rest."

She put a hand to her face as she fought the blush that clearly communicated her embarrassment that was not necessary. "I'm sorry. I'll grab my stuff and get out of your hair."

"Or..."

Her eyes swung to mine. "Or?"

"Or, you could stay here." My stomach did its own version of a flip-flop.

"In your guest room?" Her voice was now a whisper and, possibly, filled with a little heat. Possibly that was my hope speaking, or the traitor in my pants.

I nodded. "Yeah, you could stay in there. Or you could stay with me."

Her eyes widened, so I hurried to fill the silence.

"Not to have sex. I heard you when you said we shouldn't put any pressure on the kiss. I just mean, we're going to have to share a tent in Starved Rock. So this could be like..."

Now it was Allyson's turn to look amused. "Practice?"

My cheeks heated. "Um, yeah?"

Her expression said she was calling my bullshit. "Because otherwise you'd hate it?"

Talk to her! It was like Nola was screaming in my ear.

I gathered all my courage. "I don't think I'd hate it, and that scares the shit out of me, but I need to figure that out without my parents present. I'm sorry if that's a dick move."

Her expression softened. "That's not a dick move, Logan. That's a human one." She took a deep breath. "I want to be clear here. I think it's important. You want me to sleep over, and you'd like it to be in your room, but nothing is happening."

I nodded, realizing I was a prized idiot, but I thought it was all I could promise for now. "Yep, that about covers it. Is that something you could live with?"

She stood up and looked at me with a shake of her head that spoke to my stupidity. "Oh, Logan, it will be a hardship, but I suppose I can lie in the same vicinity as you for the night. If you need to erect a wall of pillows between us to protect your maidenhood, please feel free. I understand." The humor in her voice relaxed me while her statement concerned me.

"You're going to tell the guys about this, aren't you?"

Her hands met her hips as she gave me a smirk. "You mean during my morning chat Monday with Max and

Drew when they come to get a breakfast sandwich? I'd never."

"Jesus, they will never let me live this down." I shook my head while reaching for her hand and heading toward the stairs.

Ally's hitch in her breath when our hands touched told me that her humorous words were masking some feelings of her own. Good to know I wasn't alone in this.

Up the stairs with a glance to Levi's room. He'd closed the door, thank goodness. I didn't want to deal with an *I told you so* right now. I led Allyson into my room, letting Charlie trail in after us, then shut the door.

Allyson was still against it, watching me, and I inhaled what I can only assume was her perfume. I didn't want to even discuss how I could smell it on the pillows after the last time she stayed or how one of those pillows made its way into my room until I'd finally washed the sheets the other day.

I was thankful Levi hadn't figured that one out. There was no explanation.

"Logan," she breathed out.

I longed to step forward, press her against the door, and kiss her until we incinerated on the spot. Instead, I held my ground, hovering a step away like some creeper.

"Yeah?"

She closed her eyes and took a big breath before opening them to look at me. "How about you show me your room?"

Her voice was even, like she'd willed herself to calm down. Nice trick. I wondered if she could teach me?

I took a step and gestured for her to proceed me. The lamps on the side tables of my bed were on, casting the room in a warm glow. I glanced around with some apprehension. This place was the first place that I'd ever lived as an adult on my own. In some ways, it had helped that I had no memories of Nola here. At the same time, I had no idea what I was doing. I hadn't wanted my mom's help. I'd just wanted a space to disappear into. And when I'd seen this house, with views of Highland Woods from the back, it seemed like it had been made for me.

Now, however, watching Allyson look at it? I felt a weird anxiety that she wouldn't like it.

Her fingers trailed over my white comforter as she walked around the bed, her eyes glued to the floor-to-ceiling windows that overlooked the woods. She stood still on the other side of my bed and finally looked from the view to me. "You've created a sanctuary."

I shrugged and tried to put the words together to express what this place meant to me. Looking into her eyes, I felt safe to do so. "It was necessary."

She nodded, then looked to the bed—my California King that now looked like the size of a postage stamp. "What side?"

"I sleep by the door."

"Of course you do." She glanced down at her clothes, then my way. "Any chance I can borrow a T-shirt to sleep in? And possibly a toothbrush?"

I turned on automatic pilot to grab her a worn Highland Woods tee from my drawer. Handing it over, she followed me to my bathroom where I produced an extra toothbrush.

"Dang, that bath is no joke. I might have to use it in the morning."

I worked to stop the visions that assaulted me at that statement. "Um, sure, of course you can."

Allyson's snort told me she knew what affect her words

were having on me. She pushed past me and closed the door.

I moved back in the bedroom and changed myself, folding down the bedding and wondering how I got myself into this situation. I wanted to try out sleeping together before the camping trip? I mean, yeah, I didn't want to be awkward around my parents, but was this any better? And how would I survive the woman being naked in my tub? I mean, I know I was the one that originally told her that she could borrow my tub, but I'd kicked myself then too.

Then again, what kind of friend was I? I hadn't even asked how she was feeling after the race this morning? Shit, was she sore? Had she stretched enough?

While I was lost in my thoughts, sitting on the edge of the bed, the bathroom door opened, and I worked to school my expression. My T-shirt was far too big and hit her a little below midthigh. She clearly wasn't wearing a bra, and I couldn't even remotely decide what to do with that information.

Instead of dealing with that, I raced to the bathroom to brush my teeth. I also grabbed a glass for water and a bottle of ibuprofen. Maybe that could make up for my earlier negligence.

Coming back into the bedroom, I saw that she had slid under the covers already and was waiting for me, Charlie curled up by her feet.

"Feeling awkward?" she asked.

"Hell yes," I said, grateful that she was being blunt. I held out the bottle. "I'm an ass and haven't asked how you're feeling after the race. Did you stretch? Do you need any of these?"

She shook her head. "I actually feel good. I really might use that bath tomorrow, but right now I'm fine."

"Not a bad idea to take one preventively."

She nodded and held her hand out. After settling that, we turned off the lights and slid down in the bed. The moonlight was just enough to see her silhouette, which made my heart race. Charlie was at the foot of the bed between us; maybe he could be considered our chaperone.

"Logan," she whispered, looking up at the ceiling.

"Yeah."

"You sure you're okay with this fake relationship? At least for this week?"

I closed my eyes. Part of me wanted to say fuck it, let's just try this thing out. Another part of me said there was no chance in hell I was ready for that, and that wasn't fair to Allyson. So fake dating it was.

"Yep, I'm good."

We lay there on our backs, staring at the ceiling in silence. I was just beginning to drift off to the background noise of Charlie's light snore when Allyson spoke again.

"I really like your family."

I thought about that for a moment. What she'd told me of her sister, whom she loved but didn't see enough, to her parents who hadn't shown her any affection growing up but instead judged her over and over. I'm sure that, while overbearing at times, my parents were the polar opposite of what she'd experienced. My heart broke for the little girl who had looked for acceptance or validation that she was seen, never to get it.

I reached out and grabbed her hand over the top of the sheets. "I really like them too." And I fell asleep just like that.

Chapter 14

Made of Glass

llyson

Bessie and I were headed down the crown of the country road en route to town when my phone rang. I glanced to the phone mount poking out of my vents to see who was calling at the ungodly hour of predawn and was shocked to see Maeve's name. I quickly accepted the call.

"Are you dead? Do you need bail money?"

"Such confidence you have in me." The lilt in her voice belied her mood. As always, Maeve was chill. She moved through life like Teflon; nothing stuck, nothing bothered her, including our parents. Maeve had been in tune with herself from birth. I'd always marveled and admired her, and at the same time was patently jealous. While I was working hard to do everything right so that they could finally *see* me, be proud of me, Maeve did not give the first fucks whether they saw her or not. Not the last fucks either.

I appreciated her ability to ease her way through life. Always had, always would.

"Sister, you know I love you. Just cutting to the chase.

My commute in Highland isn't New Haven. I've got five minutes, and this drive is over."

"Why are you headed to the café this early?" Maeve questioned. "I thought you opened later on Sundays?"

I was grateful this wasn't FaceTime. I was certain my cheeks were red as I debated how to answer this. I hadn't needed to worry, however; she figured it out before I could make up my mind on an answer.

"Oh damn, Allyson Elise Murphy, are you headed *home* right now? Like is this a drive of shame?" Her laughter enveloped me and made me long for home—and by home, I meant my sister. While she might not put a lot of energy into her relationships with our parents, she was always there for me. With her, I found comfort. I knew Maeve, and she wasn't laughing at me but delighting in my situation.

"No shame, no sex." I spit out, inserting the word *sadly* before sex in my mind. I hung a left into town and slowed to a stop at one of the two traffic lights, debating what to tell her. I decided to ignore part of her question. "And we do open at eight on Sundays, but I'm hitting a yoga class at seven."

"Mm-hmm. Back to the drive, sister dear. Where were you last night? Do we need to have a conversation about life choices and how they reflect on the family?"

I growled; I sure did. Maeve didn't believe in any of that bullshit but was parroting our parents' typical concerns. It triggered an immediate feeling of irritation and a desire to flee.

"Sorry, sorry. You know I love you and want all the sex in the world for you. Let it rain all the people, take your pick. Jump anyone that floats your boat; I just want you to be happy."

"And that's why I love you. Now why on earth are you

calling this early? And where in the world are you now?" The light turned green, and I motored through the sleepy streets en route to my little duplex to change into yoga clothes, then head to Nomad Yoga for the morning flow before work.

"I'm on the move again. I was in New Hampshire at a yoga retreat for the past month, first as an attendee, then as an instructor. Now I'm headed toward Delaware."

"What's in Delaware?" I pulled into my drive and threw Bessie into park as I grabbed my purse, phone, and headed into my place.

"A friend is down in Bethany Beach and invited me to stay. Thought I'd see her, then decide where I'm headed next."

Maeve was like a fluff of dandelion floating in the wind. She didn't bother with concerns like, oh, I don't know, health insurance, retirement investments... rent. Her jobs were also fluid—yoga, sound meditation, Reiki, massage therapist, waitress, line cook, personal trainer, you name it, she'd done it.

"I haven't seen you for over a year. Maybe we could try to get together before the new year hits?" I left her on speaker and tossed the phone on my bed so I could do a quick change worthy of a Broadway performer.

"It's mid-April. Don't be dramatic."

I spoke from inside my shirt as I tugged it over my head, so I raised my voice a bit. "Have you seen them?"

"Hell no. Why would I do that to myself? Mom's voice mails about how I need to find some direction are enough." I heard the click of her blinker switch on as she drove down whatever road she was on. "But enough about the things that haven't changed; let's talk about something that has.

Let's return to the subject of where you were driving in from this morning?"

Smoothing my shirt down, I cleared my throat. "So funny story, I seem to have a boyfriend for the moment..."

Her gasp and peal of laughter were worth all of it. For the first time in the past twenty-four hours, I fully relaxed.

Two hours later, I was walking through the downtown square to the Sanctuary after yoga class. Kate and Kristine's space was perfect for them, but I did miss the days when Kristine held class at the café. That had been a large part of my introduction to this town. Meeting people while they relaxed after a class with a drink, maybe a scone, was a perfect social gathering in my world. Chill vibe, no mass of humanity, and no yelling to be heard over the noise of the crowd. So heaven on earth, in other words.

Fortunately for me, Nomad Yoga still supported my café by encouraging people to grab a drink or a bite to eat after they finished class. For this reason, I was rushing to give Andy a hand before the after-yoga crowd descended. I hit the front door at a jog and ran up the steps and into the former nave.

"Hey, Andy; hey, Flat Max," I called to the barista and the cardboard cutout behind the counter. "Much business this morning?"

"Just the church crowd after the seven a.m. mass," Andy said as she moved around behind the counter to wash some dishes. "And Max stopped by on his way to the park. Said to ask you if you were looking forward to your camping trip?"

I groaned, dropping my head to the counter, and counted to ten. Then I did it again. Where was that zen I'd had since Maeve's phone call and through my class? Gone, that's where it was.

"Don't lose your hard-won relaxed mindset. Should I

guess from this mini meltdown that you have shockingly agreed to leave town? Has the underworld frozen over?" She watched me from the sink, an amused expression on her face.

"I don't have time for your sass, ma'am." I leaned back from my comfy spot, resting my head on my arms. "I need to figure out scheduling for the park and the town locations, make sure all the orders are scheduled, and..."

"Pencil in time to enjoy yourself between ten and two on Saturday at Starved Rock."

"You're a word that rhymes with witch." I propped up my head to watch her and expend as little energy as possible.

Andy's laughter filled the Sanctuary as she finished up the dishes. "You've never struggled with curse words before."

"Bitch seemed severe."

"And you love me for it. We didn't get the chance to catch up yesterday. How was the race? Did you frame the medal yet? Did it make you more or less stressed about the marathon coming up?" She slid a scone my way as she continued some prep work.

Sinking my teeth into the delicious chocolate chip goodness, I let out a noise of pleasure. Damn, this recipe never failed. With a mouthful, I answered Andy. "Race was good. Medal is in my purse for now. I'm sure one day I'll think of something to do with it. To be honest, I was just happier knowing I finished and that the marathon is doable."

Andy nodded before glancing over to give me a serious look. "You've been running at full tilt. Think about the weekend, I'm glad to help."

Dammit, I knew she was. Why was it so hard for me to just let go? "Thanks. We can talk soon." I sighed, frustrated with myself, but then startled when a hand came to my back, rubbing down my spine. My body told me it was Logan before my brain snapped into gear as I fought against leaning into the man and waving a white flag.

A peek under my arm confirmed that the man himself was standing by my side and giving me a light massage.

"Hi," I said softly.

"Hey," he replied, his eyes warm and, dare I say, heated?

Andy didn't let this nonsense stand. "As titillating as this conversation is, I'm going to get ready for the swarm of chilled-out yogis that are going to descend momentarily. You two feel free to continue your sweet little greetings. Allyson, I'll shout when I need a hand." Andy moved to the register and began to get out some cups to prep. Glancing my way, she raised her voice. "And pencil in some time to fill me in on whatever this is going on here." She gestured between Logan and me with a portafilter in hand.

I turned and faced Logan, questioning why I suddenly felt shy with this man whom I'd been friends with for two years, running partners with for months. I mean he'd seen me sweaty and unable to get up off the ground.

"So I woke up this morning and you were gone."

Oh yeah, there it was. The whole "sleeping with him but not having sex" situation might be messing with my mind.

I'd woken up this morning after the best night of sleep in, I'm not sure, ever? It had been a glorious Logan/Charlie sandwich that made me feel safe, warm, treasured. Logan had been the big spoon, his arm flung across my belly. Charlie's chin had rested on my legs. The feeling of security was one I felt like I couldn't allow myself to get used to. So what did I do? I'd snuck my way out of the little spot, letting Charlie slide next to Logan, and had gotten the heck out of Dodge. Yep. Big chicken, party of one, that's me.

Meeting Logan's gaze, I answered him. "Yeah..." My voice trailed off. What did I even say? I'd taken the coward's way out.

"You get spooked?" Logan just laid it out for me.

I decided to embrace the truth. Maybe I was growing up? "Kind of."

"I understand that. I was kind of spooked myself." Logan was tracing the back of my hand that was resting on the counter between us. Part of me wanted to turn my hand over and link it with his. The other part of me clued into what he just said as my stomach sank.

"I'm sorry. I feel like an insensitive ass and a terrible friend. Have you had anyone in your bed since Nola?" My conscience was at war with the idea of avoiding this conversation in case it made him uncomfortable but knowing it was important in the long run to face the issue of his wife head-on. Had he been with anyone in the past three years? We weren't the type of friends to have had that conversation in the two years we'd known each other. It was fine either way of course, but as far as I knew, he hadn't dated. Lord knew I paid attention to him. Far too much attention if we want to be honest.

Logan picked up my hand and linked it with mine, so it looked like everyone was getting what they wanted today. "Nola never slept in that bed at my place because, to be honest, life was too hard after she passed. I saw reminders of her everywhere. So when I got the job at the woods, I sold most of our furniture before coming down here and decided to start fresh."

"Is that why I didn't see any pictures of her in your house?" Yikes, Miss Nosy, party of one, reporting in. I was overstepping ten ways to Sunday. Darn it. I started to tug my hand from his, wanting to go help Andy to get the heck out of this conversation.

"Noticed that, did you?" Logan gave me a painful half smile. "Levi has gotten on me about that multiple times, as have my parents." He continued to rub his thumb over my hand before looking up at me with wet eyes. "I loved her, Allyson. I don't know what this is"—he gestured between us —"but you have to know how much I loved her. I'm so grateful to you for trying to help me with my parents. I've only realized recently how much they, along with Levi, have been walking on eggshells because of me. If I can alleviate any stress they are carrying because of me, I'm willing to do it. But I know this is a big ask."

"Shhhh." I leaned forward, placing my free hand on his chest. "Relax. You just spit out so many things I want to address I should have taken notes. Do I regret helping you? Heck no. My idea, remember? Now I'm assuming from some of what you just said that there are no pictures up of Nola because it is too hard to see her?"

"Yep." His voice was barely above a whisper.

"I'm no therapist, but I think it might help you to see her, actually see her, and remember that she's still with you. Maybe that would help you move forward. Nola was a big part of your life, Logan, and of course you loved her and still do. I would be concerned if you didn't."

"For what it's worth, my therapist Ashley would agree with you."

"Because we're smart ladies. When you love someone, you need snapshots of your lives together around you. It reminds you of that love, whether they're here or not." I took a deep breath because this next part was going to require some vulnerability which we already knew I didn't excel at. "Now as to what's going on here..." I mimicked his gesture between the two of us. "Remember what we've said about not defining anything."

He nodded but then tugged me forward so we were just a breath apart. "Not defining, but can we acknowledge there is something there?"

My heart skipped a beat. Jesus, I was worse than a lovesick teenager. "Definitely something there." I sounded more breathless than I had yesterday after thirteen miles.

Logan's smile was visible within that gorgeous beard that I wanted to comb my fingers through. "Well, we're agreed on that, at least. That's a start." He squeezed my hand and looked a little regretful. "I just don't know what I can give you, Allyson, and I feel like that's not fair."

I tilted my head back to look up at him. "How about you let me worry about that? We're friends. For the next week, we're friends who hold hands, especially when your parents are around."

"And sleep together. Don't forget that. I typically sleep like shit, and last night was amazing."

"It was."

He took a step closer. "And friends that have kissed."

He pressed a kiss to my temple. Everything in me melted. Why was that so sexy? He held me to him as we swayed together. Rihanna's "Stay" was playing at a low volume in the background. A few people from yoga had come in, and the room was filled with a low hum as they all talked, giving Andy their orders. There was the hiss of the espresso machine, and the velvety smell of coffee was in the air.

"Yep, we're friends that have done that." I was going to incinerate right here on the spot, wasn't I? Poof. I'd be gone. The smart move would be to take a step back, breathe, sort my brain. Did I do that? Nope. No part of me wanted that life. Instead, I laid my head on his chest and let myself enjoy this moment. Swaying with this man that I was in strong like with while faking a relationship for the benefit of his parents. Absolutely not examining life choices right now but going with my gut on what was the right call.

Logan started to pull away, and I tightened my arms around him. "Stay," I whispered, along with Rihanna. She was my girl.

He relaxed in my embrace, and his lips were near my ear. "Okay."

"Really?" I asked. My cheek was still on his chest, but I didn't look up at him. I felt like every single fiber of my being was right where it was supposed to be.

Logan ran a hand through my hair, smoothing it as he went. "Ally, you have to know, if I can, I'll do anything in my power for you."

"Except for run a race with me, asshat." It came out before I could stop, just the normal banter we would have traded before I knew about the shit he carried.

For a moment, he froze, and I was immediately awash with regret. And then the most glorious sound washed over me. Logan threw his head back and laughed a deep laugh. One that sounded a little bit rusty and a whole lot beautiful. I tipped my head to watch, soaking it all in.

Finally, he looked down at me, wiping a tear from the corner of his eyes. "Sorry, that just seemed so much like something Levi would say. It just really got me, you know? I mean, I love that you don't treat me like I'm made of glass. You never have."

I slid my hand back to his chest. "I want to hear you laugh like that a hell of a lot more. Maybe on this camping trip?"

He shook his head, giving me a knowing look. "Oh, you've met Linnie and Frank, babe. This is going to be an interesting weekend for sure."

A cleared throat caught my attention. Turning to the side, I saw Emma and Maggie standing a few feet from us. Maggie had her phone aimed in our direction, the least shocking thing I'd seen today.

"Aren't you two looking cozy?" Maggie said, putting down her phone and heading our way.

"Picture for your scrapbook?" I asked.

"Video for Lou," she replied.

Super. I'd hear about that one later.

"I'll note"—Maggie did a sweeping gesture to encompass the whole café—"there is not a Traub family member to be found. So that little moment we just witnessed was for the benefit of you two and no one else."

"Coffee?" Andy called over to them. She'd gotten through the yogis with zero issue. There were small groups at the tables and the murmur of happy customers, none of which seemed to take an interest in my life as much as these two women.

"Please, you beautiful goddess," Maggie called.

Andy made quick work of making drinks for all of us. Within minutes I was sipping a lavender vanilla latte while Logan stood my by side, arm around my waist while he drank his own.

Maggie took a big sniff of hers before taking a drink. "God, this gets better all the time, doesn't it?"

Emma shook her head at her childhood friend. "You usually overexaggerate, but not today. This really is that good." She gave me a look. "You know how amazing Andy is, don't you? I mean, you keep saying you can't hire a manager, that you'd have to do too much training, but maybe you could promote one?"

"You been talking to him?" I pointed to Flat Max. I mean, I figured she got my drift. "Or him?" I nodded toward Logan at my right shoulder. "Or her?" I pointed at Andy. "Because she and I have begun talking about staffing for this weekend when I'm gone."

He tipped his head down to whisper in my ear, "What are you waiting for, babe? Andy is amazing. You love her, you trust her, and she could use extra money."

I met his gaze with what I knew was a worried expression. "But what if it's too much? What if she's overwhelmed and quits? Then I'll be worse off than I am now."

"Fair," he said. "But why don't you let her make that decision?"

"Or," Maggie said, taking another happy sip, "you could ask her to act as the manager when you go on your camping weekend. If she likes it and it goes well, you could make it a permanent thing when you get back."

I looked at Maggie with what I knew was a shocked expression, then to Logan, then back at Maggie. "Um... That's a brilliant idea."

She shrugged. "I'm full of them. just ask Sully."

"Full of something, for sure," Emma muttered with a smile.

"Well, babe, what do you think?" Logan asked.

I gave him a tentative smile, then looked behind the counter, "Um, Andy? Remember what we were talking about?"

<h1 style="text-align:center">Chapter 15</h1>

<h2 style="text-align:center">Out of the Darkness</h2>

L_ogan_

I stood in the Ryan library, scanning the display of new releases. My mom had mentioned wanting to read the new release from Lucy Score this week, and she was, as she put it, old school and preferred the print version. While I'd be happy to buy it for her, she was a big proponent of public libraries, saying they were the foundation of a civilized society and must be supported at all times.

That and the woman read, on average, five books a week. If she bought copies of all of them, they'd have to add on a wing to the house.

As a result, I found myself at the library because when I'd seen Emma at the woods earlier today, she'd pried herself away from Max to mention they'd just gotten another copy and she'd set it aside for my mom to borrow it this week.

This place set me at ease from the moment you walked in. Unlike most libraries, this one was in a small home that had been donated to the town by the Ryan sisters decades ago, and the vibe you got when you walked inside was a strong desire to curl up with a book.

I'd arrived five minutes ago, and as soon as she saw me, Emma had headed to the second floor to grab the book. From previous visits, I knew that there were offices and a conference room housed on the second floor in the former bedrooms. While I'd waited, I considered if I really needed to check out another book for myself right now. Need versus want was always the dilemma, right? I was midway through a new mystery, but I had a bad habit of picking up new books and then having far more to read than I had time for.

"See something you just have to have?" A teasing tone pulled my attention back to the room, and I looked to see Tim, one of the part-time librarians. He and his partner Eric were part of the battalion of volunteers that took care of the gardens out at the woods with our crew. Eric was Tim's opposite, a calm port in a flamboyant and joyful storm. Tim was currently petting the beautiful tiger cat Aslan that was often here at the library while he rocked a T-shirt that stated SUPPORT YOUR LOCAL DRAG QUEENS in rainbow font.

I nodded to his shirt, "You all having an issue with anyone over the drag queen story hour?" I knew a friend of Eric and Tim's came in once a month to host a story hour. As far as I knew, it had been a huge hit.

Tim gasped and put a hand to his chest. "Highland Falls would *never*. No, only love thrown our way here, no hate. I figure better to be up front, you know. Remind people that support is needed elsewhere."

I nodded, then before I could tell him that I was just waiting for Emma, the front door was flung open and another librarian, Nate, rushed in with his girlfriend Elle being pulled right behind him.

Tim murmured quiet reassurance as he rested his hand on Aslan's back as if to tell the cat that all was well with the new visitors. Not that she looked bothered in the slightest. "Where's the fire?" he asked.

Nate pulled Elle in front of him and looked from Tim to me. "Hey, Logan." With a glance to Tim, he said, "Where's the boss ladies?"

Tim gave him a curious look. Then, without moving a muscle, he called out, "Grace? Emma? Young Nate has something to say."

Nate shook his head at Tim. "Young? I'm barely two years younger than you."

"Life experiences, *mon chérie*." Aslan wound her way around Tim's arm, vocalizing her desire for him to keep giving her attention. "Elle, looking gorg as usual."

"Thanks, Tim." Elle tipped her head on Nate's shoulder.

"When are you going to publish that book, my sweet? I want to hand sell it to everyone I know, or I guess hand borrow since we're in the library, though that doesn't roll off the tongue in the same way," Tim said, still giving Aslan the attention she felt she deserved.

Elle let out a secretive smile that led me to believe I might know what their news was. Elle and Nate had both moved to town in the past year. They'd met, fell in love, and Elle had begun to chase her dream of being an author in the past few months.

"Grace?" Nate called. Clearly this library didn't believe in the silent rules of the past, though I seemed to be the only patron right now.

"Keep your pants on, son." Lou came around the corner, followed by Grace, the library director, and Emma.

Emma gave me a wave and passed over the book.

Grace, the director here and a good friend of Emma's, shook her head at Tim. "You know, at some libraries shouting is frowned upon."

Tim looked her up and down. "You're lucky you're preggers or I'd have to tell you what I really think of people who keep libraries silent like a tomb."

I raised my eyebrow and turned to look at Grace. I didn't know her well, just enough to talk when we were out in a group. Her husband Aidan was a deputy for the sheriff's department. I hadn't heard that she was pregnant, but her fitted T-shirt dress showed her small bump.

"Congratulations," I whispered.

She shot me a wink. "Thanks." Looking at Tim, she said, "If me being pregnant causes you to *not* share your opinion on the regular, watch out, I'm having a ton of babies."

"Oh please. If I was married to someone who looked like Aidan, I'd figure out male pregnancy for sure."

"I'll be sure to mention that to Eric." Nate spoke up.

"He'd say the same," Tim fired back.

I chose to ignore the crazy and leaned over to give Lou a hug. She was essentially the town matriarch and sassy as could be. She'd been invaluable in introducing me around town when I'd arrived. I credited much of the volunteer force we had out at Highland Woods to Lou. She'd met me, decided she liked what I stood for, then vouched for me with everyone in Highland Falls. Breaking into a small town wasn't easy, I knew, but with someone like Lou Williams blazing your trail, things were a hell of a lot easier.

"Hey Lou," I murmured.

"I'll deal with you later, sonny." Her tone indicated some displeasure.

"Uh-oh, what did I do now?" I asked. Valid question. I

made sure I never got on Lou's bad side. I mean, she was a sweetheart, but it didn't do to piss her off.

She peered up at me from under her cap of gray curls as she gripped my forearm. "What's this I hear about you and our Allyson?"

Shit. I mean, a fake relationship for my parents was one thing, but our friends were all in on it, so they wouldn't have told Lou, which left... "Where'd you hear about us?" Sweat was beading up at my temples, the back of my neck.

"Maggie cared enough to share a video." She shook her head at me. "And also, your mother."

No, no, no, no. This wasn't good. Lou and my mom had never met, and to some extent, that was by design. Not that they wouldn't get along. Oh no; they would get along famously, I just knew it. And in the past, I was terrified of the two women joining forces and setting me up on some blind date. Now I had just wanted them apart by principle. The world was not ready for this duo.

"Um, where did you meet my mom?" Valid question while I was working to calm my heart rate.

"She volunteered out at the woods this morning with the gardening group. Nice lady. Told me all about how excited she is for you to be seeing someone after the loss of your wife." Cue another curious look. "And how she and your dad have been looking into a rental property here in town..."

"Rental properties?" I hissed.

Lou gave me a considering glance before breaking into a grin that, I don't mind telling you, looked a little calculating. "You didn't know? She said that she and your dad wanted an easier way to visit because, you know, the grandchildren..."

Jesus.

Grace called us to attention. "Hey guys, let's give Nate the floor. I have a call scheduled with Ivy in twenty minutes planning some upcoming activities for our community read this year."

Apparently, I had somehow joined a staff meeting, plus Lou, while trying to get a book for my mom. Small towns.

Nate and Elle held hands as he told his coworkers about their news: they were officially engaged, *and* Elle had received the news from her literary agent sharing that her book had sold. Everyone surrounded them with words of congratulations all while I spiraled with Lou's words.

My parents might be moving to Highland?

After sharing my own well-wishes with the happy couple, I checked out the book for my mom and fled back to the Woods. There was only an hour or so until the end of the workday. I'd picked up a few things we needed for the park while running errands in town and was going to wrap up some items on my to-do list, then get a run in with Allyson. She was still working toward the marathon that was drawing closer each day. Me? I was ignoring the reality of the race. Denial was a healthy coping mechanism, right?

And now I was penciling in a conversation with my brother about dear old Mom and Dad.

Walking into the mansion that housed the café and so many of the staff offices out at the park, I ran into Blake, one of our interns. He'd been here full-time last summer and was part-time during the school year while he finished up his degree. I was hoping we'd be able to keep him after graduation and he wouldn't want to head off to some place bigger.

Blake was looking at a crudely written list on a whiteboard of our conference room. We'd met late last week with a team from the university in Champaign-Urbana and discussed what possible research projects we wanted to work together on. The one that we were most excited about involved the Northern Saw Whet Owl. This fall we planned to work in conjunction with the university to capture and tag these owls as they were migrating to help scientists learn more about the population.

Since I'd joined the park here, we'd reached out to the local university and other groups working in the state to see how we could help them out. Our acreage gave us a unique opportunity to see animal and plant life that wasn't common around here anymore.

Heck, Blake had set up a trail camera by a river crossing in the park from June through December, and the animals he caught on film were surprising to much of our community when we'd shared the video on our social media feeds. Some were to be expected—raccoons, possums, deer, owls— but also some that people didn't expect like river otters, minks, and weasels. The video was so popular that we were currently creating another one to release this summer. Blake was great about using social media to draw people into the park and highlight what we were doing out here.

"What are you dreaming up?" I asked him, coming in the room.

He looked over his shoulder in my direction. "Hey, man. Not much. Just wondering if I should schedule another one of those birds-and-brew hikes?"

Blake and Max had a popular series of bird hikes here at the park as part of our event calendars. Drew had also volunteered to lead some of them. Blake had the idea while at the Homestead one day after work that we should do a collaboration, offer up some of the local beer along with a hike. It had sold out within hours.

"Absolutely," I said. "I think it was a hit. Maybe talk to

Max and Drew, see who wants to lead and what day would work best."

Blake looked to the calendar, seemingly lost in thought. But after almost a year with the man, I knew his synapses were firing. You just had to wait.

"What if the Homestead created a beer inspired by this place? We could build a hike around it."

"Did someone say beer?" Allyson walked in, trailed by my brother.

I glared at Levi, sharing my displeasure.

His look back told me he didn't know what was up my ass.

"Whoa," Blake said, looking between the two of us. "Are you doing some twin telepathy thing?"

"Weird, isn't it?" Allyson murmured. Then, with a clap of her hands, she got both of our attention. "Let's return to the topic of beer. What's going on?"

Blake ran down his idea.

Allyson nodded her head. "I love how you did that collaboration with the brewery in the fall. I was thinking about it recently and how I could do more of that. You know, lifting other small businesses up? What was it that senator from Minnesota said? Something like 'We all do better when we all do better.' I want to live that motto and shine the light on all the folks in town. There's a woman, Anita, who just started making biscotti. Her business's name is adorable, Aneeda Biscotti. I reached out to her to see if she'd want to make it for my two cafés. I mean, I could, but why not feature someone local *and* take a bit of work off myself? She has so many flavors and is going to make a signature one just for the Sanctuary." She rubbed her hands together and did a little dance. "I'm thinking something chocolate."

Her joyful expression hit me in the gut. I wanted to see that look more, not the exhaustion that seemed to seep from her pores. As if drawn by a magnet, I moved next to her and slid my arm around her waist. "Nice job delegating, babe."

"I'm learning from the best," she murmured.

Being with her felt natural, right, and that made me feel unbalanced. Ignoring it, I focused on the issue at hand. "And Andy's still on board for this weekend?"

"Yep."

That was an understatement. While I knew Allyson still had some concerns that she'd never be able to promote someone else to manage the cafés with her because it would be so much work for Allyson or that Andy would hate it, Andy had none of those worries. When Allyson had asked her to take over for the weekend, Andy beamed and accepted immediately.

Looking to Blake, I continued our conversation. "I bet Sully and Jake would be in on the beer, but to make a new one is time-consuming and would have to fit in their schedule. Maybe it could happen in the fall? I can ask them, or you can."

"It's all good. They were telling me about a pale ale they were tinkering with last month. Maybe that might fit the bill? I can ask." Blake grabbed his phone and headed for the door. "I'll shoot off a message this afternoon and keep you in the loop. Later."

Blake headed out, and that left the three of us staring at each other. Levi's eyes were locked on mine as he clearly noted that I was carrying something worth a discussion or maybe an argument.

Allyson noticed the tension filling the room. "Um, maybe I need to head back to the café." She began to walk backward toward the door. "I'm sure that I'm needed there and not here with whatever this scary Traub brother stare down is." She gestured between the two of us.

"I'll be over in thirty for a run, just need some info from this guy," I said, not breaking my stare with Levi.

"Save me a muffin please," he said to her, not looking away either.

We stood in silence, waiting for her to clear the room. I wondered for a moment if we should station ourselves on either side of the table. Less chance of a headlock happening. I mean, we hadn't fought in years, but that didn't mean a throwdown wasn't a possibility.

"What crawled up your ass?" Levi said, his tone indicating he wasn't in the mood to beat around the bush as he took a step toward me, and I began to pray for furniture after all.

"Did you know Mom and Dad are planning on moving to Highland?"

Levi froze. "Are you shitting me? Planning it or considering it? Are they leaving Aurora for good?" His confused expression allowed my irritation to seep out. This was just as much news to him as it was me.

"No idea. Heard from Lou—have you met her?"

"Tiny gray-haired woman who looks like she could control the House of Rep if not the entire government?"

"Yep, that's her. Lou said she met Mom at the gardening group out here this morning, and Mom said they were looking."

Levi took a moment, processing what I'd said, then gave me a shrewd look. "So it's a given here, right? You're fucked. End of story. One, she's apparently found a gardening club and been here what, four days? And two, she met Lou? Those two could rule the world and we'd all just have to line up to do their bidding."

I groaned. I mean, he wasn't wrong. "I've got to tell them there isn't anything between Allyson and me." It would kill them, and then they'd begin to worry about me all over again which I hated, but this was too much.

"Or you could stop lying." Levi took a step to lean against the wall, now the picture of calm, sliding his hands in his pockets as he watched me.

"Yeah, that's what I said. I can tell them this was a bunch of bullshit."

He shook his head like he was disappointed that I wasn't getting it. "Not the lie I'm talking about, baby bro. I mean lying to yourself about nothing happening between you and Allyson."

I exhaled some frustration. "We've gone over this, Levi. I don't think I can give her what she needs." And damn if it wasn't something I thought about every night when I went to bed. I had one night of Allyson sleeping in my bed on Saturday, and every night since, I'd fought messaging her and asking her to stay. Again. That alone told me I was torn up about the woman.

"Maybe she can give you what you need. You think about that?" He watched me for a moment before continuing. "And then, once you're whole again, you might be in a place to finally give back. Relationships, at least the healthy ones, involve a lot of give and take. You know who taught me that?" His expression was one that bordered on exasperation.

"Who?"

"Nola." Pause. "And you." His tone said he was done treating me as if I might break, which was both reassuring and scary as hell. "You know this. You two had an excellent one, and I think that's what making you want to run. Right now, you don't think you can give back to anyone. Am I right?"

I gave a nod.

"Maybe start with taking? Crazy thought. Allyson wants to be there for you. I see it and I know you sure as hell do. Lean into it and see where it takes you."

I looked down at the floor, not sure if I could even give voice to the fears I held deep inside. "That doesn't make me a selfish ass?"

"Well, you're that anyway."

I looked his way to see he was moving in my direction. "Fuck off." I said it, but without any heat behind the words.

Levi reached out and pulled me in, holding me tight against him as he spoke against my ear. "Lean into it, Logan. This fake relationship, for the rest of this week, including the camping trip. Let Allyson help you heal. Then we can talk about this again."

I left my head resting on his shoulder because I didn't think I had the energy to stand alone. And Levi knew that. After a few moments, I took a deep breath. And then another one. "Okay."

"Okay? Really?"

I nodded against him. "I think so."

He slapped my back and then said the words I needed to hear and hadn't realized it. "You've been in a darkness for three years, man, but did you ever wonder if maybe Nola sent someone to pull your ass out of it? Because I sure as shit think she did, and I think Allyson is it."

Chapter 16

Walls

Allyson

Logan's house was positively alive with energy. Lamps glowed from every room, Charlie bounded from person to person looking for attention, and Van Morrison poured from the speakers, reminding us all that there would be *days like this*.

After an excellent dinner, we were relaxing as we put the place back in order. Linnie and Frank danced by with a kitchen towel thrown over Frank's shoulder as they swayed with his hand on her hip, him singing into her ear. Levi and Logan faced off in the kitchen, going round after round regarding the chances of the Blackhawks moving on in the playoffs this year. While their voices were raised, the amusement on their faces belied their enjoyment of this clearly familiar conversation.

I'd come over three hours ago and walked straight into a version of controlled chaos. The four of them had all been cooking in the kitchen, Linnie directing everything, Frank chopping and washing like a champ. Levi and Logan moved in a way born of years of cooking as a family, almost anticipating the next direction that Linnie was going to toss at them. And for a while, I'd stood and marveled at the noise level as well as the mountains of dishes on the counter; I was more in awe of the laughter and expressions of love.

Not once, not in my entire childhood, had I ever experienced anything like this.

Finally, I'd left the safety of observation and waded in. Linnie had given me a cutting board, knife, and a bowl of apples, instructing me to peel and chop.

There had been conversations pinging from sports to politics to people back home that I didn't know to relatives to concerts to food and on and on and on. Every once in a while, someone would break into song with the music that was coming from the speakers. The songs ranged from current hits to ones I'd place around Linnie and Frank's generation. Whether it was Neil Young or Pink, all members of the Traub family could sing along.

The feeling I had was positively electric, and I never wanted it to end.

Ostensibly, I'd been invited over because tomorrow was D Day, also known as our camping trip. This week had been filled up with quick meals or time with Logan's family. And if I was being completely honest, I'd loved it all.

We were leaving in the morning at dawn to get up to Starved Rock in time for an early-morning hike. Linnie had said that it *just made sense* for us all to stay at Logan's tonight. And thus I was here and freaking way the hell out when I had a moment to process. Why was I freaking out, you might ask? Because your girl was trying to ignore the feeling that this all felt right, which was just a recipe for heartache that I was working to ignore.

Returning to the present, I was reminded once again how wonderful this family was. Frank spun Linnie another time as they moved through the open living room, laughter following them in a wake. They were freaking adorable. I wanted that. All. Of. It. Every fiber of my being stretched toward them, wanting to capture that for myself. I wanted the relationship, the clear love on each of their faces after all these years. I wanted the easy humor with each other mixed with hefty doses of sarcasm and giving each other shit. And more than anything, I wanted parental figures that loved me enough to uproot their life on the regular to check in with their kid and make sure that all is well and when it clearly wasn't, love on them to help hold them over until all might not be well but a damn sight better. Green-eyed monster, party of one, over here.

Instead, I walked my sorry self to the windows that overlooked Highland Woods at the back of Logan's house. The Traub clan was over by the kitchen now, cleaning up from an amazing dinner of marinated pork chops, sweet potatoes, salad, and apple crisp. I had no idea what we'd eat while camping because, though I hadn't shared this with the group, I'd never camped—but it couldn't be equal in any way to the meal we'd just shared. I mean, restaurants my parents had taken us to in New York hadn't held a candle to this delicious meal around a table with people that filled me up in more ways than one. More of that please. I was here for it.

Standing at the window, looking out at the trees that had a warm glow from the white lights that Logan had strung from his house to the posts extended from his porch, I felt joy and sadness intertwine. Joy that I had this moment, these people. Sadness that I couldn't keep them. Now that I had just a taste of what this life could be like, it would be even more empty once I went back to my own because, let's be real, Logan wasn't ready to move on, and I didn't blame him.

Maybe it was time to look into getting a cat.

Lost in thought, I was pulled back to the room when Logan came up behind me and snaked an arm around my stomach. I knew he was just acting the part of this fake relationship, but I leaned into it, soaking it in. God, I wanted it to be real. I knew we were just letting things run their course, but I also knew with one hundred percent certainty that he wasn't ready and *run their course* meant parting as friends.

I had two nights and two days left to soak this relationship in because come Sunday evening when Frank and Linnie were home, Logan and I would return to the way things had been before with me lusting over the man from afar. And the more I heard about Nola from Levi and his parents, the more I understood why. She wasn't someone you got over quickly, if ever.

"Hey," he said, pulling me out of my depressing thought pattern as he held me in his arms.

We stood there, swaying together as the music changed. I recognized the song "There Will Be Time" from Mumford & Sons. The lyrics talked about walking around a darkened land, and I felt Logan stiffen, then relax.

What must the past three years have been like for this man? I thought about finding someone as amazing as Nola clearly was and losing them in an instant. It would have been a shock to the system, and I understood the hesitation to ever begin anything again. How could you trust that whatever came next would last any longer than what you had before? I needed to remember that because the more that Logan and I acted out this relationship for his family, the more I forgot we were acting. I worried my heart wouldn't survive this weekend. This needed to end with all parts of me intact.

With a gentle push toward the door to the deck, Logan stepped around me, snagged my hand, and pulled me outside, closing the door firmly behind us.

"What's going on?" I asked. He took a step toward me, then another and another. The music was flowing out of his outdoor speakers as he pulled me into his arms and we began to sway back and forth on the deck.

"I needed a moment with you, away from my family." His voice was husky, and I closed my eyes as I rested my head on his chest, not wanting to glimpse the windows to the living room for fear that his family was pressed against them watching us.

"Why's that?"

"Because I'm a bit concerned that my feelings for you are more than I can handle." His heart under my cheek was threatening to thunder out of his chest. How did I respond to that? What did it even mean?

"Is that so?" Pat on the back, Allyson, way to encourage the man.

"Mm-hmm," was his only reply.

We moved in a small circle as I racked my brain trying to think of a way to get the information I wanted, no, needed.

The night song of Illinois in early spring surrounded us, the sun long since set and the birds calling out to each other with the occasional hoot here and there from a wayward owl.

"You warm enough?" he asked.

"Mm-hmm." It was my turn to lose the ability to string together words. And I was warm enough, though my brain power wasn't focused on comfort. One, I was fine. It was cool, but my joggers and long-sleeved T-shirt were plenty warm enough even with bare feet. I would have been mortified at my dress at a family dinner—Lord knows my mother would—if Linnie hadn't been wearing an almost identical outfit. More importantly, I was working up the courage to broach a conversation around this pseudo relationship based on his words moments ago.

I had this. I did. Maybe. Or maybe after the next song.

"The Weight of Lies" from the Avett Brothers came on, and it felt like God was sending me a message. Or maybe that was my grandmother. She always did have a sense of humor. Certainly more than either of my parents would dream of.

"Can we return to something you said earlier?" I asked his chest because like hell was I making eye contact for this conversation. Unlike me? Yep. But I was rolling with it.

Logan stopped swaying and tipped my chin back with his hand, his eyes meeting mine. Well, I guess that hadn't worked out quite how I planned.

"What's on your mind?" he asked.

"Are your parents watching us?"

He let out a small laugh as his face relaxed. "Levi will distract them."

My brows drew together. "How do you know? Did you ask him to?"

He shook his head. "Because I know him."

My brain pinged away from the conversation at hand to his relationship with his brother. What would it be like to know someone like that? To be able to always trust them to have your back. I mean, Maeve loved me, and she'd be there for me if I needed her, but I had another pang of longing, wishing we were closer. It had been so long since we'd been in the same state, much less spent any time together.

"So again, what's on your mind?" He brought me back to the moment, swaying to the music as he refused to look away.

"Um, well, you said something about your feelings for me being, well, a lot," I stammered as I broke our staring contest and looked out into the woods.

Logan stopped moving just as Neil Young began singing "Falling Off the Face of the Earth." "Are you asking me how I feel about you, Ally?"

I felt the flush begin at my chest and race up my neck to my face while I gave a small nod.

He paused and brushed a hand over my cheek. Lowering his head, he stopped when his lips were just above mine. "Can I kiss you, Ally?"

Deciding it was now or never, I reached up and pulled his head to mine, letting that suffice as my answer. His lips parted over mine, a warm caress.

I took a step into him, my body becoming flush with his. His arm tightened around my waist. His other hand moved to rake through my hair, angling my head as his lips opened and his tongue slid into my mouth.

I melted into his embrace.

My heart raced as the kiss went from a level one to a hundred as he devoured my mouth and I his. I slid my hands around to his ass and pulled him against me, feeling just how much he was enjoying this kiss as he hardened against me. Yum. That was a shot of confidence that I'd needed.

Before I could hop up and wrap my legs around his waist, I heard the door open behind us and jumped back. Levi stood there in the doorway, wiping his hands on a kitchen towel, and his smile spread into a wicked grin.

"Kids, there is only so long I can keep these two from

the living room and these giant windows with a view, so you might want to move this party of two somewhere else or take a breath." His voice held a trace of humor as he moved to let us pass.

I took a step toward the house, but Logan pulled me against him, my back to his front, as he bent down and pressed a kiss into my neck before dropping his mouth to whisper into my ear. "We're returning to this conversation later, Ally, but in case you missed what just happened, the answer is yes. My feelings scare the fuck out of me, but they are there, shining like a bright beacon."

I froze on the deck, closing my eyes for a moment to soak that all in. We were still a clusterfuck of things that weren't working, and there was zero guarantee that any of this would go where I wanted it to, but at least I knew I wasn't alone in this. There was that, and I'd take both of us being a mushy ball of feelings ten times out of ten.

Before I could get my shit together and move into the house, Frank was at the door with Charlie and had an expression on his face that indicated a touch of guilt combined with some humor.

"Charlie needs to go out. Boys, keep me company?" Frank took a step or two past them, without waiting for a response, and headed into the backyard, Charlie bounding ahead.

"Uh-oh." Levi looked at Logan, then to me. "You get this means Linnie wants to talk to Allyson." He paused, clearly for dramatic effect. "Alone."

My stomach flipped, and I turned to look at Logan, panic I'm sure written all over my face.

Logan rubbed his hands up and down my arms. "Ally, it's fine. I've got you. I'll go in there and tell her that whatever she needs to say, I can be there for it too."

A spring breeze suddenly came off the woods, and goose bumps broke out on my upper body. The scent of lilacs hit me, and it was as if they woke me up out of a trance. Looking at Logan, I could suddenly clearly see how he was ready to take his mom on *for me*. Just as he was shouldering the burdens for all the people he cared about. He worried about his family's grief over Nola as well as their concern for his own. He worried they still felt the need to hover over him—not because he didn't think he was struggling, but because he didn't want them to have to change their life for him. He was the most selfless man, person, I'd ever met, and I just wanted someone to take care of him and, most importantly, for him to let them. I decided then and there, that was my new goal.

Standing up straight, I looked up into his eyes. "Go with the guys. I've got this."

Logan looked at me like he might want to argue, but Levi clapped him on the shoulder. "Your girl has this, bro. Let's go."

Levi ambled off the deck. Logan looked at me, waiting.

"I've got this," I whispered.

"I know you do." He leaned forward, pressing a kiss to my forehead, lingering for a moment, then followed the path his dad and Levi had blazed.

I took a deep breath, then walked into the house.

Linnie was sitting on the media lounge chair in the back corner of the living room near the wall of windows on the way to the kitchen. The kitchen's lights were dimmed, everything had been cleaned and put away, and candles dotted the counters and tables. Their pockets of light added a warm glow to the open living space as well as the wooded sage scent that reminded me of Logan.

She patted the spot next to her, and I crossed over. The

white circular chair was plenty big enough for two, and she had a bottle of wine on the table to her side.

"Rosé sound good?" she asked, waving the bottle at me.

I nodded and sank down in the chair, tugging up the ridiculously plush white blanket Logan had thrown over the side. I stroked it mindlessly, wondering how he kept this clean with Charlie, the furniture or the throw.

Linnie handed me the stemless glass as she said, "Washable."

I looked up. "Excuse me?"

She gave me a soft smile as she pulled her legs up and sat cross-legged facing me. "From the expression on your face, I thought you were wondering about how a guy like Logan keeps white furniture and blankets clean, and I was just saying they're all washable."

I nodded, taking a sip of my wine.

"And apologies if you're a wine purist, but I actually like ice in my wine. I don't drink terribly fast so always throw a few in there. Well, if I'm drinking white or rosé. For whatever reason, that seems like it wouldn't work with red." She was a bit rambly, which I found comforting.

I met her gaze and gave her a reassuring smile. "I like ice in those cases too."

"Good." She let out a big exhale, then grasped my hand. "I'm sorry if this feels like I'm putting you on the spot, but the boys don't call me Momma Bear for no reason."

I chuckled. "Did you want to warn me away from Logan?"

"Heavens no. I wanted to beg you to stay."

I choked on my wine, splattering some on my shirt. "Excuse me?"

Linnie put down her wine and grasped my one hand with both of hers. "It won't be easy, Allyson, but that boy has so much love to give. He's been so closed off for so long, and I truly understand. I do. We loved Nola. He loved Nola. We'll never forget her. But this is the first time I've seen him alive since she passed. And I'd just hate you to give up because his walls seem unsurmountable because I promise you they're not."

I soaked in those words with the attention they deserved. I nodded for a moment, then looked at Linnie. "And you think I can scale those walls?"

Linnie gave me a conspiring smile as she leaned over and picked up her glass. Holding it up to me, she said, "Oh, my dear, I don't think you'll scale them, I think you'll bull-doze those motherfuckers down."

I laughed and leaned forward and clinked my glass to hers. "Oh, Linnie, I think you and I are going to get along so well."

"My darling girl, I know it."

Chapter 17

Leather and Lace

L*ogan*

As we approached the end of our afternoon hike, I marveled at how our day had unfolded, how natural it had felt having Allyson with my family. Last night we'd come into the house from walking Charlie to see my mom and Ally curled up together in the big chair, laughing at something they wouldn't share.

We'd spent the next hour pouring over family albums. For the past twenty years at a minimum, my mom had given my brother and me an album every year for Christmas filled with the pictures she'd taken throughout the past year. When I was younger, I'd just said thanks and moved it aside. As I grew older and saw my parents less than when I lived with them, I grew to appreciate this photo documentation of the year that passed.

I'll be honest, the first Christmas after Nola passed, I don't think I cracked the spine of the book. Heck, I hadn't looked at any of those albums again until this past Christmas. After I'd gotten home that weekend from my parents', I went to add another album to the shelf. And then, after staring at them like they might bite, I'd pulled them all down, going through album after album.

It had been a kind of exquisite torture at first. Not the albums in middle school and early high school, of course; those were just the mortifying amusement they always are as you watch yourself grow out of the awkwardness that was the early teen years. What was painful was slowly watching Nola emerge into our lives in our college years. Then our marriage. Then holidays, family vacations, races…

That night four months ago, I sat on my couch, noting that it was all there, spilling out in front of me. My life, the good and the bad.

After many years of Nola being in photos, goofing with Levi, sticking her tongue out at me, she was suddenly gone. And those photos that came after? I barely recognized myself in those pictures. Looking at it through the lens of time, I saw how I was trying to hold it together, the shadows under my eyes, the tension in my body.

Slowly, after about a year, some of that left too. I could easily compare myself preaccident and postaccident. I wasn't where I'd been, but I didn't know if I'd ever get there again.

When I'd shared with my therapist that I'd gone through those books after Christmas this year, she'd congratulated me, stating that I was experiencing some growth. In looking through the albums, I'd allowed myself to experience the joy as well as the grief of my life with Nola. She'd also encouraged me to do exactly what Allyson had suggested, hang up some pictures of Nola. That seemed to be one step beyond what I was ready for, so I'd resisted.

Last night, watching Mom, Dad, and Levi hoot with laughter and fill in Allyson on all our stories, I realized without me noticing it, something seemed to be healed up inside me. Like a jagged tear that had been there was suddenly being sewn together. It was still tender but on the mend. I didn't want to examine it too closely for fear that my emotions couldn't handle it, so I'd simply watched.

Allyson must have sensed that I was feeling emotional, because she hadn't said a word when we'd left everyone to go upstairs but padded up in front of me and asked what time we needed to get up as she set her phone and climbed into bed, curling up and going to sleep like this was something we did on the regular. I was working to ignore how natural it all felt. And while part of me had wanted to pull her into my arms and kiss her to see where that might go, I was afraid.

This morning we'd all headed north as the sun rose. Levi had given me an obvious wink before jumping in the car with our parents, leaving Allyson and me to drive together with Charlie who had quickly made himself comfortable in the back seat. It made sense to have two vehicles; after the weekend, they'd be heading on to their place, and the three of us would be coming back down to Highland. I hadn't gotten my parents alone yet to ask about the rumor of their house hunting, but I penciled that in for a conversation around the campfire tonight. I'd had a lot of time to think about it and the weekend that stretched ahead. When we got in the car, Allyson had barely been able to keep her eyes open and asked if I minded if she got some more sleep, which I hadn't of course, and she and Charlie had snoozed all the way up. The woman was up early on a regular basis, so to me, this just spoke of the crazy hours she'd been keeping. That was true always, but while trying to train for the marathon, it had only gotten worse. My goal was with this weekend away, I wanted to take care of her. She deserved it.

Arriving at Starved Rock, we'd set up, had some food, and hit the trails. The beauty of nature always helped me find my center once again. Levi and I had hiked trail after trail in that first year after I lost Nola, first up here, then downstate once I moved. My problems didn't seem insurmountable when surrounded by all this.

As we wrapped up our first hike of the trip, I paused to soak in the beauty of this place. Not only had I worked here for several years, from an early age my family had installed the love I had for camping at this very park.

Allyson looked over her shoulder in my direction and came to a stop. "You good?"

I scanned her face and noted I wasn't the only one enjoying myself. She seemed relaxed as she turned her face toward the sun and closed her eyes with a blissful expression. This was good for her and for me. My heart felt lighter than it had in years. "I am. Really good actually."

"This place is gorgeous. In case I forget to say it later, thanks for bringing me." She reached out for my hand. "We're nearing the campsite, right? Your parents and Levi will surely be there by now."

She was right, but I didn't want her to only grab my hand to continue this fake relationship in front of my parents. We'd both admitted to some feelings involved; why not just hold my hand for that reason? But I couldn't be mad; she was just trying to protect me. Still, the small frustration was there.

Stuffing it down, I nodded. "Yep, they should be just ahead."

Mom, Dad, and Levi had done the shorter loop, taking Charlie with them, while I'd taken Allyson on the longer trail, eager to stretch my legs after the early-morning drive. We'd arrived, and instead of heading out immediately as my mom had originally wanted, we set up camp and had some lunch together. Then we'd decided on a late-afternoon hike before dinner, which had been exactly what I needed.

As we headed down the trail, the space opened to the camping area that we'd claimed just ahead. We were lucky; mid-April wasn't as crowded as it would be by summer, so we had a prime spot under the trees right next to the lake. No one else was even in the vicinity; the area was ours. My parents and Levi had their tents under the trees, right next to the lake. My asshole of a brother had made a big production of moving my tent farther away, still near the lake, but a more secluded location. My parents had laughed, Allyson had been red as a tomato, and I'd wanted to pummel him while hoping that maybe the distance would be necessary.

As we drew closer, I heard the strum of a guitar before I could see anyone and smiled. My dad loved playing the guitar and singing with my mom. Memories of them singing around the campfire over the years were imprinted on my soul.

Allyson turned to me and whispered, "That's your dad?"

I cocked my head as I listened for a moment. "I believe this is one of their classics, 'Leather and Lace' by Stevie Nicks and Don Henley."

"Nicks is a goddess," Allyson said, her eyes scanning for my parents. Judging by the direction the sound was coming from, they were just out of sight, sitting on the rocks by the lake.

"So you've mentioned before."

"Did you know she originally wrote this song for Waylon Jennings and Jessi Colter but took it back when they broke up so she could sing it with her boyfriend at the time, Don Henley?" Allyson had tugged me along, and we moved quietly into the camp. She stopped to lean against a tree where she could see my parents, Charlie spread out and lounging on the ground by their feet, but not intrude on their moment.

"Is that so?" I said, brushing her hair from her face. "Why did she take it back?"

Allyson tilted her head and smiled in my parents' direction as my dad played and they started the song all over again, my mom belting out the first verse as she sang right to my dad.

I thought for a moment about her parents, what she'd shared about them. Had she ever had a moment like this with them? Where love between your parents was so visible that it was like fireworks?

"I mean, I suppose she could have taken it back for any number of reasons, but the interview I read said she worked so hard on it she wanted it to be sung by two people in love."

"What is the song about?" I asked, more to myself though I said it aloud. It was something Levi teased me about when we were younger. I'd listen to a song, know all its words, but not have given a lot of thought to the meaning behind those lyrics.

Allyson's head was nodding along to my parents as they continued to sing to each other, swaying on the rocks where they were sitting. "I mean, I'm not exactly sure. I think it's about two people in love that have their own journeys to follow. They each need to rely on the other, to let down their walls and see each other for who they are, vulnerability and all. The song is about whether they're strong enough to do that." She turned her head to meet my gaze.

I stepped closer to her. "So they need to trust each other, even with what makes their heart feel hollow."

She nodded. "That's what they need to trust each other with the most." She linked her hand with mine.

"And if he trusts her with that, will she stay?" I brushed an errant hair, tucking it behind her ear before tracing her jaw to tip her chin up to me.

"I think so." Her breath hitched. "She's been waiting to walk alongside him; he just needs to ask."

"Are we still talking about this song?" I kissed the tip of her nose, then began to pepper kisses over her cheeks, jaw, and down her neck.

"Kind of," she said with a moan as she tilted her head to allow more access to her collarbone. "Is your heart hollow, Logan?" She raked her fingers through my hair, holding my head where it was, devouring her neck.

"Honestly?" I tugged on her ear lobe with my teeth. "I think it's becoming less so by the day."

She let out another quiet moan. "I'm so glad."

"Well, well, well." The voice of my brother was the last thing I wanted to hear, but there it was nonetheless. "Seems like a good time to remind you of the hell you're going to catch if a love bite ends up on the beautiful Allyson's neck. To say nothing of the visible beard burn."

I closed my eyes and dropped my head against her shoulder, which was shaking with laughter.

"It's not funny," I mumbled loud enough for her to hear.

"It is a little," she whispered.

"Oh, it's a lot funny," Levi said. Apparently, he had supersonic hearing, or we weren't as quiet as we'd thought.

Levi continued to my parents, patting Charlie as he passed, then he joined them in their sing-along, which had now moved on to "Heart of Gold" from Neil Young. Levi sat next to Mom, his arm wrapped around her waist, as they sang to Dad's accompaniment.

"I want that," Allyson whispered.

I pulled back to look at her. Levi was right, beard burn was real, but no hickeys, thank you very much. But it was her gaze that took my breath away. She was looking at my family with a very real longing visible on her face.

"My family?" I asked, stepping into her space again and tightening my arms around her waist.

Without looking away from them, she answered. "No. I mean, I do love your family. But I want what your parents have. That relationship. Honestly, I don't know if I'd seen that before coming to Highland Falls. But so many of our friends have found that." She gestured to my mom and dad. "Or what appears to be that, just the younger version. Were they always like this?"

I rested my head on hers and watched them. My mom had thrown her head back, laughing at something Levi was saying. The sunlight reflected off the still lake, dancing across Levi's face and bathing my family in a warm glow. "Yeah." I knew my love for them could be heard in my tone. And before I knew it, I wasn't stopping there. "I thought I'd found it." My voice caught.

"You did." Allyson didn't waver, just pulled her arms tightly around me.

"How can you say that? You didn't know Nola." I whispered, like this answer meant a lot, though I couldn't say why.

We stood there in silence for a moment, the only sounds the strumming of my dad as they decided what song they were singing next. Then Allyson spoke.

"I might not have known Nola, Logan, but I know you. I know what you've shared and the little I've heard from your family. And I know with certainty that you had found what your parents did. You two just didn't get to have it for as long, but that doesn't make it any less special." She ran her hand up and down my back. "And I'd love to hear more about her if you ever want to talk about her."

"It doesn't bother you?"

"Absolutely not." The firmness in her tone said she was serious.

I paused, but this place, the beauty, the closeness of my family, made me lay it out there, being surrounded by the trees that Nola loved, though she'd rather hike through them than camp. "Sometimes I feel guilty, but I feel her here." I gestured to the woods all around. "Nola loved the trees. She felt they were our ancient sentries."

"I love that." She looked around us, then back to me. "Why are you feeling guilty?"

Say it. I told myself. I closed my eyes, remembering Nola's face. It was warm and understanding, which I knew she would be, but it didn't make it any easier for me right now. "Because more and more, I think I might be ready to move on."

Allyson felt tense in my arms for a minute before she let it go. "With me?" she asked with some hesitation.

I nodded against her.

"I'll never rush you," she said. "Fake relationship or more."

"I know you wouldn't." I took a breath and then laid it out there. "I might be ready to be rushed though."

She took that in. "You say when."

We watched my mom shove Levi off the rock so hard he fell into the lake. My dad howled with laughter as my mom stood, all five foot two of her, hands on hips, lecturing Levi with a grin on her face. Levi sat on his ass in the shallow water, looking up to my mom with a wide smile.

I leaned down and whispered in Allyson's ear. "When."

Chapter 18

Never Let Me Go

Allyson

The firelight danced into the night sky as Frank told another story about a time he'd taken Levi and Logan on a fishing trip as kids. It had been a fly-in trip to the Boundary Waters, and they'd seen some older gentleman traveling with a group, and he'd been wearing wingtips and lugging a Samsonite.

Frank was howling, recounting the amount of luggage the group had been taking as he and his boys had stood there with only the barest of essentials. However, they'd enjoyed that group and even kept in touch a bit after their trip because of course they did. Frank didn't seem like the kind of person that would miss the opportunity to get to know someone new.

Linnie stood up, stretching. "That's all for me, kids. I'm not as young as I once was and need my beauty sleep."

"Thanks for dinner." I spoke up from my bundled-up spot in my camp chair. It wasn't cold, just cool, and I was more comfortable that I ever remember being. "Let me know how I can help tomorrow."

"You're a sweetheart, Allyson, but these boys will tell you my love language is cooking for the people I care about. So biscuits, eggs, and bacon are happening tomorrow, bright and early. All you need to do is bring your appetite."

"That won't be hard, Mom. We need to get a long run in tomorrow before breakfast, if that works out timing wise." Logan spoke up from his spot in the camp chair beside mine, Charlie's head resting on his foot.

"That works out just fine, son. I'll take a hike with your old man before setting up shop." I didn't miss the moment of happiness that passed Linnie's face when Logan said we were going to run. "Oh, we ran into Susan and Jack last week. They said to tell you hello and they'd love to catch up some time soon." Linnie's words were benign, but her assessing glance at Logan and his sudden rigid posture indicated there was more to this conversation than was obvious.

"Mom." Logan's tone was one of resignation. "You know—"

My attention was pulled to my phone where I had a text from Andy. Seeing her name on my lock screen made my heart rate immediately skyrocket as did the opening line of *small problem...*

"I knew I shouldn't leave town," I muttered.

I felt Logan turn my direction. "What's up?" he asked.

I ignored him to focus on my phone and quickly opened my texts.

Andy: *small problem...*

Andy: *But totally have it handled. Caydence had a family emergency and is out tomorrow. Called in a favor and Lou is picking up the apron again for the day. She's heading up the town location and I've got the café at the park. Relax, soak in nature, just wanted you to know about the shuffle.*

I snorted out a relieved laugh. Lou loved subbing in when we were in a pinch. Said it kept her skills fresh.

Logan was reading my phone as well. He leaned over to kiss my shoulder. "So it's all good?"

I slid my phone aside. "All good. Sorry I panicked."

"Totally understandable."

I realized Linnie and Frank had waited to see if I was okay, which was kind and not unexpected. I gave them a brief rundown of my apprehension about being away from my business and explained what happened tonight.

"I'm just glad you could get away," Linnie said. "It's good for you and gives you a fresh perspective. Think of the new energy you'll have at work after some time outside this weekend." She moved around the fire to kiss all three of us good night and headed toward her tent, Frank saying his goodbyes and following right behind her, grumbling about how he wasn't that old.

"So Allyson. How has the first day of camping with the Traubs compared to camping experiences of the past?" Levi asked as he tossed another log onto the fire.

I pulled the blanket up higher that Linnie had handed to me an hour ago after a delicious dinner of grilled chicken and what she called pocket potatoes but was sliced potatoes with cheese, butter, bacon, and green onions wrapped in foil. I had a feeling that if I hung around this family more, all future meals on my own would be a huge disap-pointment.

Peering over the edge of my blanket, I stared at the fire. "Well, considering this is my first camping trip, I'd say you all have the top spot by default, but in truth I'm having an excellent time."

Logan and Levi looked at each other, before looking back to me.

"Um, what?" Levi asked.

"You've never camped before?" Logan said.

I laughed. "Nope. Connecticut born and raised, remember? New Haven. Not part of my normal day-to-day life as a financial analyst. Maybe some people from home camp, but no one I know." I chuckled to myself, thinking about my mom looking around this campsite. She'd hyperventilate and race off to the nearest hotel. Instead, I thought I might like to move here. Could one live comfortably out of a tent in the winter? Probably not, but any stress in my life seemed to evaporate under the night sky. Linnie was likely right. This was good for me even with the minor anxiety.

"I can't believe you didn't have a million questions for us before you agreed to come, the least of which I would have thought would be where do you go to the bathroom." Logan said, reaching over to link his fingers with mine.

God that felt good.

Instead, I shrugged. "I mean, I figured the worst-case scenario was I was hovering and squatting over the ground."

"It's a little better than that," Levi said with a wry grin.

"A huge step up. You guys have it so easy," I agreed, dropping my head back to look at the millions of stars dotting the sky above.

"That we do," Levi agreed. "And with that, I'm turning in. You two still good with me joining you for the run tomorrow?"

"Of course," I said while Logan murmured his agreement.

"I'm claiming your pup," Levi said, whistling for Charlie to join him.

"Sounds good," Logan said with a pat to Charlie's head before the pup trotted after Levi.

"Night," Levi called, walking toward his tent, with a wave to us and a murmured conversation with Charlie.

"And then there were two," I said, which made Logan bark out a laugh.

"That there are," he said as he squeezed my hand. "You doing okay?"

Other than a pesky elevated heart rate, I'm great, I thought. Instead, I said, "Sure, why?"

His gaze locked on mine, and it made my entire body heat up. Damn.

"I'm sure it's a lot, being with a family you don't know well on a camping weekend..."

"And spending time with a guy that you're in a fake relationship with but have also admitted to having some very real feelings for."

He squeezed my hand again. "Did you admit that? I remember *I* said something, but not sure about you."

"My mouth admitted it for me when it crashed into yours." I winked in his direction, thankful for the darkness because my winks tended to be awkward, but the moment seemed to call for one. Maybe the light the campfire gave off would make me look sultry? Doubtful, but a girl could dream.

"Maybe that's how your mouth was feeling last night, but I noticed there was no follow-up on said feelings when we went to bed," he commented lightly. His words sounded neutral, but I thought I could detect some concern behind them.

It seemed like everything with Logan was a bit of a cha-cha, that dance they taught us in middle school PE classes, one step forward, two back. Would I like to devour the man? Heck yes. Was I worried about his frame of mind? Also, yes. Did I think it was fair to dive into something with him when he was clearly still grieving, and frankly, my life was a bit of a mess? I had next to no flexibility in scheduling a moment of self-care—please note how much I hate that term, but it does apply—much less time for a relationship. So was that fair to him? Probably a resounding no.

Sigh. So many sighs. And yet I was drawn to him and absolutely wanted more. Contrasts and contradictions all over the place.

I stood from my chair to move to Logan's, still holding his hand. "May I?" I nodded at his lap.

"Please."

Straddling his legs, I slid down until we were pelvis to pelvis. Not the most comfortable of spots in a camp chair, but we could make this work. I wound my arms around his shoulders and toyed with his hair.

"So last night, I did think, briefly, about seeing if you wanted to continue what we started on the deck before your brother interrupted." My palms were sweating; this was a bit insane how my body reacted to his.

"Hmm, but you didn't." He started toying with the ends of my hair. I really wanted to lean into that, Lord knows I loved having my hair played with, but the lingering concern in his voice reminded me to keep going.

"No. I wasn't sure if you wanted more, and I didn't want to push you." I bit my lip while noting that his hands froze, and he looked directly at me.

"You didn't want to push me?"

I shrugged. "I mean, I'm pretty sure you're attracted to me. You said something about your feelings for me being more than you could handle. I thought that might mean that you had things you needed to sort, and I didn't want to add to that." I paused before deciding to lay it all on the table. "I'm also a bit of a mess and maybe not good for you."

Logan's hands moved from my hair to either side of my face as he tugged me toward him. I lowered my mouth to his for a kiss. This wasn't an I'm-going-to-devour-you-in-a-punishing-but-amazing kiss. This was a sensuous kiss, filled with feeling, longing, and a desire to get horizontal. Like, yesterday. This was a kiss that made promises and inspired dreams. And I wanted more of it. I wanted to have a kiss like this every day for the rest of my life, and I knew how dangerous that line of thinking was.

Pulling back, I looked into his warm gaze, noting the relaxed but heated expression on his face. "That was nice," I whispered.

"I want you to put yourself first," he said as he moved to pepper kisses along my jaw, down my neck, a nip to my collarbone that caused a pulse of pleasure at my core, and then to the other collarbone and up my neck and spoke between soft pecks on my neck. "I want you to take care of yourself. I want you to let me take care of you."

I mean, if this was what putting yourself first consisted of, I was one hundred and ten percent in favor of it. Sign. Me. Up.

That being said, I needed some clarification. "How does me making out with you—"

"Or more," his tone was firm. Nice.

"Or more constitute me putting myself first?" I smoothed down his eyebrows and placed my own kiss on his neck.

"Did you want more to happen last night?" he asked, tilting his head to give me better access.

I nodded as I contemplated just tucking my head into his neck and sleeping right there. I mean, it should be uncomfortable, but it felt safe, like home, and I didn't want to leave.

I'm not sure if Logan could sense my thoughts or what, but he pulled me forward just a bit so that we were chest to chest, and my body acted on instinct before my brain could decide that it was a bad choice and did exactly what I wanted. I melted into him. His arms circled my body and mine were tucked against his torso. Safe. Home.

"Allyson, you were right. I was likely too much in my head to be there for you last night. I appreciate you looking out for me. But I'd also like you to feel comfortable telling me what you're thinking or what you want. I don't want to be so selfish that I ignore all your feelings. That's not fair to you." He pressed a kiss into the side of my head before continuing. "You matter. Your feelings matter. I want you to know that I see you, and I am grateful you saw me last night; I just wish we talked about it."

I nodded, soaking those words in. He was right, but...

"Why didn't you say something last night?" I asked. This went both ways, after all.

He paused. I listened to the sounds of the night. An owl hooted in the distance, the fire crackled.

"I was scared."

I sat with that for a moment. I understood that, felt it too.

"And now?" I asked.

More sounds of the night flooded my senses while I waited, feeling like this was a bigger conversation than I'd thought at first. It felt like we were on the precipice of something, and wherever this conversation ended up would determine, I don't know, everything?

"What are you asking me, Allyson?" He trailed his fingers up and down my spine.

I breathed in deep, the scent of Logan mixing with the campfire and the woods. Pulling all the courage I could, I spoke into his ear. "I'm asking if we want to continue what we started last night." Leaning back, I watched him for a response.

"Now?" Logan raised an eyebrow at me. Why that made me want to jump him immediately, I couldn't tell you. His fingers continued their dance along my back as he growled his response. "What do you have in mind?"

"Are you asking how far I want to take this?"

"Yes."

Yep. That was a growl. More pulses in my core at that. Interesting.

"Honestly, can we see where this leads?" I whispered. I mean, his parents and Levi were at least one hundred yards from us, but I still felt the need to whisper this conversation. I burrowed into safety.

His fingers stilled, but he still responded. "Yes."

I thought about that for a moment. Maybe he took my reply as in I wasn't sure what I wanted, which absolutely was not the case. More bravery and bluntness were needed. I closed my eyes, pressed deeper into his neck, and spilled my truth. "Logan, what I'm saying is I'd be happy to go into that tent and have sex. I'd also be happy to go down on you, delighted if you returned the favor. Hand jobs are on the table. As is kissing. Or a night of cuddling. I don't want you to feel pressured. I'd be happy with any and all of the above list." Yep, eyes were staying closed. No looking at each other after that little speech.

Logan's body was tense for a moment before he barked out a laugh. "Babe, that all sounds good. And I can't guarantee my mindset, though right now I am firmly in favor of some horizontal time with you, clothes optional. But what did we just talk about? What do *you* need or want?"

I laughed lightly into his neck. "Can I add a last option

to my list of all of the above? Not that all have to happen tonight, but truly I'd be down with any of them." My cheeks were red; I knew they were. There was zero percent chance that I wasn't blushing at this moment. I was counting on the darkness to conceal that fact from him.

"Okay, babe. Then I'm going to need you to return to your chair for a minute." He squeezed my ass and slid his hands from me, allowing me to push back and come to standing.

I took a few steps to my chair. "Do we need cooling-off time?"

"Hell no." He stood up. "I need to put this campfire out before we hit the tent."

I nodded because that made sense and curled up in my chair. Watching him move around in black sweats that hugged his ass and a long-sleeved T-shirt from the Homestead that stretched across his shoulders was no hardship. He poured water over the fire, using some stick to mix the ashes and embers with the soil. He flipped some of the logs that remained, dousing them with water as well all while I stared like the stalker I was. Finally, he tossed the stick to the side and turned to me. He looked confident and sure. I wanted to wrap myself around him and never let go.

The moonlight illuminated him, barely, as he reached his hand out to me. "Ready?"

Chapter 19

All of the Above

Logan

Was my heart threatening to beat out of my chest? Yep. But I knew that it was not only from nervousness but also excitement. Yes, there was some trepidation with what we were about to do, but I was ready. Still conflicted about a lot of what came next but working to be present in the moment, and I knew with complete certainty that I wanted this.

To be fair, there was a part of me that wished I had gotten to this mindset last night when we were in my home with an actual bed instead of a tent by a lake with my parents some distance away, but I was letting that go.

Allyson and I made our way to our yellow tent by the lake. It was still, the moon reflecting off the water, and a sense of tranquility filled the air. Give it two months and all the campgrounds around this park would be humming. Late spring, however, we had the place essentially to ourselves.

I unzipped the tent, gesturing for her to go first, then climbed in behind her and zipped us in. Allyson was kneeling next to the sleeping bag that was spread out on top of the mattress. She pressed down, testing the cushion, I assumed.

"Think that will work for us?" I joked.

"I'm impressed we have any type of mattress," she said. "I assumed we'd be sleeping on the ground."

We both sat on the edge, taking off our hiking boots and putting them inside the zipped door. Allyson immediately crawled onto the mattress and let out a sigh of comfort.

I crawled on top of the mattress, pulling her with me to lie facing each other. "We used to. As Levi and I got older, we began researching mattresses. My parents used to use some other style, not terrible, but we wanted them to be as comfortable as possible. We finally found these. Not cheap, a beast to deflate, but almost like being in a bed, so we got three."

"And it sleeps two," she said as she ran a hand down my arm. "Just wish I could see you better."

I thought about that. "I can unzip the sides and let the moonlight come through the mesh. I'll just do the top part, not that we are much more insulated with the sides zipped or not, but it helps."

"Is it too cheesy if I say I'll keep you warm?" she asked.

I laughed as I crawled around, unzipping just a little of each side, and the tent filled with moonlight. Crawling back to my spot, I was grateful Allyson had spoken up. Seeing her lying there on my mattress and pillow, her red hair fanned out around her, would be a memory I would hold dear. Somehow I knew that to the depths of my core.

"Come here, Logan," she whispered. It was like a siren's call and spoke to something deep within me. "Let me take care of you," she said.

Coming to rest next to her, I brushed her hair from her face. "But I wanted to take care of you."

She leaned up to lightly kiss my lips before lying back down. "Maybe we can take care of each other."

With that, I knew that we wouldn't just be stopping at hand holding tonight. I was ready and I wanted this, more than anything.

"You still good with the all-of-the-above option?" I asked.

Her smile was breathtakingly beautiful when she looked at me. "Yes, teach."

"Oh, sweetheart, there are plenty of things I can teach you," I said with a growl as I lay down completely to hook one leg over her and tug her body to mine.

"I bet you can," she whispered. "But maybe we could shed some of these clothes first."

I reached back and fisted the top of my shirt, tugging it over my head and tossing it to the side where my flannel from earlier was already resting.

Allyson hummed her appreciation while her fingers went on a journey from my abs to my chest and back. They landed on the waistband of my joggers, which she began to push down to indicate her desire to move this along.

"Oh no, babe. We need to get you undressed too," I said as I helped her pull her shirt off. She immediately rolled to her back and kicked off her leggings. I took her in for a moment, stretched out over the sleeping bag in her bra and underwear, and worried I wouldn't last long. They were sheer, nude, and left little to the imagination, even in the low light. I groaned.

Allyson let out a low laugh. "See something you like?"

"You know it."

"Then shed those joggers, sir, and get your ass up here."

I kicked them off and crawled up to her in my boxer briefs.

"Hey there," she whispered.

"Hey," I said. Any hint of uneasiness about what we were doing had disappeared, and I was grateful for it.

I dipped my head to meet her lips and fell into her embrace. Allyson tugged at my hair as I slid to my side and held her to me, our legs intertwining. Her mouth parted, and I slid my tongue to meet hers as we traded kisses. I felt like I could do this forever.

Allyson's breathing became more erratic as I traced a path down her neck.

"Like that?" I asked, nipping the base of her neck at her collarbone.

"Love it," she said.

"What else do you like?" I murmured as I caught her earlobe between my teeth.

Instead of telling me, she pulled my head toward her chest. Message received. I lavished the top of each breast in open-mouthed kisses before tugging down the sheer cup and sucking one nipple into my mouth and biting gently. Judging by the way she sounded, that was most definitely the way to go. I loved learning her body, finding out what worked for her.

"Good, babe?" I asked, wanting to see her eyes, or as best I could in the low light, on me.

Those beautiful eyes met mine, and I fell for the expression of arousal that lit up her face. "Absolutely perfect," she whispered before pulling my head down to devour me in a kiss. After a minute or two, we came up for air. "Just saying you don't need these either," she whispered as her hand slid into my briefs, and she traced from my side to my back, giving my ass a squeeze.

I let out a moan of pleasure as I moved myself down the

mattress, kissing her beautiful body as I went, her hands sliding from my underwear to my back, to my head.

"I'll lose them in a bit; I need to do this first." I reached for her underwear and tugged them down, letting them join the pile of clothes in the corner for the tent.

Her smile was secretive, a bit seductive as she looked down at me, crooking a finger to urge me up.

I shook my head and tugged her legs to part them enough for me to kneel between them. I picked one up and kissed her inner thigh, my mouth trailing until it reached her pussy, then lowering her leg and doing the same to the other side.

Her hums and moans increased as she fought to stay still. God, she was gorgeous.

Finishing the descent from her other leg, I finally reached her core. Looking up her body, I noted that her back was arched, and her breathless pants had increased. Looks like we were on the right path. I leaned forward, parting her lips with my thumbs, and licked up her slit right to that tiny bundle of nerves.

"Oh," she whispered. "Yessssss."

Damn, why hadn't we tried this weeks earlier? Months? I mean, I knew, but I think I could happily stay down here forever.

I traced that path over and over with my tongue, flattening it out, sliding it around her clit, paying attention to the noises she made until I knew we were close. She rocked into me, again and again, until I stayed focused on her clit and sucked it into my mouth slowly, no longer teasing. Her hips immediately rose, and she began to whisper words indicating I was on the right path, which her body was already telling me was the case. I kept a consistent pressure until her hips shot up and her body stilled as my name shot out of her mouth. I kept at it until I could tell she was oversensitized, and I crawled up her body.

Rolling her to her side, I noted the blissed-out expression on her face, which made me want to do this again and again and again.

I leaned forward, capturing her lips. With a soft kiss, I pulled back. "No regrets?"

Her warm eyes met mine. "Only if we're stopping." Then the meaning of her words clearly clicked in as she followed up. "Unless you want to stop."

"Fuck no," I said. I rolled to the side, feeling for my bag.

"What are you doing?" Allyson asked, pressing kisses into my back.

"Looking for my bag with the condoms," I said, feeling the edge of it and tugging it toward me.

She laughed. "So you weren't kidding when you said you'd thought of this last night? You came prepared."

"That I did," I said as I found the zipper.

She put a hand on my arm. "Totally up to you, but I know you're clearly clean. I am too, and I have an IUD."

I stilled, then turned toward her. "Promise you'll be up for round two because if I'm bare this first time, it might be over rather quick."

She laughed and pulled me onto my back. "I'm good with that."

As she swung her leg over and straddled me, I fought letting go before we even connected. Allyson reached for me and stroked my cock, locking her eyes on mine.

"You know, we haven't hit everything on my list." She noted with an impish smile.

"We've got time, babe," I said, fighting not to thrust into her grip. "But not much if you keep doing that."

She nodded and placed me at her entrance, then

lowered herself onto me. Sweet Lord, her walls gripped my cock, and I took a breath to let her set the pace she wanted.

When she was fully seated, her eyes opened and met mine. "Wow," she whispered.

I nodded back to her and touched her hip to indicate she needed to move. Now.

She leaned forward, planting her hands on my chest as she took charge, and damn, it was a sight to behold. I kept my eyes open the whole time, not wanting to miss one minute of this. As the sensations continued to build, I worked hard to hold back as she rode me to the climax she wanted to claim.

"You close?" I grunted out, meeting her thrust for thrust.

"Mm-hmm," she said, increasing her pace.

I worried that I was going to get there before her, but right as I reached up to find her clit, she stilled and dropped her head, letting out a low moan as her walls clamped down. I grabbed her hips, flipped her to her back, and increased my own thrusts, riding her through her orgasm and into my own.

Collapsing to her side, I consciously kept most of my weight off her as we both worked to catch our breath. After a few moments, she turned on her side facing me and grabbed my face, bringing it to hers.

We kissed, her lips opening sweetly for mine. It wasn't a frenetic kiss but a leisurely one like we had all the time in the world to lie there. Pulling back, her eyes scanned my face.

"You okay?" she whispered.

I could play dumb, but I knew what she was asking. "I'm good," I promised because I was.

Allyson's gaze didn't waver, like she was searching to

make sure I was telling her the truth. Clearly, she seemed to like what she saw on my expression, because she nodded before curling up into my shoulder and throwing her arm across me.

My brain kicked in, thinking of sex without a condom and what I knew from before. "Hold on," I whispered, sitting up and grabbing the bag that I'd pulled over earlier. I reached in, feeling around until I found a washcloth for our shower tomorrow and grabbed my water bottle. Wetting it, I turned and held it out to Allyson. "Can I?"

She looked surprised, but nodded anyway, parting her legs, and allowing me to help clean her up. Mission accomplished, I tossed the towel to the side and helped her get under the sleeping bag. She once again rested her head on my shoulder, and I toyed with her hair as her hand lightly traced a mindless pattern over my pecs.

"I don't think we're getting to the rest of your list tonight," I whispered. "I'm exhausted."

"Me too," she said. Even her voice sounded sleepy. "But I'm glad we didn't fight this anymore."

"Same."

"I've felt like I've been running on empty for so long," she said in a hushed voice. "The cafés are amazing, and I'm so grateful for the business, but they have been the focus of all my time, and I needed more."

"More being what?" I asked, trailing my fingers across her shoulder and back.

She leaned over and pressed a kiss to my chest. "More being time with friends, time on the trails running, and time with you."

I smiled thinking of how she was opening herself, even when she'd often rather curl up at home. It was good for her.

"Well, for what it's worth, clearly I was operating on E

too." I pressed a kiss to the top of her head, then lay back with my head on the pillow.

"And you're feeling okay about being filled up with a relationship, or whatever this is, again?" Her voice faltered a little, which was not okay.

I turned on my side, tilting her chin to meet my eyes. "It's okay to call this a relationship, Allyson. I know it started as a fake one to get my parents off my back, but I'm in this with you and want to see what comes next."

"I'll be honest, the marathon still gives me extreme anxiety. I alternate between wanting to run and wanting to hide. Not sure either will get me to a point of healing." I leaned forward, kissing her nose. "But I'm absolutely okay with being filled up with you, or..." I paused and gave her a small smile. "...filling you up again."

"Don't think I didn't notice change of topic there. I don't want you to stress about the race, but I'll allow it for now." She ran her hand up my chest and moved forward to snuggle into my neck, nuzzling into my beard, just like she had out by the fire. "But I am glad you don't feel empty," she said into my neck.

"Back at you, babe." I pinched her ass, which caused a surprised yelp followed by some laughter, and curled my arms around her, falling asleep faster and harder than I had in three years.

Chapter 20

Family Conversations

Allyson

A magical weekend with the Traub family hadn't helped my mindset. Instead, it felt as if I was living in a fairy tale that I didn't want to wake up from. I'd woken in a tent, cuddled up to a solid wall of a man. Before I could suggest an encore from the night before, his eyes snapped open and he whispered we were about to have company, right before Levi had started singing Pink's "Just Give Me a Reason" at the top of his lungs. Logan had said that there would be no stopping him until we got up, so that we did.

Leaving the tent, I fired off a quick text to Andy to confirm all was well for the day. She reiterated that she had it—she was working at the park, Lou was manning the café in town, and I was to chill the fuck out. Message received.

After that I joined the Traub twins on a long run, and frankly, I don't know when I've enjoyed exercise more. True, I often told Logan that I'd started running as a form of torture, but over the months that I'd taken up the sport, I'd found a peace in setting out on the trails, with him or alone.

So while I appreciated what exercise did for me mentally and physically, had even begun to look forward to it, I'd never consider it fun by any stretch of the imagination.

And yet the twenty miles winding through Starved Rock had flown by. We'd headed out, running the first eight with Charlie. Swinging by the campsite, we'd dropped the pup off with Linnie and Frank. Logan was careful to keep Charlie's mileage low, so we'd done the first loop, then headed on to a longer one without him.

Levi and Logan had traded insults as we ran, teaching me that it was indeed possible to run while thinking you might pee your pants from laughter. They seemed to notice in some instinctive way when my energy was lagging and then choose the exact moment that I needed some levity to lighten our conversations.

Even better, though they had a shared history thirty-three years long, they never made me feel like an outsider. They shared stories, including many from being here in the past. But also hilarious memories from college and some true treasures from their younger days. I saw why Logan was so happy to have Levi stay in Highland a little longer now that he knew it hadn't been as a spy for their momma bear.

As we wrapped up the last mile, slowing to a walk to cool down before hitting the campsite, I looked to Logan. Good Goddess, as Ivy would say, he was a treat for the eyes. He and Levi were both wearing ridiculously short running shorts, but that just served to showcase their long muscled legs. Each of them had worn a light long-sleeved shirt which was now sticking to the backs with sweat. My leggings and shirt had done me well, but I couldn't deny a little added heat from watching Logan. Spring in Illinois was fickle in

April. Our run was warm enough for shorts, but our hike later might need layers because there was a breeze.

While the distance had been a chore in some ways, though we'd come close before, the two of them seemed at ease at the pace. I knew Logan could run faster than I did, but he never seemed to mind running alongside me and my shorter legs. If I'd been paying attention for the past five months of running together, I would have noticed more than the tension in his face as we approached the half. He hadn't been as relaxed as we ran, I now realized.

That wasn't a factor today.

Was it due to the addition of Levi or the exercise we'd participated in last night? I wasn't sure. Whatever it was, I wanted more of that for him. And selfishly, I wanted to continue what we'd started, but a nagging part of me warned that this was too easy.

"So what's on the itinerary today?" I asked to double-check, hands up on my head as I worked to even out my breathing.

"Brunch, which will be a spread. Another hike with Mom and Dad. Pack up later to head home, guessing around late afternoon." Levi was walking backward up the trail as he relayed the schedule to me.

"And don't forget a conversation with Mom and Dad about their newfound interest in real estate in Highland Falls," Logan said from my side.

I chuckled, wondering how that conversation was going to go. It had been a few days since Lou apparently dropped that news bomb on Logan. He told me about how he'd thought Levi might have been holding out on him, but he'd been wrong. He'd debated bringing it up the past few nights but decided against it, wanting to save the conversation for the end of the camping trip in case it left him with the need to cool off afterward.

"Have to say, you two, for running twenty miles today, both of you are looking surprisingly relaxed. Anything you want to share?" Levi's voice was alight with amusement.

"I hope you trip on a tree root," Logan quipped, though there was no heat in his words. I fought a satisfied smile.

"Mm-hmm. I think that answers my question." With a look at me, he gave me a brilliant smile and nod, indicating his approval, turned, and headed to the camp site.

"Momma Bear, feed me," he called.

Linnie was working on a positively glorious buffet of food. Camping with the Traubs included a Blackstone griddle, so it wasn't exactly roughing it. Logan said if they had to hike to a camping spot, they packed lighter. Here they drove right in, so the weekend had been pretty easy. While I was a fan of this type of camping, I wasn't sure I'd be able to do some of the longer trips they'd gone on with fewer creature comforts.

"Grab a plate; it's all ready to go." Linnie stacked some more pancakes on a plate on the table they had set up. Bacon was already stacked. Fruit cut up and in bowls. Some eggs and hash browns were also available. After our run, I wanted to eat it all.

Logan passed me a plate, and I followed Levi through the line. There was a picnic table next to the water, so I joined Frank and Charlie there while Logan and Levi debated who was going to eat more pancakes.

Finally, Logan and Levi joined the table on either side of me, and Linnie sat down next to Frank, passing him a plate she'd filled for him. He shot her a wink and dug in, breaking off a bite of bacon and handing it to Charlie under the table. Darn it, his wink didn't look awkward either. Maybe I needed to practice.

Just as I took a large bite of pancakes, Levi spoke up. "So *mis padres*, Logan and I were wondering what's up with looking for a house in Highland and not telling us? Are you two planning to up and leave me all on my lonesome in Aurora?"

I can only assume I was startled by the notion of having an honest conversation with your parents with no one icing out the others in displeasure as a result because my food went down the wrong pipe and I immediately began coughing. Levi and Logan both reached over to slap my back, apparently trying to help or kill me—jury was still out.

I finally got control of myself and looked up to see the entire table watching me. Grabbing my water bottle, I picked it up to take a drink, waving in a gesture to keep going as my eyes streamed with tears. "Don't mind me."

Linnie and Frank gave each other a look that clearly spoke volumes before Frank gave her a nod. Linnie took a breath and turned to us. "Well, it's like this. My friend Donna fell and broke her hip last week."

Color me confused, and apparently, I wasn't the only one.

"Mom, I'm sorry to hear about Donna. I think I can speak for Levi and me when I say that one, I want to know if she's okay, and two, I'm failing to see how that is connected to you looking for real estate in Highland."

I slid my hand on Logan's thigh. I could feel how tense he was, and I knew he was concerned that his parents were reacting out of a need to take care of him.

"It's like this, kids. We're not spring chickens anymore," Linnie began.

"You don't say," Levi said, heavy on the sarcasm.

"Hush," Linnie gave him a mom look. "Donna's kids moved after they got out of college. She and Mike are only ten years older than your dad and me. Her kids had to upend their lives to come home and make sure she was on the road to recovery, and she was lucky because she is. Before too long, she's going to be right as rain. But that put me to thinking—"

"Dangerous," Logan muttered. Levi reached over, and they knocked fists.

"Shut it," she said without missing a beat. "Levi isn't sure where he's going to land, but I wouldn't be shocked if it ended up being down here. And Logan, you're here and settled. Now that I see you with Allyson, I know that for certain. We'd love to be here, closer to you all, for good times and the hard times to come."

My gut clenched. Linnie was such a sweet lady, but she was invested in believing this relationship had staying power. I prayed to Ivy's goddess that she was correct.

"Way to be morbid, Mom," Logan said with a shake of his head. Apparently, he wasn't as freaked by the comment about the two of us as I was.

"Yeah, Linnie. Should we go pick a burial plot?"

"Done and done," Frank said with a grin. "Just might need to transfer it down here, but I'd like a spot with a view."

"Maybe we can put in a firepit in the cemetery?" Levi asked. "Then I can come hang out and have a beer while I tell you stories once you're gone."

"Just pour one in the ground for me, and we're good," Frank fired back.

Holy wow. The humor and love wrapped up in this his conversation along with a side of sarcasm and irritation made my mind spin. What was this?

"So you're moving to Highland?" Logan asked.

"Are we ignoring the fact that Mommy Dearest thinks I am?" Levi asked, reaching over to steal a piece of bacon from Logan's plate.

"Dude, that should have already been a thought in your brain. You love being near me, and you've made friends with the guys. Besides, what's keeping you in Aurora?" Logan asked, leaning behind me to hit Levi upside the head.

"I mean, truth, but maybe let me come to these types of decisions in my own time?"

"Are you there now?" Linnie asked.

"Are you picking a house that has a space for me?" he retorted.

"Heck no. You're a grown-ass human. Find your own spot." Linnie gave him a disapproving headshake, then she looked to Logan. "I'm sorry we didn't mention anything to you sooner." She looked to Levi. "Or mention anything to you either. It was just something we've been considering. When we were down here, we decided it wouldn't hurt to see what was out there, but we're not in a rush. Nothing has called to us yet, and we're not moving for anything that doesn't feel right. So you have time to get used to the idea."

Logan slid his hand on top of mine on his thigh and squeezed. "Sounds good. We just want you guys to be happy."

I wondered if this would be a setback to him, thinking of losing his parents, though hopefully not until a way into the future. Would that make him think of Nola more? How would that impact anything going forward with us? Part of me wanted to protect him from everything, to wrap the man in Bubble Wrap. A larger part of me wanted him to face it all but have me to come back to and deal with the hard stuff. In reality, I couldn't force that; it was all on him to decide. All I could do was be there. And I would if he'd let me.

The rest of the day was peaceful. My fingers itched to text Andy again and see how she and Lou were getting along. Logan had made me promise not to, so I hadn't, but that didn't mean I hadn't thought about doing it about a million times since we left. I was praying we wouldn't return from the two days up here to find that she quit, that it was too much. I relied on her far more than I'd realized. And while the idea of asking her to come on to manage with me was appealing, it would set me back significantly if she didn't need this kind of pressure in her life. I mean, she could likely find an easier job that paid the same in a heartbeat. I just hoped it worked out and she had a great weekend.

After a long afternoon hike where Frank pointed out more species of birds than I knew was possible, it was time to say goodbye.

Linnie hugged each of the guys while Frank double-checked that everything was packed up to his satisfaction, murmuring something about the old video game Tetris and how you needed to pack a vehicle in a certain way. When he finished, he moved to Levi while Linnie came over to me.

"No big goodbyes because I know we will see you again soon," she said, pulling me in.

"Thanks for treating me like family," I whispered into her hair.

"Sweetheart, you are family." She stepped back, looking me in the eye. "You take care of both my boys, but especially that one you're crazy about."

Her gaze was warm, and I could only meet it with the truth. "I am crazy about him."

"I know. He feels the same about you too. It will work

out, Allyson; just keep being there for him. Make sure he meets your needs as well, in the bedroom and out of it."

My eyes widened as Logan's hand slid onto my hip.

"Mom, Allyson isn't used to the blunt talk about sex," he groaned.

"Well, open communication about sex is the foundation of a healthy relationship," she retorted.

Levi, overhearing this, laughed, and said, "Typical."

"She's not in a relationship with you," Logan said, not moving away from his mom.

"No, but if she needs someone to talk to, I'm here." Linnie put her hands up and shrugged.

My cheeks were pink. I knew they were; how could they not be?

After that embarrassing moment, we got through the goodbyes and were quickly on the road. I offered the passenger seat to Levi—clearly my short stature didn't need it as much as he did—and curled up in the back with Charlie. The hum of the road immediately put me to sleep.

Two hours later, Levi's voice woke me up. "Sleeping Beauty, we're home."

I sat up in the back and saw we were driving through the downtown of Highland.

"Your place or mine?" Logan asked as he navigated by the courthouse.

Butterflies fluttered in my stomach. I'd hoped after last night that we were continuing to see how this thing between us unfolded, but I'd feared I might have to fight him on that.

"How about we swing by my place for some clothes, then head to yours?" I asked, stretching in my seat. My back and neck were not happy with the position I'd slept in. Some yoga might be in order when I got to Logan's, or maybe a soak in the tub. I leaned over and rubbed Charlie's side, and he stretched out happily, laying his head on my lap.

"Sure." Logan clicked on his blinker, heading down Main to my duplex. Levi talked to him about what we'd want to make for dinner. I swear the man only thought about food. A song came on the playlist, and Levi cheered, turning it up.

"What is it?" I asked.

"'Murder in the City' by the Avett Brothers." Levi sang an opening line to Logan.

Logan glanced back at me. "We used to sing this one to each other all the time."

"Aww, you two have a song?" I smiled at them as they sang a couple of lines to each other before Logan pulled up in front of my place.

"Allyson, you expecting anyone?" Logan asked as he came to a stop in my driveway, turning down the radio.

"What?" I asked, looking out the window to see a woman step out of a car parked in front of my house. She turned in our direction and I gasped. "Maeve."

Chapter 21

President of the Fan Club

Logan

Watching Allyson run at her sister, I could only marvel at the difference between the two women. Both were shorter, hovering above five foot like my mom. Allyson's long hair was strawberry blonde, and she was slightly curvy, although less so than when I'd met her. In the past year she'd lost some weight; I was assuming due to stress. The muscle that she'd gained from running helped, but she still weighed less than when we'd met, which concerned me for her stress levels. Her face was a billboard for her current mental load, with thinner cheeks and shadows under her eyes, although those were absent right now. High five to my camping trip and time with the Traubs.

Having never met Maeve, I felt like you could sense the woman's personality from a distance, and it was one that said, *Back up, I am my own woman.* She had curves for days and her hair was blond, I'd assume long like Allyson's though it was in some messy knot, wrapped with a bandanna around it, and aviator sunglasses shoved up on top of her head. She was wearing some sheer type of dress thing with a low V-neck on top of jeans with boots. And I was pretty damn sure she didn't have a bra on.

"Jesus," Levi said from my elbow where we stood leaning together against my 4Runner. "Who in the hell is this?"

I looked to my right and saw that Levi's eyes hadn't left Ally and Maeve for a second. Interesting. "Putting two and two together, I'm guessing that's Ally's older sister Maeve."

Levi turned to meet my stare. "So many things. One, we're going with Ally now?"

"Fuck off."

"Two, that's her *sister*? You sure it's not some hippie rolling into town to do a tarot card reading?"

"Well, you heard her in the car, and I know that her sister's name is Maeve. So yes, that's her sister. And I'm pretty sure she would absolutely give you a reading. From what Ally's told me, she also teaches yoga, does sound meditation, massage, and whatever else interests her. And let's go back to *that's Ally's sister*. Don't piss her off. Don't hit on her." I felt my heart rate increase and was fascinated that I was feeling the need to protect a woman I'd never met from my brother who might be a dumbass at times but was overall a good guy.

"Interesting," Levi said, looking to the two women embracing.

After a moment of rocking back and forth together, Allyson stepped back and looked at Maeve. "I cannot believe you're here." Grabbing her arm, the women walked in our direction.

"Maeve, this is Logan and Levi Traub. Um..." Her cheeks heated, and I could tell she wasn't sure how she should qualify our relationship. I chose to do that for her.

Sliding next to Ally, I wrapped my left arm around her waist and made sure she was pressed up against me as I extended my right hand to Maeve. "I'm Logan."

She slid her hand into mine, her eyes locked on me. "Mm-hmm. So you're the fake boyfriend who is absolutely more." She gave me an assessing glance that told me she put up with zero bullshit and she was judging me ten ways to Sunday. I liked her already.

"Fair assessment."

She then gave Levi a once-over. "And you're the lesser twin."

He looked to me then back to Maeve in shock. "Excuse me?"

Maeve looked to us and shrugged. "I mean, it's hard to measure up to perfection, am I right?" She sent me a wink. Oh boy, this woman liked to mess with people. I wanted to sit and watch because it was going to be fun.

"Did I miss the gene for a good wink?" Ally said, watching Maeve. "Dammit, I did."

Levi was busy grumbling to Maeve about how he was older than I was and, if anything, was the greater of the two of us. Maeve looked like she was bored by the conversation. Charlie spun in a circle and let out a bark.

Suddenly, Maeve clapped her hands to get everyone's attention. "Okay, as much as I love a good family drama, someone is going to need to feed me and soon. So sis, sorry to show up unexpected, but can we talk about that over dinner?"

"The Homestead?" Levi said, apparently deciding whatever this was, he was here for it.

I glanced at Allyson who was now worrying on her lip. She needed comfort and peace, not a night in a brewery, even if Sundays weren't packed like other nights. Nope. I wanted her in my place. Preferably spread naked on my bed, but sitting comfortably on my couch under a blanket talking to her sister would work for now.

"Let's go to my place. Maeve, you're welcome to bring your stuff and stay the night. Ally was going to, if that's still the plan. And Levi, how about you and I whip up dinner while these two catch up?" I looked at the group and realized my quiet nights from months ago had changed without me realizing it.

"You have wine, Twin One?" Maeve said, a glint in her eyes.

"You bet your ass I do."

Allyson shook her head at the entire situation, which wasn't an unrealistic response. "Okay, let me grab some clothes and we're out of here. Maeve, do you want your car at Logan's?"

"Absolutely. Always have an exit strategy." Maeve said.

"Need to run at a moment's notice?" Levi said, trying to get under her skin.

"There have been times," Maeve replied, unfazed. Looking back at her sister, she said, "I'm assuming you know where the God of Sexy over there lives. How about they go ahead, and we'll follow once you have what you need?"

"I'm the God of Sexy," Levi said in a hushed, but still audible, voice.

"In your dreams," Maeve replied.

"Mae, they're pretty much identical," Allyson said, fighting a smile.

"You don't say," she said with a drawl. "Somehow I don't find it difficult to tell them apart."

"Neither do I," Ally said with a shrug.

"All right. I like Maeve's plan. Don't be long, though." I tugged Allyson forward and captured her with a soft kiss.

Her lips let out a small sigh, which I took as the opportunity it was to slide my tongue in her mouth alongside hers. We kept it slow, lingering, until a whistle broke the moment.

"Nice," Maeve said, either to the kiss or the flushed cheeks on Allyson. "Now you two, when I say I'm hungry, I'm not one of those girls who want to pick at a salad. I mean it. So hop to, we'll be around shortly."

"Yes, ma'am," Levi said.

"You're growing on me," she replied.

"Like mold," he said to a sharp burst of laughter from Maeve.

"Allergies, any food to avoid?" I asked, walking around the car to open the back door for Charlie as I got ready to jump in.

"I love all food unless it tastes like cardboard because you've removed all the good stuff," Maeve said.

"Ditto," said Allyson. "And maybe make sure there is a dessert."

"There's always room for dessert," Maeve replied as the two women turned and headed into the house, arms around each other, conspiring.

I closed the driver's-side door of my car and looked to Levi in the passenger seat.

"What in the world was that?" he asked.

I took a breath, looked back to Allyson's duplex. "Maeve." Enough said.

Two hours later, my house was filled with noise. Music was rolling through the speakers. That's just the way Levi and I were raised; something was always playing. Tonight it was the Avett Brothers and Mumford & Sons—or had been until Maeve had gotten ahold of my phone. It seemed that Ally's love of Stevie Nicks came from her sister, so we'd had a heavy dose of Stevie as well as Fleetwood Mac in general for the past hour while she debated the greatest songs and bands with Levi.

Leaving them to it, I picked up the plates from dinner and headed to the kitchen. The lasagna pan was still on top of the stove with the remainder of the homemade garlic bread. A bowl that had held a Caesar salad was nearby, though empty now. Beer cans and a wine bottle needed to be dealt with. I debated leaving it all till tomorrow but decided I could tackle this while they all visited, then we could move to the couch by the fireplace. There was a chill in the air tonight; a fire would be good.

As I dealt with the leftovers, moments from the past flashed through my mind. Nola and I had hosted so many dinner parties over the years. She loved having friends and family over until the midnight hour, a counter filled with glasses and plates to clean up the next day that told you that your friends had a good time. It was something I gave up in the past three years, not sure how to return to it, not wanting others to intrude on my inner sanctum that this home had become. Somehow with Levi, Maeve, and Allyson though, it just felt right. It was like slowly my soul was whispering *more*, and I was just now able to hear it.

Moving onto the dishes on the counter by the sink, Allyson appeared with the remainder of the plates from the table and immediately began rinsing and handing the plates to me to load the dishwasher.

"Sorry about my sister crashing," she whispered.

I laid my hand on hers to stop her, getting her to look at me. "Why are you sorry?"

"Well..." She bit her lip and looked to the dining room table where Maeve and Levi were gesturing with their hands, their voices rising, but amusement evident. "She can be a lot."

"So can he; it's fine. She tell you what made her want to come out here?" I asked as I resumed loading.

"Yeah," she handed me a plate. "You."

I stopped, turning to stand, and took the plate out of Allyson's hand. "You mean you told her about us?"

She looked away, so I moved and closed the dishwasher. Allyson looked resigned and moved to jump up, sitting on the counter, bringing us closer to eye level.

"Yeah, I said something to her."

I stepped into her space, and she widened her legs to allow it.

"When I was headed to yoga in Bessie two weeks ago. She was en route to Delaware, and she knew I was driving home, and it was early in the morning. She laughed because she said I was having a drive of shame." She dropped her head to my chest; I kissed the top of it.

"When's the last time you saw her?"

"At least a year."

I nodded for a moment, thinking of the conversations we'd had about Maeve over the years. "You said you guys were close, you just don't see her a lot."

"Mm-hmm."

"Do you want Levi and me to make ourselves scarce so you can spend time together one on one?"

She leaned back, tilting so she could meet my eyes. "That's sweet. We're in your home. But no. Please stay. I just want to warn you, Maeve is blunt. She knows that you were married before, that Nola passed. She's not mean, but I don't know how anything she says will come out." The worry was evident in her eyes.

"Babe, that is not your concern. I can handle it."

Her voice was hushed as she leaned forward, clenching the sides of my open flannel in her hands, "I don't want you to *have* to handle it." She looked at me, then licked her lower lip as she thought of what she wanted to say. Her eyes pleaded with me as she whispered, "I want her to like you. And... I want you to like her."

I smoothed down her hair and put a finger under her chin to tilt her head up so she could meet my gaze. "Didn't you say Maeve and your grandmother were the only two people to stand up for you when your parents were being dicks?"

She nodded.

"And that Maeve waived all her portion of the inheritance to you from your grandmother because she thought you'd do something amazing with it and she just wanted to travel, allowing you to be able to buy the Sanctuary?"

Another nod.

"And that at every low moment of your life, she has told you that you have it, you are capable and smart, even when you've doubted it yourself or your idiot parents have made you doubt it?"

Final nod.

"Then babe, you've got no worries. She can be as blunt as she wants, but in the fan club of Maeve—middle name?"

Allyson looked at me with a grin. "Claire."

I gave her a nod. "Well then, in the fan club of Maeve Claire Murphy, you're looking at the president. If she is your champion, then I am her biggest fan."

Allyson's smiling was blinding. "Really?"

I nodded the affirmative. Holding her chin in hand, I leaned forward to press my mouth to hers. Her lips immediately parted as she tugged me to her, pressing her chest against me, moving to wrap her arms round me. Our tongues tangled while my hands found her ass and pulled her forward on the counter, wondering what excuse I could make for the two of us to go to my room for an hour—or two.

Maeve spoke up from the table. "Oh, Logan, think you can pry your face off my sister to come over here and tell me all about your wife? Want me to try to do a reading so she could talk to you? I'm thinking she might have something to say about the fact that I see zero pictures of her around here. Thoughts?"

I stepped back and let my forehead drop to Allyson's. She met my eyes and whispered, "President of her fan club, remember?"

I shook my head and decided I probably shouldn't toss Allyson over my shoulder and leave the room, though I couldn't say I wasn't tempted.

<h1 style="text-align:center">Chapter 22</h1>

<h2 style="text-align:center">Balls in the Air</h2>

A_llyson_

Bessie and I left the country roads behind us as we turned in to Highland Woods, the tall evergreens flanking the road like sentries as we drove up to the mansion. I'd already been to the Sanctuary in town this morning, opening it up, conversing with Flat Max about what a great job Andy had done over the weekend out at the park, how Lou had kicked ass doing the job she'd retired from in town, and spent some time visiting with our regulars. The place had run this weekend just as if I'd been there, which was something to consider.

According to Lou, who'd stopped in for her Monday morning coffee along with Emma and Maggie, everything had been seamless when I was gone. She had chastised me a bit, reminded me that she'd had more staff in one location than I'd had in two, and told me I was living the analogy about burning the candle at both ends and I needed to get on it. Yeah, yeah, I knew and was working on it. It didn't help that so much of Lou's staff had been friends her age that all retired from the café when she did.

After Caydence clocked in, healthy once again, I'd hopped in Bessie to head out to the park. I needed to be in both locations today, reassuring myself that all was well and nothing had fallen apart in my absence, though there was already clear evidence that everything had gone according to plan. I knew I couldn't continue to run between both locations, so I penciled in a conversation with Andy. I had this, I did. I needed to grow up and have a conversation with her about expectations—hers and mine—and get on with it.

Flat Max told me that I was putting too much importance on my presence to steer the ships, or cafés, as it were. The cardboard Yoda might have a point.

But I digress.

It would be a lie to say my heart wasn't doing a little pitter-patter at the notion that I'd likely see Logan shortly. Last night solidified his good-guy status in my heart. He'd handled Maeve with the patience of a saint, or a man used to dealing with a twin brother who was a lot in his own right. When Maeve had asked for details on Nola, Logan had given them without censure. He was honest about why her picture wasn't spread across the house. He told her upfront that he had feelings for me while also worrying that I deserved more. I wanted to applaud and hug him in equal measure.

I also had a nagging feeling I was missing something, but for the life of me I couldn't think of what that would be, so I worked to move on.

It was probably good that I ended up sleeping with Maeve on the couch. Logan and Levi had gone up early. Logan had kissed my forehead and told me that he understood, and he'd see me in the morning. Part of me had wanted to go up and have a repeat of the previous night in the tent. A larger part of me was afraid of how much I'd wanted that and what I was going to feel like when he decided we needed some space because that was sure to happen. In short, I was a hot-mess express, party of one.

Maeve and I stayed up late talking about her journey to Highland. The last time we'd talked hadn't given me any indication that she planned on visiting. Turns out she'd stopped at her friend's place in Delaware as planned and then said her gut instinct said she needed to see me. Maeve strongly believed our ancestors spoke to her, and they were the intuition that she used to guide her life, her inner wisdom. So when those hunches came up, she followed them. Full stop.

I was just glad that this time that feeling led her to me. How long she'd be here was anyone's guess. I'd take her for as long as I could. Until I'd seen her standing outside my duplex, I hadn't realized how much I'd missed my big sister. In that moment of looking out the car window to see her, I had an ache that bubbled up inside me, and I ran to her, needing to hold her in my arms.

I'd told Logan I needed her to like him and vice versa. If my parents had been here, I wouldn't have had any strong feelings on what they thought about Logan or he them. But Maeve? She was so different than me, but she also *was* me, or a part of me. I knew she rubbed some people the wrong way—Levi, for instance—though their dislike of each other last night also morphed into a mutual appreciation, so who the heck knew where they'd land. But Logan? I wanted Logan and Maeve to get along.

I swung Bessie in the parking space at Highland Woods and hustled to the café. I'd left Maeve doing some yoga on the back deck at Logan's before I'd headed to the coffee shop in town this morning. She said the surroundings were good for her soul and she'd see me later. Maeve was not one that you needed to help get adjusted to a new place, provide a list of directions, or dispense intel on her surroundings. If she stuck around for more than a day, she'd have more friends than I did here and probably be able to list off the best places to eat that I'd never even heard of. Judging as it was now a little past nine in the morning, I hazarded a guess that I'd see her in the next hour or so with a story or two about people she'd already met.

Walking in the back door, I sang out, "Andy, my love. Are we still speaking?" Coming around the corner to enter the café space, I saw Andy standing at the POS ringing up one very much not flat nor made of cardboard Maxwell Harp.

Andy was rocking a sleeveless tee today to keep those tattoos visible for all, looking very much like the badass she was as she gave me a look with an arched brow visible under her heavy black bangs.

"Who won the pool?" Max said with a nod in my direction.

Andy shook her head in my direction. "Blake was the winner," she said without a glance to Max. She seemed disappointed by that.

"Yep, pay up." Blake was standing to Max's left, already devouring a muffin.

"What pool?" I asked, stashing my bag below the counter and wrapping an apron around my waist.

"We bet on how long it would be before you called Andy this weekend to see how everything was going." Max took a swig of the coffee and nodded to Andy. "Excellent latte."

"And how long did you think I'd make it?" I asked him.

"Three hours."

"What? I'm insulted by your belief in me, or lack thereof."

"I had six," Andy said.

Humph.

"I said you'd make it until morning Sunday and won even though you texted Saturday since you didn't initiate that one," Blake said, taking another bite.

"Thank you for believing in me, Blake. Maybe you get another muffin on the house."

"Fess up," Max said to Blake.

Blake gave me a sheepish look. "Well, I figured you'd make it a full day because Logan would take your phone."

"Logan did *not* take my phone." As if that would be necessary. I fought an eye roll.

"I did have to make you promise to take some time to yourself, and you had itchy fingers." The man himself spoke up from the armchairs, *our armchairs*, by the window. I looked over to see him and Maeve sitting there, watching all of us like they were highly entertained.

"Do I still win?" Blake asked.

"I suppose," Andy replied, sliding some cash his way.

"Are you all saying my sister is a workaholic?" Maeve asked the group.

"Yes," was chorused at her.

"Hey!" I said, looking at my supposed friends. "I'm not a workaholic. I just want the cafés to do well." I stepped around the counter to the café side and leaned against it, sending a glance that spoke to what I thought about their opinion.

"Well, unless something has drastically changed in the past three years, you have a type A personality and are convinced your worth is in what you produce, thanks to our stellar upbringing." Maeve laid out her truths and then took another swig of coffee, watching me over the rim to see how I'd respond.

Drew spoke up from his seat at the counter next to Blake. "Is stellar upbringing code for asshole parents?"

"The assholiest," Maeve replied. "Or, maybe it's not assholiest, but people who have their priorities so skewed that simply providing the basic needs of food, shelter, and an adult present during our childhood were all that they had to give, along with the unflagging command that we do not make them look bad."

"Uptight?" Drew asked.

Maeve nodded. "That's one way to describe them." She gestured in my direction. "Allyson's response was to be the model daughter and keep everything on course, make them proud, keep all balls in the air, until she moved here and did the unthinkable by leaving our dad's business to run a café."

"Then the balls dropped." Drew nodded.

Everyone looked from Maeve to me. Logan's gaze heated me up inside, not with lust, though that was there, but with a feeling that he wanted to be by my side, to hug me.

I spoke to him even thought he was across the room. "Those balls needed to drop. They had to if I was going to be able to have a life I liked," I whispered.

"I feel like Jake would be really upset that I missed an opportunity for a ball joke," Drew said.

"Not the time," Max grumbled at him.

Maeve put a hand on Logan who was starting to stand, keeping him in his chair as she moved my way. Coming to my spot at the counter, she grabbed my hand. "Chickie, you should like your life—no, you should love it. That's not selfish to want that." She gave me a considering once-over.

"Have you been beating yourself up over leaving Mom and Dad?"

I was embarrassed to admit it. What thirty-year-old adult still cared what their parents thought of them to this extent? "Somewhat."

"But you don't talk to Mom when she calls."

"Most of the time." Pause. "It's easier."

Everyone else had faded away, though I knew they were still here; it seemed like Maeve and I had created our own little bubble.

"It's easier because then you don't have to hear about how you've disappointed them."

I nodded.

Maeve put her hands on her hips and proceeded to look like the tallest five-foot-two person I'd ever met. "So what you're telling me is that I need to spend some time here teaching you how to let their thoughts about *your* life and what *you've* chosen to do with it roll off your back like water. Is that right?" Her expression on her face was one of a pissed-off nature, though I knew it wasn't directed at me.

"Does that mean you're staying for more than a day?" I asked with trepidation. I hadn't dared hope for more but would welcome it if given the chance.

Maeve's expression became gentler. "I'll stay as long as I need to."

I pulled her against me, a hug that spoke volumes. It was like I'd been all alone for so long I hadn't realized I could feel another way. I'd tried to tell myself phone calls were enough, but damn did I miss my sister. And whether this was for a week or a month, I was going to soak up every minute.

"You know you kick ass, and it's their loss they don't appreciate you," she said into my hair.

"Ditto."

We stood there, rocking back and forth in a hug that was years long when there was a series of claps bringing my attention to the room.

Maeve and I stepped apart, and I looked to Andy who was standing behind the counter surveying the crowd.

"Okay, people, let's give these two some time and stop watching this show." Andy looked to Logan, Blake, Max, and Drew. "Don't you four have, I don't know, a park to run?"

"Ma'am, yes, ma'am." Blake grabbed a second muffin from Andy with one hand, his coffee with another, and headed for the door.

Max and Drew grabbed their coffees and headed after Blake. Logan just looked at me from his seat, not moving.

"I don't think Mr. Sexy is going anywhere until you talk to him." Maeve waggled her eyebrows at me.

"Mr. Sexy?"

"I still haven't quite worked out what I want to call him and his brother. Thing One and Thing Two are in contention."

"If I'm talking to him, what are you going to do?"

She tugged the strap on my apron and transferred it from my waist to hers. "I'm making muffins with Andy."

"Excellent. Glad someone wants to work today," Andy said with a wink in my direction.

"Before I go talk to Mr. Broody over there"—I gestured to Logan with a thumb, hearing his words of protest at my comment, which just made me smile—"lay it down. How did you feel about moving up to management this weekend? Even when it wasn't going smoothly?"

"Absolutely excellent. Promise," Andy said, pulling out our recipes.

"Do you still want to make managing a permanent thing?" My heart rate kicked up, waiting.

"Abso-fucking-lutely," Andy said, leaving no room for doubt. She gave me a huge smile, which I returned.

"And you're still good with being my right hand; we can alternate who is at each location daily."

"Yep, but I still think you need more staff." Andy gave me a glance.

I nodded. "How about you and I talk about that later today?"

She raised her hand for a high five.

"Yes, what are we celebrating?" I looked over to the door to see Emma walking in.

"Allyson is promoting Andy," Logan said, moving up beside me and squeezing my waist.

"Woo-hoo!" Emma said. "That's awesome. Remember I have some book club kids at the high school to recommend if you'd like,"

My heartbeat tripped a bit as I considered that. No, it was time to reclaim my life. This could be good, would be good. "Tell them to call us to set something up," I said.

Andy gave a theatrical gasp, to which I rolled my eyes.

"That's fabulous," Emma said. "I'm just here for a minute to talk to Max, but could I get a latte?"

Andy immediately moved to make her drink, and Emma leaned over the counter with her hand stretched out to Maeve who came out from the kitchen, likely to see what was taking Andy so long. "Hi, I'm Emma. Are you new?"

Maeve gave Emma's hand a squeeze hello. "I'm Allyson's sister, in town for a bit."

Emma looked between the two of us. "Yep, I see the resemblance." She paused, then her face lit up as she turned toward me. "Oh, let's go out tonight and celebrate your sister in town. I can text Maggie." She grabbed her phone and held it up, waiting for my go-ahead.

Maeve gave me a look that said she knew I'd rather curl up on a couch in my pajamas, but I was going out for a little bit no matter what. My head nod made Emma cheer again, and I was surprised to feel a bit of excitement bubble up inside me as well. Who knew?

Chapter 23

Bring Your Miley Energy

Logan

I walked in the door to the Homestead with Max and scanned it, looking to see if Allyson and Maeve were there. I felt strangely proud of her; I knew she'd rather be home tonight. And yet when Emma had informed her that they were doing a girls' night and she wasn't taking no for an answer, she'd agreed. Emma was not usually so forward, so Allyson seemed reluctant to turn her down, like she'd known she meant something to Emma. And really, there was no turning back when Maeve learned it was karaoke night. Apparently, that sealed the deal, and they were all in.

Personally, I would have welcomed a night at home with Allyson even if our siblings had been by our sides. I'd rather gouge my eyes out than stand in front of anyone and sing, but to each their own. College had been its own thing with Levi and me jumping up to sing on an occasion. We had a song that was *ours*. But we hadn't done that in years, and tonight would be no different. I'd matured from wanting to make an ass out of myself.

Looking around, I saw that the girls weren't here yet. Sully and Jake were behind the bar, Drew sitting in the stools in front of them. The brewery was slightly full for an after-dinner crowd on a Monday night. Karaoke would be starting in about half an hour. I wondered if people were out to sing or watch the embarrassment of their friends and neighbors.

Max grabbed the seat next to Drew, and I sat on the other side of him. Sully slid a beer in front of me, another in front of Max. "This is the pale ale we've been working on. Been talking to Blake about debuting it for one of our hikes. Tell me what you think."

Taking a sip, I considered the flavor. It reminded me of a beer that was a huge hit in a brewery over near Champaign that was light and a bit citrusy, perfect for summer. "That's good, man. What are you calling it?"

Jake stepped up into the conversation. "Tossing around a few names." He leaned his forearms on the bar with a bit of a smirk. "I was thinking of something bird related to go with the nature hikes. Maybe something like starlings, red-breasted nuthatch, or dickcissel. You two have any thoughts?"

"Not something about nuts, man," Max said, taking another drink.

"Dickcissel for the win?" Drew replied with a grin.

"I mean, dicks and nuts do go together. Maybe a combo?" Jake rubbed his chin as if he was actually considering it.

I took another drink, then considered. "Thinking about your other beers, maybe something music related?"

"Blackbird?" Max suggested.

"Beatles or Sarah McLachlan?" Drew asked.

Max gave him a look. "Beatles."

"I don't know; Ivy likes Sarah's version."

"What about songs with flying?" I suggested. "Learn to Fly?"

"Foo Fighters?" Max asked.

I nodded and everyone else chimed in that they agreed.

Sully raised his glass. "Learn to Fly." And we all did the same.

I finished my glass off. "When will it be ready?"

"Should be ready no later than a week from now is the plan," Sully said, moving down to wait on a customer.

I looked down the bar at Drew on the other side of Max. "What's up with you, man?"

Jake started laughing. "I just told our family group text that he's in here acting like a sad panda because his girl is out on a girls' night."

Drew was lost in his own thoughts, not even reacting to Jake's words. I spoke without thinking much about it. "Just to say, that's good to care about someone so much you want to spend time with them."

Jake and Max turned toward me, both silent. Bringing up any allusions to a dead wife often were conversation killers. I knew this from past practice. But I was slowly getting to the point that I wanted to talk about Nola more. Allyson was teaching me that keeping her locked away in my memories was no way to live and clearly had done me no favors.

After a few beats, Jake spoke up. "Sorry, man."

This was why I'd avoided this conversation for three years though. How did you bring up someone you lost without having people feel sorry for you? I didn't want any pity.

I sighed. "No, I didn't mean that like I was chastising you. Just wanted to say I was glad to see Drew got his head out of his ass with Kate even if that means he's going to be a sad sack."

"We all are," Jake replied. "And he doesn't even seem to get that they're coming here for their night out, and I can't bring it to myself to tell him." Jake's grin was reminiscent of the way Levi and I looked when torturing the other.

I could feel Max's gaze still on me, so I turned to meet his stare. "Max?"

He leaned forward and kept his voice low enough for Jake and me to hear him but no one else. We were in our own bubble. "Just saying, man, you don't talk much about your wife. We're all here if you want to."

I let that sit in me. Yeah, Allyson was right. Letting others in was healing. "Thanks. I miss Nola like hell but am working on living more in the present."

"You going to do that living by not ditching your girl for the marathon?" Jake asked, giving me a raised brow.

"I do appreciate you and sad panda over there stepping up when I didn't the other day." I jerked my head toward Drew.

"So..." Jake leaned in front of me. "The marathon is coming up in what, a week?"

I nodded. "This Saturday." I paused, looking down at my hands. "Honestly, it makes me want to vomit, but I plan on running it with Allyson. Though Levi is on standby."

"What am I standing by for?" Levi's hand clamped down on my shoulder as he took the stool on my left.

"In case this man flakes on Allyson again for the race." Jake leaned to grab a glass and held it up to our bellied-up-to-the-bar crew. "Guys, what can I get you?"

Levi and I ordered an Evolution, Max a Black Hole Sun.

"And yeah," Levi said, sitting down and leaning on his

elbow against the bar to look at me. "I'm on standby, but I think he's got what it takes and will be in that race."

Jake distributed our beers as I pondered if I really had what it took to complete my first marathon in three years. I prayed I did. I could run the distance; I knew that wasn't the issue. I was more worried about what emotions the race itself would dredge up. Would it set me back in my healing process or push me forward? A comment from my mom about Susan and Jack at the lake had unearthed some memories I hadn't found a way to deal with. Would the race just compound that?

"Good to hear, man," Max said, ignorant of my inner turmoil, holding out a beer so that we could clink our glasses.

I was grateful for a change of topic when Max leaned over to get my attention. He brought up the new program the university was going to run with us at the park this spring, and I was making some mental to-do lists when the aromas of tonight's special got my stomach rumbling.

"I'm going to need some food," Levi volunteered. Clearly, we were in sync as usual. Jake slid some menus our way only to have all of us look to Sully as he let out a loud whistle.

"Look sharp, men. This crowd just got a lot more interesting," Sully said with a nod toward the front of the brewery.

Turning in my seat, I looked across the dining area toward the door. Looked like girls' night had arrived at the brewery, and I couldn't say I was mad about it.

The whole crew, led by Lou, started snaking their way through the tables to reach the bar. A new Miley Cyrus song was playing, and Lou was clearly feeling it. She danced as she weaved her way though, arms held high as she swayed, grabbing the arms of men as she passed and flirting her seventy-plus-year-old ass off.

Lou was only the engine of this dance train that had Emma, Maggie, Ivy, Elle, Kate, Allyson, Maeve, and Tim following behind. The women were dancing, but also smiling or laughing. Allyson was glowing, which made me want to have her to myself, not that I'd intrude on this. And Maeve was clearly fitting in just fine. Tim brought up the rear, waving to the crowd as they moved through, in his element. The man didn't know how to not be the center of attention, and when he and Lou were together, it would be good to have the police on standby.

Reaching the bar, Lou smacked the counter to get our attention before she pointed to the speakers. "Let Ms. Miley educate you all, gentlemen; a woman scorned *will* emerge on top—every dang time."

Jake slid a vodka and water with ice, easy on the water, to Lou. "Now what would Verdell say to that statement, Lou?"

"I'd say she speaks the truth." Verdell, Lou's very understanding husband, spoke up from a table on the side of the bar where he was dining with a friend. The two of them were such opposites, not just because Verdell was Black and Lou was white, but he was the brake, and she was the gas pedal, all the way down. The entire town should be grateful to him. Unchecked, who knew what Lou would have gotten up to over the years?

Lou picked up her drink. "That will go on his tab," she nodded her head toward Verdell before returning to the center of the bar and raising her arms with Tim to sway to the music. Verdell sat and watched with a look of fondness on his face.

I looked around. Tim was wearing a T-shirt with a

rainbow on it that said Sounds gay, I'm in. I laughed and looked to Max. "Think we need to give Eric a heads-up?"

"Emma already did. He is feeding their dogs and then coming here to be the DD for anyone who needs it."

"Count me in for anyone who needs a ride," Verdell called over.

Man, the people in this town. They really believed in the whole takes-a-village concept, and that didn't only pertain to parenting. And in a personal way, I was so grateful that after a drunk driver stole Nola's future three years ago, I was in a town where the people I spent time with were conscientious about ensuring no one was driving under the influence. It was part of what made this group work for me when I first met them. That even with Sully and Jake's job being tied to a brewery, the entire group was conscientious about drinking and treated it responsibly. It was refreshing.

Looking around, I took our crew in. Drew was talking to Kate. Sully had his arms wrapped around Maggie and El. Jake and Ivy were swaying together as they talked to Drew and Kate. Lou and Tim danced around in circles. And then Allyson and Maeve were there.

"Who is singing tonight?" Maeve gave Levi and me a once-over.

"I'm not a huge karaoke fan," I said.

"Color me surprised," Maeve said.

"And you are?" I asked. I mean, I wasn't sure I could be less surprised by something if I tried.

"I like to sing." Maeve's expression grew from thoughtful to calculated as she looked between Levi and me. "I think we'll get you two up there before the night's over."

"I highly doubt that," I replied.

Maeve shrugged and headed to the karaoke song list to browse. Levi quickly headed over to join her.

Allyson swayed to the music in front of me. I parted my legs and tugged her to me. Her smile was bright enough to chase away the concerns I had earlier. Everything seemed easier when she was near.

"You having fun?" I asked.

"Yeah." She slid her arms around my waist and laid her head to rest on my shoulder. "I'm so happy," she whispered.

That brought a smile to my face. "Tell me why?"

She let her lips trace a path on my neck that gave me goose bumps before speaking. "Maeve's in town. I'm out with friends and not feeling itchy about it." And she waited a few moments before continuing. "And you."

"Me?" My heartbeat felt like it was pounding with both joy and a touch of nervousness.

"You." She leaned back and met my eyes. "How does that make you feel?"

I looked into her eyes. I had no doubt she wanted the truth, but I worried I would hurt her. Still...

"Can I be honest?"

"Always." Her gaze was encouraging.

I took a breath and exhaled. "It makes me excited and scared."

Allyson leaned forward and pressed her lips to mine. Pulling back, she said, "Thank you."

I drew my brows together. "For?"

"Laying it out there. It's fine, Logan. I'd be floored if you didn't feel a little scared. To be honest, I'm a little scared too."

I leaned forward to kiss her too. She'd just parted her lips, encouraging me to ramp up the heat level, when we were interrupted by Tim who whistled like he was hailing a cab on the streets of Chicago.

"Ladies, just because we've found the men doesn't mean our night out is done. My girl is singing, and we're not ignoring that. Bring your Miley energy and let's dance!" Tim and Lou were still dancing in the center, but apparently, he didn't want the night to slow down.

Allyson gave me an impish grin before kissing my cheek and wading in to dance with the group. Maggie passed the baby and sling to Sully, who headed behind the bar with one hand on the bump in front of him. I knew from past experience that baby Ellen was a champ at chilling in the sling, even at three months, but I also knew that Maggie didn't stay out too long if Sully couldn't go home early, so she was likely already on the ticking clock and going to make the most of it.

As I watched the group screaming about flowers on the floor as they danced around, I saw Maeve at her spot near the karaoke stage where some poor suckers would be getting up to sing shortly. She looked from me to Allyson, who was spinning with Tim, and then headed my way.

"Pick your song?" I asked her.

"Picked yours," she said.

"Um, hell no," I replied. "I don't sing."

"Mm-hmm, you might have mentioned that." Maeve's voice was casual, but I waited. I had a feeling I knew what this was.

We stood for a few minutes, watching my friends dance from one Miley song to another. Maggie was a big fan; she must have influenced Sully's playlist.

"Don't hurt her," Maeve said, still watching Allyson dance, not even glancing my way.

I took a breath. Even though I knew that was why she'd

come across the bar, I still felt like it was a punch to the gut because I couldn't promise anything. I looked to Maeve, and she turned and met my eyes. "I care about her."

"I know."

"I can't promise not to hurt her. But I'm trying my best."

"I know." She bit her lip, then looked to Allyson. "And she knows that."

We stood there together, the words between us, and watched them continue to dance.

A few hours later, karaoke night was going strong. The majority of our crew had sung one song if not more. Tim and Lou had done a hell of a rendition of "Jolene" that brought down the house. Maggie had left over an hour ago but sang some song called "Beautiful" with Emma before taking off to put Ellen to bed.

Levi walked over to me, and I thought he was going to say he was ready to hit the road because I knew I was. Instead, he said, "Get ready, we're up next."

"Excuse me?"

"I don't know how long I'm in town, and it's karaoke night. We're doing our song. It's been too long."

"I thought you were potentially staying?"

"Still up for debate."

"Avett Brothers?" Double-checking what I knew to be true.

"You know it."

"Murder in the City" by the Avett Brothers had been our song since college. Before Levi played the beginning of it the other day when we were coming back from the lake, I don't know if I'd listened to it since Nola had been gone. It was too closely tied to when I met her and carefree college years, though really it had always reminded me of Levi. When we were at karaoke and had had several beers, we'd sing it, saying that some of the lyrics were as close to our relationship as any we'd heard.

Levi had picked it to sing, which mean I had to wrap my brain around this quickly. Did I love karaoke? Not really. Being the center of attention was something Levi was far more comfortable about than I was. But I'd do it for him.

Allyson was leaning on me, looking exhausted, but had perked up at this conversation. "You're singing?"

I gave a long-suffering sigh. "Yep." Then looked to Maeve who was watching me with humor in her eyes. "You win, Maeve."

"That I do, Superior Twin."

"Ladies, this bus is leaving for my place as soon as the song ends. Be ready."

Allyson laughed. I wasn't kidding.

Our names were called. The crowd that was left howled their support as I followed Levi up and grabbed a mic.

"You'll love it," he said.

"Not sure about that," I grumbled.

I sang the first verse, not doing too bad, though my voice could be better. The first verse kicked off with one of the brothers singing of what they would say to his family if they died unexpectedly. I'd always loved it because the feeling of being tied to your family was one I strongly identified with.

Allyson gave a loud cheer. Levi chimed in on the second verse, which brought laughter from the crowd as the lyrics joked about which brother was better and he pointed to himself.

The last verse we sang together. I felt emotion welling up inside as Nola's face popped to my mind. What would she have said if she knew her time was coming so soon? Would the love we shared be enough? Had I been enough?

Would this ever get easier?

As we repeated the last two lines, my eyes welled up as I fought back tears, knowing the truth of those words. There was nothing as important as family. I would have been lost without mine for the past three years, and I would never forget what they'd done for me.

Levi looked like he was warding off his own tears. We ended to applause as we handed over our mics and Levi pulled me in for a hug.

"Love you," he said gruffly. "Sorry, that was more emotional than I had planned."

"Love you back, and I'm okay." I took a beat. "But I wasn't kidding. This chariot is out of here."

He laughed and looked at Allyson and Maeve, who had appeared right in front of us. "Looks like your girl knew you were serious. Let's roll."

Maeve and Levi took off through the dining room while Allyson and I followed behind. Our friends were going to have to be okay with our Irish goodbye. As we reached the door, Allyson turned to stop me before I could follow Levi and Maeve out.

Placing a hand on my chest, she rose up on her toes and gave me a chaste kiss. "That song was beautiful."

"Thanks," I said.

"Whatever emotions came up, they're good and I'm fine with them," she said, giving me a squeeze. "That was the song Levi played in the car the other day, right?"

I nodded.

"But it reminds you of Nola?"

I nodded again. "A bit."

"I'm guessing Levi and you used to sing it because of the brother and family part."

"Yeah."

She watched me carefully. Then with clear emotion in

her voice, she said, "Takes on a different meaning with the loss of your wife."

Exactly what hit me when we were signing. Like a hell of a Mack truck.

"Yep."

She wrapped me in her arms and squeezed. Pulling me down, she whispered in my ear, "I bet Nola thought it was beautiful. You know she was watching." Kissing my cheek, she turned and stepped through the doors.

I wasn't sure how she seemed to know what I needed, but it seemed to be happening more and more.

Taking a breath, I spoke out loud. "Hope you enjoyed the show. That won't be happening again anytime soon."

Shaking my head at myself, I stepped through the door, a feeling of lightness coming over me as I jogged to catch up to Allyson.

Chapter 24

Couch Conversations

Allyson

Logan was just ahead of me as we wrapped up our final run before the race tomorrow. Today was a breeze. We'd already covered the training needed, and this week had been about keeping our muscles relaxed, four days of easy runs for about a half hour each, nothing taxing. Still, I couldn't help but be nervous about tomorrow. Would I be able to go the distance in a race? Would the crowd make me go out too fast like I had in the half? I couldn't do that for a full marathon. And most importantly, would my training partner be by my side?

He said he would, and I mostly believed him, but I was also worried that maybe I should be telling him it was fine to stay home. Was this too much to ask? Was I putting our relationship, even one in these early stages, in jeopardy? Maeve pointed out I was far more concerned about Logan and his mindset than I was about my own performance in my first marathon. And while she was all in on encouraging what we had started here, she also didn't want me to revert to making someone else the priority over myself. According to Maeve, I'd done that with my parents growing up, and now that I finally was speaking up there, she didn't want to see me revert in this relationship.

She had a point, but I felt like she was missing something. Logan did care about my feelings, my dreams. My parents never had. Was I falling for him? Yep, sure was. So much so that it scared me at times, mainly because I felt he needed more time. This was his first relationship after losing Nola, and I felt the importance of treading slowly.

Since Maeve had been in town, I hadn't stayed at Logan's place since Monday night after karaoke, so it felt like I could describe our speed not only slow, but glacially slow. Was that an adjective? If not, it should be. We'd seen each other often this week, stolen some moments where we could, but Monday night had been just as hot as the tent over the weekend, and then several nights of texting while we both hung out with our siblings. I mean, I was here for my sister, but I also wanted to spend time with this guy.

But as I followed him into this parking lot today at the end of our run, I was overcome with fondness for the man. Fondness! When had I ever had a feeling for someone I was dating that I would describe that way? Not only was I attracted to him, lusted after him, but I also just really liked him. I enjoyed spending time with him. Was it because we'd spent the past two years becoming friends? Maybe. Whatever it was, I returned to the worry that maybe I'd pushed him with this marathon training and race. If he couldn't come tomorrow, I'd understand. But I had a strong feeling he wouldn't be as easy on himself.

Coming to a stop in the parking lot, Logan held up a hand for a high five. I slapped his, and he used the opportunity to grab my hand and pull me to him for a semisweaty hug.

"Your last training run. All that's left for you in the plan you laid out is the marathon." His arms tightened in an embrace as he kissed my temple. "How do you feel?"

I raised up to kiss the underside of his bearded jaw. "Ready." I stepped back and leaned against Bessie. Logan and I had parked next to each other and were two of the only vehicles left in the staff parking lot. It wasn't too late, only a bit after five, but for a Friday evening, no one wanted to hang around. Looking at Logan, who was leaning against his 4Runner, I decided just to lay it out. "Logan, if you can't go tomorrow, I completely understand."

A determined look came over his face. "No, I am ready, Allyson. I don't want to miss this."

I stepped forward and pulled his face down to me. Pressing a kiss to his lips, I let him go to return to my spot. "I know. I just need you to know I understand how hard this is. I wish I could help."

Logan brushed the hair that had fallen out of my ponytail behind my ear. "I know you do, and I hope you get that without you, I would have never gotten this far. So thank you." He tugged my hair, tipping my head, and captured my mouth in a kiss.

I sank against him, enjoying the moment. It was a gorgeous spring evening, finally a bit warmer, and the quiet of the park around us made me want to soak in this time together. Logan had other plans though as he pulled back after kissing the top of my head.

"Just saying I'm not opposed to some more of that." Why not just lay it out there?

He laughed and pulled me to him, pressing his lips to the crook of my neck where I got goose bumps every time, which the man damn well knew. "I'm good with more of that too. What are you doing tonight?"

"If it involves coming to your house, I'm down for anything."

"Hmm, that sounds dangerous." Another kiss on my neck, tingles shot down my torso, and I leaned in. "Levi is headed to the Homestead to meet Max. What's Maeve doing?"

"She and Ivy are doing some sound meditation together at Nomad studio with Kate and Kristine." I fought a moan as his mouth continued to trail along my neck.

He paused. "Think she'd mind if she was alone in the duplex tonight?"

My pulse quickened. "I think that's a brilliant idea."

"We could eat our prerace meal, do a little stretching..." He toyed with my hair as his mouth descended to kiss the tops of my breasts as far as my tank and running bra allowed.

"I'm all for stretching," I said, trying to control my breathing.

Stepping back and giving me some space, he nodded at my Jeep. "Want to hop in Bessie and go home to grab some clothes and head to my place?"

I gave him a sheepish expression. "How much of a hussy do you think I am if I tell you I already packed to stay at your place and have my stuff for the race tomorrow?"

"Not a hussy, but a brilliant woman who thinks ahead." He leaned forward to briefly kiss me again, then pulled back. "See you at home?"

I nodded, turning to hop into Bessie, and tried to work out why the emotions I was feeling were getting the best of me today.

A few hours later, Logan and I lazed on his sectional, Charlie by our side. The temperature had dropped to the fifties, which was too warm for a fire, but cool enough to cuddle under a throw. Even without a fire, the feel of his house with candles lit everywhere was cozy, music playing lightly in the background.

We'd come back, walked Charlie, took a steamy shower together, and made a pasta dish filled with vegetables and grilled chicken, light enough not to impact our digestion for tomorrow but with enough carbs and protein to ensure a good start.

Logan stretched out on the long part of his couch, me curled against him under the throw, and we continued to talk, an unhurried pace to our conversation like we had all the time in the world.

"Did you and Andy meet and talk about her taking on more responsibility?" he asked. My head was on his chest as I looked beyond the couch to his deck, lit up with white lights, and into the woods beyond.

"Actually, yeah. Emma has a few high school kids that are coming to interview in a few days."

He reached up, tugged out my ponytail holder, and finger combed my hair. "Do you feel okay about that?"

"Yeah, I do. I know I was worried about a few things— the work involved in teaching someone the business..."

"But Andy already knows it."

"Exactly. And I was worried that I wouldn't be able to pay what I wanted, but I looked over the books with Andy and Maeve, and I'm really fine." I slid my leg along his and entwined our feet together. "I can't ignore my cushion from my grandmother makes this easier, but the business is also doing well enough that I can take this step. I don't know why I didn't do it earlier."

"Do you think there's more behind that?" His voice was gentle, like he didn't want to spook me.

"Like what?" I wasn't sure where he was going with this and felt a touch of apprehension.

Logan didn't speak, so I leaned back to look at him. His face was pensive. Turing to me, he said, "I might have been in therapy too long and am overanalyzing this."

"Oh boy, this should be good. Go ahead." I wondered what on earth he could be debating.

"Is there any chance you felt like you needed to do it all without help in your business to prove something to your parents?"

Whoa. Well, that's a thinker.

My gut reaction was to say no, that I was just a hard worker, that I had to be to make this all flow. But was that the truth?

"Steam might come out of your ears any moment. Talk to me, Ally."

I looked to him. "I'm just trying to think through my reactions and wondering if you're right."

"Maybe share your thoughts and we can process it together?"

I sat with that. That sounded like some healthy-relationship shit right there. So I sat up, scooching up the couch until I was in the crook of his arm, our legs stretched out in front of us. His left arm was around my shoulders as he toyed with my hair. I placed my right arm on his lap, and he reached over and grabbed that hand.

"Spill, babe. Truth in my question?"

I tried to get my thoughts in order. "I mean, possibly? I'm thinking of my mindset when I came here. They thought it was absolutely idiotic to leave a stable job at my dad's firm and come buy a café. It didn't matter to them that it was an established business or that I was able to expand within a year. I remember my call when I told them about the second location. My dad warned me that I was spreading myself too thin."

"What was your reaction?"

I grimly owned up. "To work harder."

"Would you say your dad had a healthy work/life balance?"

I laughed out loud. "Um, hell no."

"And your mom doesn't work, right?"

"Nope."

"So you haven't exactly had a role model for what it is that you want. It's fine to be passionate about your business, but I know all too well that at the end, your job doesn't matter one damn bit. You won't regret the hours you didn't work, but you will regret the life you didn't live." He squeezed his arm around me to cushion the words, but he didn't need to, I was hearing him loud and clear.

"I know you're right. I do. And I love my job, which is a blessing, but I promise that I'm going to figure a way to work a more reasonable load."

"And what steps will you take to do that? It's fine to say the words, but you need to have a plan on how you will make this happen."

The candles threw flickering light against the walls. With only the few lamps on in the living room and kitchen, we were bathed in warmth. I cuddled into the thick throw and his arms, thinking through the best way to achieve my goals. In hiring Andy to manage and possibly these kids part-time, could I actually take some of my life back? What would that look like? More time with friends; I could potentially attend a yoga class or two when it wasn't a Sunday morning. Feeling rested would be a gift. And more time to devote to whatever this was growing between us. Yep. All of that sounded pretty wonderful.

Under the blanket, I turned and slid over Logan's lap so that I was straddling him. "Well, I need to interview these kids with Andy, then look at scheduling and ensure I'm not keeping the hours I currently have." I twirled my fingers through his hair. He was about due for a cut; it was getting wavier than I'd seen it. I pressed a kiss to one temple, then the other.

"Also consider your mental load. You want to make sure you're taking some of that off your plate too." He slid his hands around to my hips, then moved them to my ass. "Will you manage one location, Andy another?"

I shook my head. "No, she and I talked about that. I want to be at both. Maybe we'll have a schedule like one week on at each, then switch, or certain days of the week."

He nodded, considering that. "But you also want to work so that you have some days off each week. I know Andy already does, but you are typically there daily."

I leaned down, pressing a kiss to his neck. "I know," I murmured, nipping at his collarbone. "That's why I'm adding the part-time workers."

His hands tightened on my butt. "Promise?"

I gave a light laugh. "Promise." I sat up and ran my hands through his hair before leaning forward and sliding my lips against his. "Thanks for caring about me. Can I care about you for a minute?"

"You already do." He grabbed the hem of my tee and gave a chin lift to start pulling my shirt up.

"Hold on."

He paused.

"I just want to check in. I feel like you've had something on your mind since we got back from the lake. Is it just the marathon?" I rubbed at the crease that appeared between his brows.

He looked away for a moment, seeming to consider my words before looking at me. "I promise I'm fine. This is bound to stir up some feelings, but I think that's normal."

I nodded and leaned in to press my lips to his cheek. "As long as you speak up if it's too much."

"Promise. Can we get back to it?"

I smiled and nodded as he slowly tugged my tee up my arms and tossed it somewhere behind the couch. Charlie figured out that this wasn't going to be his scene and headed over to his bed in the corner.

"Hmm." Logan ran his hands over my breasts. "I'm a fan of the no-bra look."

"Saves time," I quipped.

"And is hot as hell." He leaned forward, capturing a nipple in his mouth.

My hands slid down and helped take his T-shirt off too.

"Are we going upstairs?" I asked.

"How do you feel about this couch?" Logan asked, moving to my other breast. "Or"—he nodded over my shoulder—"we can throw a few blankets in front of the fireplace."

I immediately stood up, grabbing the thick throw we'd been using and spreading it on the rug. A glance to the couch confirmed my belief that he was just watching me work topless. "Like what you see, babe?"

"I'd like it more if there were no pajama pants on your lower half."

Keeping my eyes locked on his, I hooked my pj's and underwear with my thumbs and slid them off, kicking them to the side.

His gaze went molten as he stood, kicking his own pajama pants off, and came to stand in front of me, his hard cock telling me he was just as affected as I was. Sliding his hand into my hair, we pressed our lips together, mouths parting as I welcomed his kiss. Slowly we lowered to the ground, I pushed him to his back, straddling his waist.

Breaking our kiss, I looked at him as innocently as I could. "I somehow don't remember this in my marathon training plan."

He barked out a laugh. "Babe, we'll market the shit out of it when you get a personal record tomorrow."

I gave him an imperious look. "Since it's my first official marathon, don't I PR automatically?"

"Truth."

I gave a quick kiss to his lips, then began sliding down his body. Before I could get far, he stopped me. I let out a noise of protest, but he just gave me a wicked grin and shifted me until I was headed in the right direction, but he had access to me too.

"Sixty-nining? Really?" I asked with a look over my shoulder at him.

"Far better use of our time." He winked at me. Damn it. His wink was hot too.

"You're such a giver." I said, right before he pulled my core down to meet his mouth, licking up my seam before latching on to my clit.

Holy hell. I guess I'd be all relaxed for the race tomorrow. Gave new meaning to prerace preparation.

Chapter 25

Running on Empty

Logan

Anxiety was at war with some type of melancholy in my brain as I stood with Allyson at the start line. I'd operated on autopilot this entire morning, trying to keep it light and not bring Allyson down. This was her first marathon, and I wanted her to enjoy it. We'd picked up our packets yesterday. This morning we'd got up early, had a light breakfast, and I went over the plan for fuel and hydration during the race.

She was ready, I was not.

However, that really didn't matter. I'd decided earlier this week that I was looking at it wrong; this marathon, *the first marathon after*, was always going to suck. It was just something I was going to have to push through. Like every day since Nola had been gone, there were some days, some occasions, that you had to muscle your way to the other side. I was never going to be okay today, whether it was now or in ten more years. I just needed to get it done. Running it with Allyson, helping her out, was actually perfect because it gave me somewhere else to focus my energies.

Allyson danced in place, shaking her legs and arms to get the jitters out. "Can you believe we're finally here?" she asked.

I faked a smile. "It is unreal."

She gave me a second glance. "Are you still okay? You know you can bail; I'll be fine."

My heart tugged at the notion that this woman whom I was beginning to care far about more than I was willing to examine would actually put my mental state above her own. Nope, I'd be right beside her for this entire race, for better or worse.

"I'm good, babe. You can't get rid of me. We're running this race, and I'm watching that sweet ass of yours cross the finish line in a little less than four hours. You've got this." I pulled her toward me, pressing a kiss to her temple, only to be distracted by hoots from behind us.

Allyson and I separated and looked over to the sidewalk where spectators were wishing runners well, and I saw three familiar faces. Drew, Jake, and Levi stood there with—was that Betty White on their shirts?

Allyson took one look at them and doubled over laughing. They moved toward us and pulled her to them, each of them taking a turn to give her a hug and, from what I could overhear, some words of inspiration. After Levi got to talk to her last, the three of them looked at each other, then turned as one, showing us the back of their shirts. They each said the same thing, KICK SOME A$$, ALLYSON. YOU ARE OUR GOLDEN GIRL. LOVE, THE SWEATY BETTYS.

"Aww, you guys! Thank you so much." Allyson was near tears, but I could see that was happiness through and through.

"Picture time."

I looked over to see Maeve weaving through the crowd

in our direction. The guys immediately grabbed Allyson, putting her right in the middle, arms around her. I stepped back right when I found her gaze on me.

"What are you doing? Get in this picture." She gave me a look that said to not cross her.

"But this is your thing with them," I protested.

"Ass in the picture, Traub," Allyson said with a look that told me I didn't want to piss her off.

And truly, I didn't. I wanted today to be about her, so I got my ass in the picture.

Maeve took several before the loudspeaker that had been sharing announcements over and over for the past half hour said we were minutes from starting. Everyone hugged Allyson and me, saying they'd station themselves along the route.

Levi grabbed me and turned us away from the group. "You good?"

I nodded, not trusting myself to say too much. He met my eyes and scanned my face, not believing my words but making his own assessment. I didn't blame him; if the roles were reversed, I'd do the same thing.

After a few beats, he apparently decided he agreed with me and pulled me in for a hug, then pounded my back and said, "Kick some ass."

The crew left, and it was down to Allyson and me, along with about a thousand of our closest friends. We moved to the pacer that had the sign up for the nine-minute mile, which was what Allyson said she felt comfortable with. In the half, she'd averaged a pace of eight-minute miles, which she'd managed but was a little fast for her. We'd discussed slowing down if she needed; we'd just have to watch her progress.

Scanning her, I could tell she was tense. I pulled her in

for a full-body hug and spoke into her ear. "You have this. You've trained for it. Let the rest go, and get on that course and have a blast."

Allyson reached up, put both hands on the side of my face, and pulled me down for a hell of a kiss. Releasing me, she bounced on her toes and shot me a smile that made me want to mow down anyone in her path. Then she spoke, and it was like an arrow straight to my heart.

"Logan, I can't even begin to thank you. I mean, I had no idea what I was asking you last fall when we began training together. You did it, you encouraged me, you made me believe in myself, and it cost you. I'll never know how much. You put me first, and I don't have a whole lot of experience with people doing that. I just—"

I couldn't take it a minute longer; I swept her in my arms and kissed the hell out of her. This woman drove me to madness. Her drive impressed me while it also made me want to hole up with her in my house so I could take care of her for days on end. This thing that had started out as friends, morphed into that fake relationship which, in turn, transformed into something that was quickly becoming the most important thing in my life.

The loudspeaker crackled. "Runners, it's time. On the gun, you're off. Have a great race, and we'll see you at the finish."

I broke away from Allyson, seeing that her cheeks were now flushed from a heat that I knew had nothing to do with the temperature or any exertion yet. "You've got this, Ally."

"I do, thanks to you," she said, squeezing my hand.

"Nope. You did the work, babe. Thanks to you."

"Count down," the starter called out. "Ten..."

The crowd joined in. "Nine... eight... seven... six... five... four... three... two... one." A roar of applause met the beep of the gun, and the crowd started moving. At the nine-minute-pace group, we were stationed in the middle of the pack. We waited as the surge ahead of us began, and eventually our group did as well. It took a bit to actually reach the start line. When we did, Allyson let out a whoop, and my mind briefly turned to Nola. I sent up well-wishes to her and said a prayer that she'd see me through this. It felt selfish, but I knew she'd slap me in the head if she was here and heard me thinking like that. Nola, more than anyone, would be thrilled I was running today.

Allyson ran the race like a seasoned veteran of marathons. Honestly, I had known she'd put in the necessary work, but these races can be a beast even when you've trained as you needed to. As we ran, she kept her pace and fueled when needed. Our friends had apparently planned where to place themselves along the course, so we had someone cheering us on every few miles.

First it was Max and Emma around the three-mile mark. Allyson always started off feeling the miles. For her, for the most part, it got easier midway through the race, then tougher at the end. Emma's shout caught our attention to see that not only was Max with her, but also...

"Flat Max!" Allyson shouted with laughter, surging ahead and finding her stride as we ran by Emma and Max who were waving the six-foot tall Momoa cardboard cutout.

Around mile ten, we heard Maggie and looked over to see Ellen in the sling across Sully's chest by as they cheered us on. I was in awe. Here it was her first marathon, almost halfway through, and she was joking with the crowd we were running in, waving to friends along the way.

At the halfway point, Ally pointed to the water and fuel station. "Grabbing some," she said, and I nodded in agreement. As she high-fived the volunteers, she then pointed to

Jake, Ivy, and Addie with a giant unicorn poster, looking at me with a blinding smile. I felt a push to catch up to her. She was killing this race.

"Got it," I murmured to the universe, and possibly Nola, falling in stride with Allyson once again.

As we sailed through the eighteenth mile, basking in the cheers of the library crew of Nate, Elle, Tim, Grace, and Gabby, I felt some emotion welling up inside. I worked to shove it down, but all I could think about was that plane ride to Boston to train, how Nola had shown me a spreadsheet she'd set up with a list of the states and how she'd highlighted the ones where I'd ran a marathon already. I felt myself get choked up as I considered how different my life was just a few years ago, only to feel Allyson by my side as she tapped my hand.

"You good?" her gaze was concerned.

Hell, we were so close. I refused to do anything but believe that we had this in the bag.

"I will be." That was as truthful as I could be at the moment.

Her nod said she got it.

However, four miles later I noticed that she was laboring more than she had been.

"Need to walk?" I asked. I had zero issue with walking during a marathon. Allyson and I'd talked about this. Better to walk and remain uninjured if need be. She kept running in silence as my worry grew, but then I heard someone calling our names. Looking over, we saw Drew, Kate, and Kristine, along with Lou and Verdell with a sign proclaiming that Allyson was kicking ass and taking names.

"You've got this, girlie!" Lou said, waving her sign.

Allyson laughed, and her entire body seemed to loosen

as she picked her pace up, gaining her second wind, and we headed to the finish.

As we came down the final mile, I looked for our siblings. Maeve and Levi had stayed to see us off at the start, and sure enough, they were there when we crested the small hill at the end.

About a hundred yards before the finish line, Allyson reached over to grab my hand. Shooting a blinding smile at me, she shouted, "Together." Music was blaring from the speakers, and my heart took a skip when I heard it was Jackson Browne's "Running on Empty."

Listening to Browne's words, Allyson and I ran toward the finish chute, and I thought about how empty I had been for the past three years. I'd told Allyson that at the campground, but after the past week or so with her, I knew it had been far more dire than I'd realized. I really had been just going through the motions of life since I'd lost Nola, everything had been gray. No wonder my parents and Levi had been so worried.

Allyson squeezed my hand, and I looked over and squeezed hers right back. She was gorgeous, but more than that, she was positively beaming. We crossed the line, hand in hand, and then as soon as we were free from the crowd, I pulled her toward me and wrapped my arms around her shaking body.

"Babe, you did it."

"We did it." She corrected me immediately.

We walked away from the finish to stay out of everyone's way as they wrapped up their own races. There were tables to grab some fruit, food, and drink as you moved toward the spectators and the area opened up.

I handed Allyson a banana just as I heard someone shouting our names. I saw the mass of our friends heading our way, and I nudged Allyson. "Get ready; you're going to be squeezed to death in three... two... one."

Kate reached Allyson first, and I lost track of who hugged whom as we were each passed from friend to friend, hugs, back claps, congratulations. My heart was full of the realization that some came out because they knew it was a big deal that I ran this; some others came only because they wanted to support Allyson and me. I really had made some amazing friends in Highland Falls.

When I reached Levi, he leaned down and whispered in my ear, "I had no idea, or I would have warned you." Meeting his gaze, I gave him a confused look, but then saw our parents motoring my way.

"Mom, Dad," I got out before becoming the middle part of a Frank and Linnie sandwich. "I didn't know you were going to be here."

"Of course you didn't because you didn't invite us." My mom stepped back and put her hands on her hips, giving me a disapproving look. "After I heard you two talking about running the marathon, I looked it up and told your dad we simply had to be here cheer you on."

"It's fine, Mom." I leaned down and pressed a kiss on her cheek. "I'm glad you're here."

When I pulled back, I noted her concerned expression which was mirrored on my dad's face and Levi's. I saw Allyson coming up behind my parents, I'm sure to greet them, but I focused on my mom. "What's up?"

Mom bit her lip, then stepped closer to me. "I mentioned you were running this in passing to Susan. I had no idea. Please know that I just wanted to reassure her that you were doing okay..."

The bottom dropped out of my stomach as I looked past my parents, past Levi, past Allyson, to see a couple coming up with wide smiles on their faces. I'd avoided Susan and Jack as much as possible for the past three years. Nola's parents were wonderful people, but being in their presence made me feel the guilt of Nola's death in waves that always threatened to take me down. Because they were so kind, they never pushed it but sent me cards every so often because they wanted me to know they were thinking about me.

Time had a funny way about it; I knew they hadn't forgotten me—I'd never forget them—but I couldn't forgive myself enough to let me be loved by them anymore. They hated it but understood, or I thought they did until I saw them walking toward me.

Allyson had reached Levi, and I looked at both of them, tears swarming my eyes, and whispered, "I just can't."

Levi nodded at me, understanding what I could not say.

Allyson looked confused, scanning the group, but I saw her stand up straight as she leaned toward me and pressed a kiss to my lips before stepping back and said, "Go."

Levi slid his arm around her shoulder and gave me a look that said he had her and I ran.

Chapter 26

Fuck the Contract

Maeve sat in the armchairs, *our armchairs* in the corner, giving me the eye. She was convinced I was ready to implode when I was fine. That's it. I was *fine,* and she couldn't believe me.

Levi sat in front of me as I bustled around behind the counter, restocking the pastry shelves, cleaning up from our morning wash, and he was watching me too. Finally, I dropped the towel I was cleaning the counter with and looked from one set of judgmental eyes to the other. "What?"

Thank goodness the place was empty save these two fools, Caydence in the back. The morning crowd was long gone.

Maeve stalked over to the counter to sit next to Levi and lecture me from up close, I assumed. She scanned me up and down, then looked to Levi. "I'm worried about her."

He looked from me to Maeve and nodded. "Me too."

The assholes clinked their mugs together as I threw my hands up in frustration and groaned.

Lord, please save me from these well-intentioned-but-insane souls. I took a cleansing breath, then another one. For shits and giggles, I took a third. When I felt like my heart rate was approaching more normal readings, I looked at the two of them. "I'm not going to break. I've already told both of you that. I'm fine."

"But Logan—" Maeve began.

I held a hand up. "Logan is taking care of himself. He needs to."

"You know he cares about you..." Levi started.

I held up a hand to him too. I needed to lay it all out there and maybe then these two would *finally* listen to me. "Levi, I get it. You explained who Susan and Jack were yesterday. You also told me how Logan hadn't seen them much, if at all, since Nola passed. I remember your parents mentioning them on our camping trip, and I noted his reaction at the time but got distracted. I also felt that he's had something on his mind since our trip but chalked it up to running his first race since Nola passed.

"I feel for Logan, I really do. Do I wish he would come to me and I could help him through this? Yes. But I also understand that this is not my grief to manage. He's shoved so much down over the past three years, choosing not to face it instead of dealing with it. This is necessary if he wants to grow and possibly move on. So I'm choosing to look at this visit as a potentially positive thing for us and letting go because there is not a damn thing I can do here." I leaned on the counter across from these two and tapped the counter to make my point. "You have to let me do that. I'm not going to break. I'm not going to follow Logan around, begging him to hurry up and heal—"

"Are you two even together anymore?" Maeve asked with a wince.

"He still cares about Allyson," Levi began, looking at Maeve, but I interrupted him.

I let out an exasperated sigh. Maeve and I had been over this. "I am assuming we are unless I hear otherwise. He needed time; I'm giving it to him." I blew out my frustrations. "Again, while I wish we were dealing with this together, I have a feeling there are some aspects of losing Nola that Logan still needs to deal with, and maybe that needs to be done on his own."

Maeve looked irritated. "I wish you would just speak up for your needs."

I got that; I did. "Maeve, love you lots for caring, but that isn't what is happening here. I care about Logan. A hell of a lot. But what you see before you *is* me taking care of myself. I'm not sitting around, waiting for him to figure out what he wants or needs. I'm getting my shit together, living life, and making sure to be here if and when he needs me."

As if I'd planned it, three teens chose that moment to walk in the door from the mansion.

"Um, Allyson Murphy?" The boy in the front asked.

"That's me," I said. "Come on over and have a seat." I gestured at the open stools by Levi. I hazarded a guess, based on earlier descriptions from Emma. "Gabe, right?"

Gabe nodded, then gestured at the other two kids with him. "Sam and Henry."

I went over what Emma had already told me about these three. Sam and Gabe were sophomores, Henry a senior. I reached over and shook their hands and got right to business.

"I'm here, I'm here." Andy rushed in. We had talked about interviewing together, so Lou bailed us out once again and was running the town location with Sonia. Andy came behind the counter and stood by me.

I bumped her hip with mine and looked to the kids in front of us, ignoring Levi and Maeve for the moment. "All right. Emma Sullivan has recommended each of you for a job here and the location in town for part-time work. I'm a big believer in interviewing by doing, meaning I'm dumping you into the fire here. I shared that with Gabe when we talked on the phone. Did he tell you guys to clear your schedule for two hours this afternoon?" I looked to Sam and Henry.

They both nodded.

Andy leaned across the counter, giving each one of the teens a glance. "Excellent. Caydence is one of our part-time baristas as well. She's here today to show you what to do. Allyson and I will too, of course, but sometimes it's more relaxing to learn from a co-worker, not a potential boss."

Andy looked to me, so I continued trying to reassure the boys since they all looked even more nervous than they had when they walked in, especially Henry. "Don't worry; we're not leaving you by yourself or anything, but we will all be with you every step of the way today and, if you decide this seems like a fit, for your first week or so. Please remember this needs to be a good match for us but also for you. If you don't see yourself spending some hours here each week, speak up today, no hard feelings. Now before you get started, is there anything we need to know?"

Gabe and Sam shook their heads. Henry cleared his throat, his cheeks flushing. I waited, figuring if he wanted to share, he would. Gabe and Sam gave each other looks like they knew what was coming.

"Um, Ms. Murphy—"

"Allyson, please."

He looked to Andy.

"Andy is fine for me."

He wiped his hands on his pants, rocked a bit on his stool, then started again. "Allyson and Andy, I just wanted to be upfront." He swallowed, clearly nervous. "Last year, I got in a lot of trouble. I was hanging out with some people that weren't great for me, though that was my choice and I take full responsibility for that." He looked down at his lap, and we all sat, waiting. I knew he needed to get this all out. Henry took a breath and then looked up, making some solid eye contact. "I broke into garages around town for the hell—sorry, heck—of it and then was involved at the fire out here at the barn."

Henry looked to Gabe, clearly feeling some regret. "Gabe and Emma ran in the barn and pulled me out. If it wasn't for them..."

Gabe reached over and patted Henry's shoulder.

"Anyway, I was still a jerk for a while more. But I did community service, and my parents had me see a therapist. I stopped doing stuff that was bad for me. Then I did a volunteer program out here last summer with Blake and Max. I just wanted you both to know before you thought about hiring me in case anyone in town would say anything to either of you. I don't want to reflect badly on your business." He looked down at his hands. "It's okay if it makes you change your mind."

Emma and Max had recommended these three. Emma said Sam and Gabe had been in a book club she'd run at the library for a few years, Gabe's mom had originally been a thorn in her side, but Emma had helped her get a job in town and that smoothed out. They'd also shared about Henry, and I in turn had given Andy the heads-up. That being said, I was glad he told us himself, showed a lot of character.

"Henry?"

He looked up at me.

I looked at Andy, and she clearly read my mind because she nodded. Looking to Henry, I let him off the hook. "Sounds to me like you've learned a lot in the past year. We're good with you working here if you think it's a good fit after today. Cool?"

"Cool." His relief was palpable.

Caydence appeared from the back with aprons in hand. "You three ready to get to work? We're starting with some chocolate chip muffins."

Murmurs in the affirmative from all three, they headed where Caydence pointed. She glanced our way. "You two got the front?"

"Absolutely," I said, watching as she quickly put the boys at ease, taking them to the baking area we had set up just out of sight of the front counter.

Turning to the counter, I first looked at Andy. "Looks like we might have found some staff."

"Proud of you for following through." She bumped my hip once again.

I looked across the counter to Levi and Maeve who were watching the two of us. "Yesssss?"

"You really are taking charge, putting yourself first," Maeve looked impressed.

"Told ya."

"Love that that kid owned his fuckup." Maeve nodded in the direction the boys just went.

"Yep."

"Mom and Dad would hate that you gave him a chance." Maeve looked at me with a wide grin.

"Yep." I let out a light laugh as my grin matched hers.

"Logan will be happy that you're adding some workers," Levi said, which did give me a momentary pang.

I wasn't lying; I did believe he needed this time. But I couldn't say that it didn't hurt that I'd heard nothing from him since he left the race yesterday, and what I wasn't sharing with these two was that every hour that he remained silent from me made me more worried that he was going to decide he wasn't ready for a relationship.

I was working to be okay with that. I had to be. Whatever else, I wanted to emerge from this with our friendship intact.

It was okay to fall for your friend, right? Because that was another thing I was keeping mum on but was damn certain about—I was in love with the man.

It was inconvenient, to say the least.

And yet, onward.

I took a deep breath. "Okay, you two, I'm going to need —" I was cut off with the vibrations from my phone. I pulled it out of my back pocket to see our mom's name on the screen. Holding it up to Maeve, I sighed as did she.

Well, I'd ignored her calls for two weeks. I figured I might as well get this over with. I put her on speaker as I answered the phone.

"Hey, Mom, you're on speaker with me and Maeve." I was a big believer of telling people they were on speaker and who was there. I left Levi and Andy out because she wouldn't know them and, frankly, wouldn't care. I looked at the two of them and mouthed *sorry*. Levi's shrug told me he was fine. Andy pointed that she was going to join Caydence, and I nodded in agreement before turning my attention to my phone.

"Finally decided you were done ignoring my calls?"

"Pleasant as always, I see," Maeve wasn't playing. Nothing unusual there.

A sigh worthy of an actress was audible through the

speaker. "Girls, I don't have time for this nonsense. Allyson, you haven't gotten back to me about summer plans. I sent you the itinerary for the retreat weekend with your father's company."

"Why on earth did you send that to Allyson?" Maeve's eyebrows climbed higher on her forehead than I realized was possible.

"Not that it's your business, Maeve, but Allyson helped organize the retreat in the past. Janice at your father's office has retired, and we just don't have time to train anyone new. I need Allyson to organize everything and come here to make sure it all runs smoothly. You'd be welcome, but Lord knows you wouldn't make time for us in the past..."

Levi looked at me and mouthed *wow*.

Exactly. You know what? I thought I was done before. Now, one hundred percent, call the press: I was over my parents. I'd waited around for two years for them to figure out I was successful in my own right, for them to visit, for them to care, for them to *see me*. Now? Done.

I took a breath and then laid down thirty years of baggage that I had been carrying. "You know what, Mom? I did get that itinerary, but I won't be coming or able to help plan the weekend. Dad's new hire is just going to have to figure it out, or maybe you can."

The gasp through the phone was likely heard around the world.

I was undeterred and motored on. "I have a business here in Illinois that I'm needed at. You both are, as always, welcome to visit, but if you plan on coming and belittling Maeve or me, maybe just stay home. Ditto on the phone calls. I've decided I don't need negativity in my life. I love you and Dad, but I'm taking care of me."

"Well, of all the ungrateful things you've ever—"

"Bye, Mom. Before you say anything that will disappoint me, I'm just going to let you go. Love you." And I clicked the button to end the call.

Maeve and Levi immediately cheered.

Holy shit. Yep. I did that.

"Allyson Murphy, I cannot believe what I just heard." Maeve came around the counter and hugged me, rocking back and forth.

"That felt damn good," I whispered into her ear.

"I bet it did." She stepped back and squeezed my face. "Proud of you, which seems to be a reoccurring theme today."

I laughed. "I need to use the restroom. Can you man the counter if anyone comes in?"

"Absolutely. Want me to make you a latte?"

"Vanilla," I requested, taking off my apron and putting it on the shelf.

"Can you teach me?" Levi asked, and I smiled as I heard their teasing begin and headed toward the mansion's hall.

"Think you can keep up, Lesser Twin?" I heard the laughter in Maeve's voice.

"Come on," Levi said, acting put out.

En route to the public bathroom near the café, I passed a conference room and came to a stop. Full stop.

Logan was in the room, talking to a group. I knew there was a conference here this weekend; they'd rented out the bedrooms in the mansion and the other residences around the estate. It wasn't too big, maybe fifty people?

I walked closer to the door so I would be able to eavesdrop but not be seen. Yeah, maybe not what I should do, but there was no stopping me. Logan stood in front, pointing out some locations on a map of the park that was being projected onto the wall, and telling the group what they should make sure not to miss during their time at Highland Woods.

"Before I let you all go to check out the examples on conservation we've been doing this year in conjunction with your university, please make sure you hit up the café housed here in the mansion during your stay. Allyson—"

He paused and seemed lost in thought for a few beats. I noticed it because it made my heart skip, but I'm not sure anyone else would.

"—has the most amazing pastries. Her coffee is out of this world. And the entire place just makes you want to stay awhile. A trip to the park isn't complete without a stop at the Sanctuary."

Someone spoke up from the back of the room. "Isn't the Sanctuary the café in town? I've been there."

Logan nodded. "She's an amazing businesswoman and runs both locations. She adds a lot to our community." He looked out the window, and I knew it was so that he could take a moment to get collected. "Okay, let me get out of your way. I'll be in my office if anyone needs anything."

He strode off toward the door in the back that would take him on a shortcut to his office that, conveniently, avoided passing the door to the café.

What was I to make of that? His words were beautiful; he looked like crap. Oh, Logan. I just wanted to help him in some way. And maybe, just maybe, tell the man I was crazy about him.

I made quick work of hitting the restroom and then walked into the café. I marched past Levi and Maeve and rounded the corner to see Andy, Caydence, and the boys working. "I'm going to need someone to deliver some muffins and a coffee to Logan's office."

Caydence raised a brow. "He already had his one

muffin allotted for the day, as per this year's napkin contract, before you got here this morning."

Of course he did. "He's grieving," I said. "Fuck the contract." I glanced toward the teens. "Sorry boys, but the f-word will get dropped here on the regular."

They laughed, clearly not bothered in the least.

Levi and Maeve cheered from the front. I might not be invading his space, but like hell I wasn't taking care of this man.

I looked to the duo behind me. "Levi, Maeve, I'm going to need you to help out here for the next hour. I need to get ahold of one Maxwell Harp, the real Max, not the cardboard one. I need to talk to the man about a tree."

Maeve looked concerned, but Levi just smiled. "Your wish is my command."

Chapter 27

Letting Go

Logan

A glance at my phone told me what I already knew. Time had decided to simply stand still. Just before lunch yesterday my day went from emotional but exciting to a mess that I had no idea how to sort out.

And I'd had no contact with Allyson. My heart—no, my very soul—ached with missing her.

Even Levi, when he got home yesterday afternoon, had realized quickly that I was too busy kicking my own ass; he wasn't going to add to it. He'd told me he made sure Allyson cooled down and got home from the race with Maeve, then came to me.

Last night my parents had come by, hugged me, and said they were going back to Aurora and would call later. If I had to hazard a guess, they had a conversation with Levi and decided the best course of action was to give me some distance. Was that a good choice? Maybe, maybe not. At this point, it was all a crap shoot. What was up was down, and down was up. I thought I was healing, possibly ready to move ahead with my life. Clearly, I was wrong, and I felt like I was drowning.

The worst part was, I was concerned about what Allyson would think. Would she blame herself? Think this meant that what we had wasn't special? Or, what made me physically ill, believe I didn't care about her?

Because I did. I knew that. And I should just pick up my damn phone, the one with the clock frozen in time, and call her. Hell, even text her. Anything to tell her what she meant to me. But it was like there was some block. It seemed that I was physically incapable of doing it. Even after she'd sent me coffee with a muffin today, my second of the day, I couldn't get past this block.

So I lived in my own kind of purgatory as I sat at my desk, only rooms away from the woman I wanted to run to, to say the fuck with all of this. I held back, though, because I couldn't see where I was while facedown in a puddle of despair. These feelings, this grief, were going to keep sweeping me away, keep preventing me from moving on, if I didn't deal with it.

And yet, I didn't know how or even the first place to start.

Sweeping my phone off my desk and sliding it in my pocket, I whistled to Charlie to follow me. Passing Max's office, I stuck my head in, seeing that he was also here, spending a few hours on a Sunday afternoon. The fact that we could bank hours worked outside the normal day and flex them when needed was a great benefit of being here. There were often conferences scheduled at the mansion on the weekends, so it made sense to add that perk, allowing us to leave early during the week or come in later. Max had Poppy and Winnie curled up near his desk.

"Heading out on the trail. Want me to take your pups?"

Max looked up. "Nah, I'm heading out soon." He gave me an assessing glance. "You good?"

I thought about lying, but why. "Working on getting there."

"Fair enough." He nodded in my direction and got to work as I took the long way to avoid the café. Cowardly? Yep. But at this point, I was just trying to get to a healthy place where I could figure out what was next.

Nola's parents, Susan and Jack, had texted me immediately yesterday, apologizing for coming to the race unannounced, but pleaded with me to meet up for dinner tonight. I'd agreed because I'd have to be an asshole not to, but I was dreading every part of it.

Charlie and I headed around the pond and down the familiar trail. The sky today was a brilliant blue, birds singing their welcoming notes of true spring. The trees were beginning to have leaves but weren't full. The warmth of the afternoon held the promise of the summer to come.

Where would I be come June? July? Would I still be mired in this sense of loss, mixed-up feelings? I didn't want to be. I wanted to be with Allyson.

My breath caught. I hadn't admitted that to myself yet. But I did. My feelings for this woman were so strong it scared the hell out of me.

Coming to my bench, *our* bench, I sat and looked at the river, letting Charlie laze by my feet. Surrounded by the trees, I felt safe and protected to deal with the emotions that threatened to pull me under.

Nola would hate this. I knew that. If it had been me, would I want her to feel this sense of despair for the past three years? No, never.

And when I examined it, I knew I wasn't just struggling with grief, but an overwhelming sense of guilt. That was why I hadn't been able to see Susan and Jack since Nola passed. I was sure they'd hate me. They didn't, or said they didn't, but that didn't matter. I hated myself enough for all of us.

Elbows braced on my knees, I dropped my head, tears swimming in my eyes. I'd talked to my therapist about this. I'd done the work. And I couldn't let it go. Something was stopping me.

A twig snapping brought my head up, and I looked over my shoulder to see the duo I'd been avoiding standing just off the path.

Susan and Jack.

I guess dinner plans were tossed in favor of surprising me at work. To be fair, I might have bailed on them, and they knew me well enough to anticipate that move.

I wiped away at my eyes, thinking I'd fake that I was fine, but quickly saw that wouldn't be happening. Susan's look was the one I'd been told was passed down in the female side of their family; it said she wasn't here for any bullshit, and I knew my time was up.

"Hey." Was all I could come up with. I started to get up, but Susan waved at me.

"Nope. We're coming to you. Scoot your ass over and make room; the three of us are fitting on that bench."

Jack shrugged at me with a sheepish grin. He never got in the way of Susan. Lessons learned from decades of marriage.

I did as I was told and moved down. Charlie was up, tail wagging, glad for new company. Susan, sitting right next to me, immediately patted her leg for my pup to come over and pet his head.

"Name?"

"Charlie."

She nodded, then scanned me. "I like a dog for you."

"Levi got him for me last year."

"Did it help?" She narrowed her gaze. Looks like we weren't avoiding talking about grief today.

"Some."

Sitting up from paying attention to Charlie, Susan turned to me, then Jack. "Nope," she said. "I need to stand."

Susan was an attorney and often paced as she talked like she was presenting her case to the jury. This familiar act brought a smile to my face.

She stood in front of Jack and me, pacing a path parallel to the river. As she walked, Jack leaned over and spoke in a hushed voice. "Hey, sorry for the surprise visit."

His gravelly voice was so familiar and full of regret my tears came again. "It's cool," I whispered, my voice cracking.

"Okay, I've thought a lot about this," Susan said as she paced, glancing at us on the bench, but also speaking to the trees. "Nola wouldn't want you to be here, clearly guilt ridden, three years later."

I started to interrupt, but she wasn't having it.

"Nope, don't even try to argue with me, Logan Traub. I mean, I know you also grieve her loss; we all do. When you get to be old like us, you know that loss is part of life. We will always wish we had more time with Nola—of course we will—and there are days that wishing will knock me on my ass, but I know that it's a waste of *my life* if I stop living as a result. I've spent the past few years thinking why your grief has so consumed you, and I came to the notion that you were not only dealing with grief but guilt. Like you somehow believe you caused Nola's death."

"I did." My voice was steely. I didn't want to talk to

them about this, but maybe it would give me closure if I did. If I finally got the chance to apologize for it.

"Bullshit." Jack spoke from my side.

Susan and I looked at him with surprise. Jack was always the quiet and reserved of the two.

"What?" I asked.

"What I said, bullshit. You are a smart man. You know you were not the driver. You no more caused that accident that I did." Jack looked pissed.

I scoffed. "How could you have caused it?"

"I paid for her to be there." Jack gave me a glare. "Remember, you two were saving up for a place here, and Nola didn't want to spend the money to go with you when you'd be doing a return trip in a month for the race. I gave her the cash for the ticket and told her to have some fun. Did I cause her death?"

"Well, no, but—"

"No buts." Susan interrupted. "Unless you want to blame both of us too. Because when Jack told me Nola was thinking of staying home, I called her up and told her to go. And I'm not at fault. Jack isn't at fault. You're not at fault. We don't blame you. Nola wouldn't blame you."

A guttural sob came out of my chest before I could stop it. Before I could say a word, Jack and Susan had both pulled me to my feet and surrounded me in a hug, Charlie squeezing his face in as well.

"Logan, stop blaming yourself. Nola would hate this," Susan whispered, pressing a kiss to my head.

I let the sob go. That one stuck in my throat and all the ones that followed. We stood there, holding each other up in a circle, letting the grief and guilt of a lifetime go and releasing it to the trees and the wind.

We rocked back and forth as I let the feelings run out of

me in this spot where I felt so much safety and peace. It was exhausting and necessary.

"There you go, there you go," Susan said, her arm tightening around my waist. "It's time to let it all go."

She was right. It was, and I did.

Chapter 28

Bloom

Allyson

Walking into the café, I brushed my hands on my pants before heading to the sink and scrubbing them clean. Our Monday morning rush was done as was the lunchtime crowd. Now it was just a quiet afternoon where I could consider that I hadn't seen or spoken to Logan since Saturday morning. Distractions were needed.

"Hey Gabe," I greeted my new employee. All three boys had hired on when Andy met with them yesterday as I'd gone on a journey to find Max and set my idea in motion. I was surprised at how happy our new staff members made me. "How goes it today?"

Gabe was restocking the pastries and gave me a sheepish grin. "I might put on several pounds working here. How do you look at these muffins all day and not want to eat one of each?"

I laughed. "It does get easier." I dried my hands on a towel. "Andy said all three of you asked to be added to the schedule."

Gabe nodded. "Yep." He looked around, then took a

step toward me, lowering his voice. "Thanks to you both for giving Henry a chance." He glanced away from me as he continued. "Emma helped my mom once, giving her a new path. I think everyone deserves it."

I reached over to squeeze his arm, which brought his gaze to me. "I couldn't agree more, and we're glad to have you all." I gave a rueful glance at the dirty dishes from this morning. "You have no idea how much."

"No problem. I have cleanup; Caydence is on the counter."

"Aye-aye, Captain," Caydence said to us before turning to Mrs. Tuck to take her order.

I looked around the café, realizing Mrs. T's book club was gathering. It had been a month since they'd last met. That day my mom had driven me crazy, calling over and over, Mrs. T had been kind enough to spend some time giving me advice. What a difference a month makes.

Mrs. Tuck slid down the counter to a spot in front of me. "Allyson, how are you? I haven't seen you since the last time I was here."

I put the towel down and walked around the counter. "Mrs. T, can I give you a hug?"

She didn't hesitate to pull me in. Mrs. T was solid; her hug filled me with comfort.

I stepped back and smiled up at her. "Thanks. When you were here last month, you got me thinking. So did several friends, and well, I've made some changes."

"Proud of you, Allyson," she said with a beautiful smile.

"Your retirement is coming up at the end of the month, correct?" I asked.

Mrs. T nodded.

"Are you ready?" I had only been in this town for a few

years, but even I knew that Mrs. T was the backbone of the high school.

"Well, as you have seen firsthand, I don't need to be in the school to help others. Somehow, I have a feeling that I'll do just fine." Mrs. T placed her hand on mine, her brown skin a contrast to my own, and squeezed my hand.

Mrs. T headed over to her book club as I brushed some dirt off my leggings. I'd been grateful for the help this morning; it was only twenty-four hours ago that inspiration had struck, and for the most part, a day later my dream had been realized. Max didn't mess around. After sending the coffee and muffin to Logan yesterday, I'd stopped by Max's office to explain what I wanted, and he snapped into action. He knew of a nursery the park used for all their trees and had called immediately. They'd been happy to help me out and worked quickly, meeting us here this morning to get it planted.

Blake had helped with the project too, whipping up a temporary plaque for the area and installing it where I'd asked. Standing with the two men along with the guys from the nursery this morning, I'd been overcome with emotion.

I still hadn't heard from Logan, but I was choosing to believe he was doing the work he needed. Max said that yesterday afternoon he'd given directions to Logan's favorite trail to the couple who'd come to the race on Saturday. We all knew from Levi that they were Nola's parents and that Logan had avoided them, for the most part, for the better part of three years.

I passed over a plate of muffins to the book club crew and went to wipe down some tables from this morning as I let the happy hum of the café along with the sounds of the espresso maker soothe my soul.

To put it plainly, I was worried about Logan. I was no

therapist, but losing Nola the way he did and his avoidance of racing since then had already been set up to make Saturday a lot, emotionally. But then this strained relationship that was shoehorned back into his life the same day? It was concerning.

Was I worried for him and his own mental state? Sure was. But was I also distressed as to what this meant for our little fledgling of a relationship? Yep times a million.

As a result, I was putting my head down and proceeding as if we were fine. Healthy, I know. I'd been honest with myself on Sunday; I'd fallen for Logan. No buts about it, that's where I was. In my mind, what that meant was that you care about someone, good times and bad, when they're emotionally stable and when they're a mess. Logan was currently a mess, so that meant it was time to buckle down.

My mission, that I was a touch nervous about, was that I was taking care of this man. I was ensuring he got a muffin, scone, and/or coffee from the Sanctuary every day, even if he was avoiding me. Eventually, he and I would talk. I would let him know I was okay with moving slowly, wading through this grief, but that we could do this together. That right there was where I felt like he was making a mistake. He kept trying to tackle this all on his own; he didn't want to put anyone out. That wasn't what relationships—hell, that wasn't what love was all about.

What it really came down to, therapy wise, was that Maeve was right; it was time to prioritize myself. I knew what I wanted. Whether that was in my business or relationships, I was done feeling like I wasn't seen or not important enough. I was worth it, and so was Logan.

Now I just had to convince him.

A throat clearing behind me made me turn, assuming

one of my book club ladies needed more snacks. Today they were discussing a new steamy romance from Kate Canterbary. When they read romance, they liked to tell me they were peckish, then howl with laughter as they whispered *peckish, peckers* to each other.

Bless.

The person in front of me wasn't one of Mrs. T's friends, but Logan Traub, looking, well, rough. There were shadows under his eyes, his hair was disheveled, and his beard was in serious need of some beard oil or something.

However, there was something about him that seemed... different. I thought about it, trying to pinpoint what it was as my eyes drank him in.

He was at ease. The indentation between his brows was gone. He wasn't tense, but relaxed.

"Hey, Allyson." His voice was gravelly. "Is there a chance you could get away for fifteen minutes or so?"

"You can take her," Caydence called over from the spot at the counter where she stood with Gabe.

Logan seemed to take that moment to realize that, while the café was busy, we were relatively caught up, unlike the days in the past. Gabe came out from behind the counter and was spraying down tables. Caydence was singing as she made some coffee, and Sonia came from the back with restocks.

So yeah, I could take fifteen. Hell, I could take an hour. Because what he couldn't see was that the town location was also fully staffed. And Andy and I had a meeting scheduled for this week to look over our books and sched-ules to decide if we needed more staff or were comfortable for now.

Another step forward, another step telling myself that I had this. And I knew I did.

Logan's face when he turned to me took my breath away with a beautiful smile. "You've added some staff."

I nodded. "Three high school workers."

He tilted his head as he considered my words. "And Andy as manager."

"And Andy."

"Proud of you."

I could barely hear his voice; it was a whisper.

"Where do you want to talk? I can take a break."

He pointed behind himself to the doorway where Charlie sat patiently waiting. "Is a hike okay?"

I smiled to myself. Hopefully this was a good-news hike. Because otherwise, maybe my gift would be a goodbye gesture. No, I couldn't think that way; this would be fine.

"A hike would be wonderful."

We headed away from the mansion as Logan walked by my side and Charlie trotted ahead. It was another beautiful spring day, not too warm, and being a Monday, not too crowded. I kept quiet, knowing he'd asked me out here for a reason. I didn't have to wait long.

"I have to apologize for Saturday."

"No." I put a hand on his forearm to stop us right inside the trail head. We turned to face each other. This I needed to say while we weren't walking. "Logan, before you say anything, let me tell you this. There is no need to apologize. I told you to go. I didn't know who that couple was at the time, but that doesn't matter. I care about you, a lot. And your pain was all over your face." My gut clenched when I thought about how anguished he'd looked at the end of the race. "Do not apologize for that. My only wish, if I can be selfish for a moment, was that I would have loved to help you through that, to hold you when you were hurting, but you do not need to apologize for doing what you needed."

Logan stepped toward me and pulled me into his embrace. His mouth found my ear. "We have stuff to talk about, but thank you for supporting me."

"Anytime."

I wanted kiss him, to go to his place and find our way back to each other in his bed, but that was likely not the path to a healthy relationship, as much as I wanted it to be.

He stepped back first and gave me a sheepish smile. "Can we keep walking?"

I nodded.

As we walked, Logan told me how he met with Susan and Jack. They'd worked through a lot of pain and guilt on his behalf, which was an amazing gift. "They asked if I'd finally take Nola's ashes."

I looked his way, not realizing this was a thing that had been up in the air.

"Her ashes?"

He nodded. "I knew she wanted to be cremated, but she wanted her ashes scattered. She was so young; we'd never discussed where. It was just too much, so I'd asked Susan and Jack to keep them years ago or scatter them themselves. They held on to them instead. But when we talked yesterday, we think we picked a spot. I want to run it by you."

He looked hesitant, but strong. So strong. God, he was beautiful.

"Me?"

He reached out, linking his hand with mine as we walked up the trail to his favorite spot in the park. "This might seem like it's too fast, Allyson, but I realized when I was talking with Susan and Jack that you were the other half of me now. I wished you were with us yesterday and last night. I felt like something was missing when you were gone. And it's because, without realizing it, I'd fallen in love with you."

I pulled on his hand as I came to a stop, the canopy of trees above us creating an arch, the quiet birdsong the only background noise beyond the rolling water of the stream below.

"You love me?"

"Yes." He watched me, a confidence I'd never seen before apparent.

I could feel my smile spread across my face. "I love you too."

The shock that washed over him was visible. "What? No, you don't have to say it just because I did."

I laughed, moving to wrap my arms around him. "You silly man. I do love you. I only realized it yesterday, but that's how I feel."

Logan bent his head, hands on either side of my face, as he brushed his mouth over mine. Our lips parted for the sweetest kiss. It wasn't filled with heat like others had been. This one contained the promise of moments just like this from now until forever.

Charlie barked to express his disapproval of our lack of progress on this hike.

We stepped back and looked at each other. I brought my hand up to my mouth and took a breath.

"Wow," I whispered.

Logan grinned. "Wow is right."

Linking hands again, we returned to the trail, and Charlie bounded ahead.

"So like I was saying, I talked to Nola's parents. We were thinking we could scatter her ashes up here." He gestured ahead of us on the trail, where the bench and his favorite spot were coming into view. "I think..." His voice trailed off as he came to a stop. Scanning the area, he looked puzzled. "Is that a new tree? We didn't have anything scheduled for this spot right now."

My heart was hammering in my chest. Surely he wouldn't be upset, but I was nervous.

"So I did something," I said, squeezing his hand.

Logan looked from the tree to me, then back to the tree. "Did you plant this?"

I nodded. "With help from Max, Blake, and some company Max approved of."

Logan was clearly trying to puzzle this together. "Okay, I don't mean this in a rude way at all, so please know that. But why?"

We started up the hill, and I wanted to get this said before we got to the tree, so I spit it all out. "I asked Max what species of trees we had out here or what we typically planted. He gave me some options. I looked up the meaning behind them."

"Meaning?"

"Like what each tree was supposed to represent. It's actually kind of cool. Sycamores"—I pointed to the tree—"represent strength, protection, eternity, and divinity. I thought that with those qualities, Nola might approve of it. So not only did I order a tree yesterday, which fortunately they had and were able to bring over today to plant, but also a plaque to be made to go by it. It's on order and will arrive in a few weeks, but Blake created this temporary one."

Logan was silent as we came to stand in front of the young tree. The makeshift plaque from Blake was a piece of slate on a stake. He'd used some type of paint to make the sign.

In Memory of Nola Traub

Take a look, Take a breath

BLOOM WHERE YOU ARE PLANTED

Logan read the plaque and then looked to the cloudless blue sky. From the spot here between his bench and the tree, we were just feet from the bluff over the river. Hawks soared overhead, woodpeckers could be heard all around, and Logan tipped his face up, closed his eyes, and breathed deep. A breeze rustled the trees, shifting his hair on his head before he looked back at me.

"My God, Allyson. This is more than I have words for." Tears welled at the corner of his eyes.

"So it's good?"

"It's great."

We stood, just soaking in the moment as Charlie lounged in the sunshine. Finally, Logan looked at me. "I feel her here."

I thought about that for a moment. "Maybe that's why you've been drawn to this spot for so long."

He let that roll around in his mind. "Maybe."

I took in our surroundings. "I think this is the perfect place to spread her ashes."

"I'll call Susan and Jack. Maybe we can do it next week."

"Sounds good."

"And Allyson." He looked at me with mischief in his eyes.

"Yeah?"

"I'm not going to ask you to marry me today, but I will be one day soon."

I laughed and tugged him to the bench, sitting down and throwing my legs over his as I nestled as close as possible. "You will, will you?"

"Yep. Locking you in."

I leaned over, pressing my lips to him, but then I pulled

back, our foreheads touching. "Only if we can get engaged right here."

He kissed my forehead before resting his head against mine again. "That's a promise."

We sat there, listening to the birds talking to each other as the breeze floated on, peace in our hearts.

Chapter 29

Snapshots of Our Lives

Logan

The May Garden Market was in full swing on the streets surrounding the courthouse. Our Main Street program organized this event every year, closing off streets and bringing in vendors—both local and from nearby towns. There were booths for gardening, food, and a variety of local businesses. Highland Woods had a booth set up. We had brochures of trail maps, large displays of scenic spots around the park, and information to share on camps and upcoming events as well as current projects we were involved in. I'd manned the table for the past hour, but I was off now and in search of my girl.

Allyson had scheduled her shift at the Sanctuary to coincide with mine so we could check out the market together. It had been twelve days since we'd laid it all out at my spot on the trail. I felt like a different person.

Last weekend Nola's parents, my parents, Maeve, and Levi—neither of whom had made any moves to leave Highland Falls as of yet—and our closest friends joined us at our spot. I'd said a few words, as had my family and Nola's parents. Together we'd scattered her ashes. It had been a beautiful day, and a weight I'd carried around for years was just... gone.

I heard my name and looked up to see Allyson running toward me. Her red hair was streaming behind her, and she had on a loose T-shirt, jeans rolled up, and her Birkenstocks. She'd never been more beautiful.

She jumped up in my arms, laughing as I grabbed her, letting her legs circle my waist as we spun around.

"Aidan, why don't you carry me around anymore like that?" I looked over to see Grace, Emma's boss at the library, walking with her husband Aidan.

Aidan laughed and put a hand on her belly. Grace's belly had popped a little more in the past few weeks. Earlier this week, I'd met some of the guys out at the Homestead when Allyson had gone to yoga. Aidan was close with Max and had confided to the group that it had taken longer for them to get pregnant than they'd planned on, so he was working to curb his overprotective streak. It seemed that Grace didn't like being told what to do.

"Babe, you can jump all you want when this little one is on the outside." He tucked a strand of her blond hair behind her ear and kissed her neck.

Grace rolled her eyes as she looked up at Allyson in my arms. "Jump while you can, Allyson. Because if that one gets you pregnant one day, he too will want to wrap you with Bubble Wrap."

Aidan shrugged without remorse.

The two of them walked past us, heading to the wood-fired pizza food truck.

Allyson glanced down at me. "Do you plan on becoming an overprotective caveman when I'm pregnant?"

I tightened my arms under her butt, keeping her tight against me. "You saying you're good with a baby?"

"Or two."

"Then yes, absolutely I will be overprotective." I kissed the underside of her jaw.

She smiled and kissed the tip of my nose. "I'm good with that."

Lowering her to the ground, I asked, "What do you want to see?"

She scanned the crowd. Levi was sitting on the half wall that framed the lawn that led to the courthouse. Charlie was on the leash by his feet, Maeve was talking to him and, from what it looked like from here, arguing. Her hands were flying as he looked down at her, a smirk on his face.

In other words, their usual.

"Charlie staying with Levi today?"

I nodded. "He'll bring him home later."

Allyson looked my way. "Maybe we should escape out of here while we can?"

Yep. Sounded like a perfect plan. "My place or yours?"

"Yours. We've been at my place all week." She glanced toward our siblings and our group of friends that were gathered near the pizza truck. "Should we say goodbye?"

"Hell no." I tugged her hand and headed in the opposite direction. "It will take us another hour if we do that."

She laughed and we turned and motored to my car.

Just twenty minutes and a handsy ride home later, we spilled through my front door into the cool silence of my house.

"It feels weird to be here without Charlie," Allyson said as I closed the door behind her.

"Yep." I locked the door, not that Levi didn't have a key, but at least I might hear it if he got home earlier than expected. "Now ass to the bedroom," I said, slapping her behind.

Laughing, she walked ahead of me, hips swaying, shedding clothes as she went. I did the same, leaving a trail in my wake.

Entering my room, Allyson turned just before the bed. It wasn't even lunchtime; sun flitted through the windows, bathing the room in light. Allyson's back was to the bed, and she crooked a finger as she gestured for me to come to her.

I moved her way. There was nowhere I'd rather be.

I nibbled my way down her neck, drunk on the scent of her. She shifted against me, and I pulled her body to mine as I lowered us to the bed.

Allyson arched her back as I made my way down her body. As my mouth moved past her belly button, she tugged on my hair. I looked up to see her heated gaze locked on mine.

"Can we do more foreplay the second time around?"

"You don't want it now?"

"I don't need it, I need you."

I slid my fingers between her slit, and she was clearly ready. I worked my way up her body, running my tongue around the underside of each breast before sucking on one nipple, then the other, finally reaching her mouth which immediately met my own.

As we kissed, I rolled us to my back and let Allyson straddle me so she could set her own pace. She wasted no time, reaching down to grab my cock and set it at her entrance. Pulling back from our kiss, she raised up, bracing her hands on my chest as she lowered down until she was fully seated.

"Damn," she exhaled, a small smile on her face. "Never gets old."

I laughed and gave a small shake of my head, then reached up to tweak a nipple. "And I hope it never will."

She looked at me. "I believe you're right, Mr. Traub."

"Set the pace, Ms. Murphy."

"I want slow," she said, beginning a languorous slide.

I sat up, allowing her legs to circle my waist. "Slow sounds great," I whispered, my hands finding her ass.

It was small kisses, little nibbles, and easy movements. Sex with Allyson was everything I needed and more. Sometimes it was so much I could barely breathe or keep a thought in my head. Others were languid, like we had all the time in the world to explore each other and soak in the moment. And there was everything between. She kept me guessing, and I wanted to continue that for the next fifty years or so.

"I'm close," Allyson said as her internal grip on my dick began to tighten.

"Mm-hmm, I can tell," I said, wrapping my arm around her to shift her to her back so I could thrust deeper. As soon as we switched positions, her legs tightened around my torso, allowing me to find a new angle that took her over the edge.

"Logan," she breathed out, finding her climax.

Three thrusts more and I joined her.

Dropping to her side, I rolled her with me. We were still connected, and I slid her hair behind her ear, tipping her chin up to press a kiss to her lips.

"I love you so damn much," I whispered against her mouth.

"Ditto," she said. Looking into my eyes, she started to say something else when her stomach spoke for her.

I kissed her nose and then looked at her with as stern of

an expression as I could. "Allyson Elise, what did you eat today?"

She wore an expression that said she knew she was in for it. "In my defense, we were swamped preparing for this morning."

"What was the point in hiring all this help if you don't take time to eat?" I shook my head at her like I was disappointed.

"Hey, Mister, I'll have you know that all that work made for some delicious muffins you will likely be eating tomorrow. If you're good, I might even let you have two."

"I thought that contract was void now that we were together." I raised a brow at her to express my seriousness about this subject.

"Can't have you getting a belly now that I've got you, can I?" She ran a hand over my stomach, and I pulled away.

"If you start that again, we'll never get you fed. Eggs good for a quick lunch, then we can grill out for dinner?"

"Perfect." She slid away from me after giving me a quick kiss. "I'll meet you in the kitchen."

I grabbed my clothes as I moved down to the kitchen, getting dressed again in a reverse order from the way I shed them. Once I reached the kitchen, I pulled out everything to make an omelet and some toast. I'd just started to whisk the eggs when Allyson made her way over to the island, coming around to my side and wrapping her arms around me.

"I've got something for you," I said, leaning into her.

"What?" she said, swaying against me.

I nodded toward the envelope on the end of the island. "Take a look."

She moved across, meeting my eyes before sliding out the photos I'd had printed. She looked from one to the next, taking her time with each. There were several pictures of

Nola and me, an action shot of the two of us running the marathon, one Levi had taken of Allyson and me on the deck when we were dancing together one night, some of our friends at the brewery, one of a young Allyson and Maeve with their grandmother, and a few more of Allyson and me.

Laying the stack down, she moved my way, not bothering to wipe away the tears spilling down her cheeks.

"Where did you get all these?" She asked, winding her arms around my shoulders.

"Over the past two weeks. After the marathon, before Susan and Jack left, they gave me an envelope of pictures they'd been saving. I went through those, then asked the guys to send me a few to print off, and I asked Maeve for some too, though I didn't print any of your parents. Maybe one day."

"That's fine," she said. "But what made you do it?"

I brushed a thumb over her cheek. "You."

Her gaze was unwavering.

"You once told me that when you love someone, you need snapshots of your lives together."

She bit her lip and nodded.

"Well, you know I love you, Ally. I want our life all over this house. And I want to put Nola's pictures up because you were right; cutting her out of my life didn't help. However, I am really hoping that one day soon, like tomorrow, this will be our house, not mine. I'm not sure how you feel about having Nola's picture on the walls..."

Allyson put her finger against my mouth. "Shhh. Nola's pictures are *always* welcome in our house. Loving her doesn't mean you don't love me. I've never been jealous of her, and I never will."

God damn, this woman. "That's excellent to hear

because you have nothing to be jealous of." I paused, then decided to just ask. "Want to help me hang some photos?"

"I'd love nothing more." She tilted her head, then whispered. "And I'm good with tomorrow."

"What?" Now I was trying to follow this conversation.

"Moving in. Tomorrow works for me."

I laughed, reaching down to pick her up and sit her on the counter. She immediately parted her legs and let me in. "That works for me too."

Leaning in, she opened her mouth for a deep kiss that had me going from slightly interested to ragingly hard within seconds.

Shifting from side to side, her eyes crinkled with clear amusement. "Why, Logan Traub, does old BA want to come out to play?"

I pulled back and looked at her with confusion. "BA?"

With a wicked smile, she slid her hand down along my cock. "I thought Levi told me this guy was a traitor at times —Benedict Arnold, was it?—that he knew long before you that I was the one for you?" She gave me a devious smile as she lightly squeezed my length.

"That's it," I said, tossing her over my shoulder with a slap to her ass. "Lunch will have to wait."

From her spot upside down on her shoulder, I could feel her stomach tensing with her laughter, and she slapped my ass as I moved us to our bedroom. "BA can't wait, babe?"

"No, Ally, he sure can't." And wouldn't have to, ever again.

Epilogue

Four Years Later

L*ogan*

It was a warm day in late May that made the long, coolish Illinois spring days that came before worth it. Summer was in the air after weeks of it feeling like it would never come. Charlie was trotting down the trail ahead of us while Allyson was behind, singing "Old McDonald Had a Farm" and just in general loving life. We all were.

The past four years had been magical and, no other word for it, healing. Allyson hadn't wanted a long engagement, so we'd headed to the courthouse on a sunny day in June, just a month after the marathon, and got married. My parents, Levi, and Maeve had been there. Maeve had their parents on FaceTime. They didn't seem too broken up about not being there, which I worked to let go of my anger about. Allyson wasn't upset; she'd been full of sunshine, enough for us all.

We'd celebrated at the Sanctuary that afternoon with our friends—Allyson and Andy had a crew scheduled. We'd devoured anything they had whipped up plus the beer and apps the guys had brought over from the Homestead. It was low-key and full of joy, exactly what we'd wanted.

One year later, William Traub had been born, and I felt like I understood the character of the Grinch, my heart had grown that day, far beyond what I thought I was capable of. Mom said God knew what he was doing, and Will was going to be a handful, just like Levi and myself. I'd say Ally didn't deserve that, but she loved him to pieces and didn't care one iota if he was trouble personified; he was ours.

And then God gave with both hands again this year because this little girl in the sling on my chest came along just three months ago. We were sleep-deprived and blissfully happy.

Behind me I heard three-year-old Will shouting about animals, then joining Ally in singing the noises that animal made. As we came around the curve in the trail, he called out, "We're almost there, Daddy."

That we were.

Our bench was just up ahead, my favorite spot in the park, and by it, our sycamore that Allyson had planted.

I got there first, placing my hand on the trunk as I always did, feeling the warmth of the bark and the energy that I felt each time flow through me.

"Down, down," Will cried from his spot in the pack on Allyson's back.

I quickly moved to them, pulling him out and down. Charlie quickly came to his side, ready to play or, hopefully, find a snack that Will dropped.

"We might need to switch on the way back," Allyson said, stretching a bit.

"Absolutely." I had a feeling that wouldn't happen. Allyson loved talking to Will as they hiked, making up stories and singing songs. But I'd gladly take a turn if it worked out.

The caw of a bird came from above, and we all looked up into the brilliant blue sky as Will cawed in response.

"It's a beautiful day," Allyson said as she spread a blanket out for Will to play on here by our bench, our tree, our spot.

"Sure is." I marveled at the sense of peace that was in me now, that had been there for a little over four years. I knew a large part of it was this woman in front of me, but I wasn't selling myself short; it had taken a lot of work on my own to get here, and I'd done it and was damn proud of myself for it.

"Charlie," Will said, looking at me with pleading eyes.

"Only one," I said as Will happily handed Charlie the first of what I knew would be several dog treats. The two were best friends, and Charlie had found a champion in his campaign for more snacks.

"Lewi?" Will asked, looking behind us for his uncle.

"Not today, bud, next time." For this little one's first visit to our spot, we'd left Levi and Max at the mansion with Max's dogs. They were getting coffee while they waited for us. They knew we'd wanted today to just be about our little family but wanted to be here for us when we were done.

Will nodded, then grabbed a car that Allyson handed him and drove it around his blanket, Charlie settling in beside him.

My wife's shrewd gaze scanned me. "You good?"

I nodded. "Better than good."

She watched me for a few beats, then dipped her head before stretching out near Will and our pup. "We'll be right here."

God, I loved her.

Taking a few steps over to the tree Allyson had planted, I toed off some debris that had blown over the plaque on the ground in the past week. My hand rubbed over the bundle against my chest who hadn't made so much as a peep since we started our short hike. The fresh air did that to her every time. Allyson liked to joke that I'd passed it down to her in my genes. A love and peace to be found in the outdoors. I could get behind that.

Stepping up to the tree, I put my hand back and centered myself, one hand on my little girl, another remembering my first wife. For all the things I loved Allyson for, the fact that she included Nola in so much of our life was somewhere at the top. Pictures of her were all over our house. Her parents knew our children; they had an open invitation to visit. Allyson had taught me that moving on was not forgetting or leaving Nola behind. I did the work—I knew I did—but she had healed my soul.

Taking a deep breath, I thought about Nola. I was grateful this was where we'd scattered her ashes; so were her parents. They visited us, and this place, often. So while there was no headstone, we didn't need one. I felt Nola here. Heck, Allyson said anytime she wanted to strangle me, she came out here to ask Nola for advice and patience. Somehow, I could vividly picture Nola, wherever we end up, being absolutely thrilled with that.

Finally, I was ready. I said the words I'd been ready to share with her for three months but hadn't wanted to say until we were here, though I knew she already knew.

"Nola, I wanted to introduce you to your namesake, Fionnuala. She's only three months, but she's just as beautiful as you were. And before you ask, it was Allyson's idea. Heck, she probably came out to tell you about it. We're not going with the nickname of Nola, though, because that's yours. Instead, meet Fiona, or Fi. I know you will be looking out for her and Will. Showering them with your love. Please know we are sending some out into the world for you too."

A warm breeze washed through at that moment, making the leaves dance and flutter as a group of starlings rose out of the trees and flew together just above our heads. And I felt her, I felt the love, and knew that I was no longer empty but filled with absolutely peace.

I tapped the trunk three times, then moved to sit down next to Allyson, who leaned over to pull Fi out of the sling and nurse. I pressed a kiss to her head, the baby's, and grabbed a car to play with Will.

"Love you," I said to Allyson.

"Love you, babe," she said, reclining against the bench.

The starlings continued their formations and the sun beamed down. All was as it should be.

Acknowledgments

Good gracious, I thought book five, *Starting Over,* was difficult to write. The universe decided that was highly entertaining and set me back a step or two.

Before beginning this one I had a Zoom call with my editor, Sue, and remember telling her that the book was about Logan's wife who had passed away, but he had already coped with the grief and was ready to move on.

Fast forward many months and Sue sent me a note after reading the book - what happened to low-grief storyline for Logan?

Life, friends, life happened.

I'd written about twenty thousand words of this book when my mother-in-law had two major life-impacting events. All of December and January of 2022 and 2023, this book sat in the computer, no words being added, as my husband and I learned about strokes and the recovery process. My mother-in-law moved from a month in the hospital to a nursing home, relying on their expert care when just weeks ago she'd been living independently: driving from place to place while moving through life like normal.

I remember telling my therapist it was strange to grieve for someone who was still with us, but also wasn't.

What preceded and followed were some of the hardest and loneliest weeks and months, of our lives.

As of the typing of this acknowledgments, she's doing

great and has moved to an assisted living facility in town. I dedicated this book to her because I am in awe of how hard she's worked to get where she is. Also, Logan's story is forever shaped by hers. It changed this book because though my life is not in the books, the shadow of my life impacts my writing, always.

Thanks to the usual suspects for the ongoing support that surrounds me like a worn and comfortable blanket. Friends that listen to my concerns, writing colleagues that answer my odd emails, family that allows for my sporadic writing schedule - knowing when I decide to finally sit down, everything else falls to the wayside.

And thanks to readers. It's weird to write and no longer be in my own bubble, but have people send messages of support, post beautiful reviews, or contact in some way. Writing is isolating. Thanks for making it less so.

All my love,

Kat

About the Author

Kat Ryan is a middle school teacher by day and a budding romance author in the free time she steals for herself. She loves to write about small towns, found families, strong women, and cinnamon roll heroes that love them. She's a sucker for a HEA and more than a bit of steam in the stories she writes.

Kat lives in the Midwest with her husband and her two sons where she consumes a steady diet of coffee, chocolate, and romance books. And while her students and sons plan to never read the books she writes, her husband has and continues to cheer her on.

Want more from Logan and Allyson? Subscribe to Kat's newsletter on her website, https://katryanwrites.com. All "extras" for each of Kat's book are linked in the newsletter that comes out every month.

Also by Kat Ryan

www.ingramcontent.com/pod-product-compliance
Lightning Source LLC
Chambersburg PA
CBHW030148310726
48970CB00005B/1644